"My lord," she gasped.

In the light from the sconce his face was all hard angles and smooth planes. There was a loneliness about him. She was sure of it this time. An impossible bleakness as he stared into her eyes. His lids lowered a fraction, and his mouth softened and curved in a most decadent smile when she nervously licked her lips.

A flash of hunger flared in those storm-gray eyes.

An answering desire roared through her veins. Shocked, heart pounding, she stared into his lovely face, waiting, wondering.

Slowly he bent his head, as if daring her to meet him halfway. Unable to resist the challenge, she closed the distance and brushed her mouth against his. His hand came behind her nape and expertly steadied her as he angled his head and took her lips in a ravenous kiss.

On a soft groan he broke away. His chest was rising and falling as rapidly as her own. His gaze was molten.

"Would it really be so bad to be married to me, Miss Wilding?" he asked in a low, seductive growl.

* * *

Haunted by the Earl's Touch
Harlequi‌n February 2013

Author Note

I have always loved the spooky Gothic novel and mysterious old houses. Clearly the secrets in Bane's and Mary's pasts made them the perfect couple to spend time in a house haunted by a ghost and riddled with passages behind its walls. But how, I wondered, did my earl make his money? Then I made a discovery.

Tin mining has a long and ancient history in Cornwall, and was at its height of profitability during the Regency. It was quite a thrill to visit a tin mine, where I was able to go underground and see and hear what those miners of old would have seen and heard. I learned a lot more about tin mining than would ever fit within my story, and if you are as intrigued as I was you can learn more about it on my blog, www.regencyramble.blogspot.com, as well as finding out about the other places I have visited.

If you want to know more about forthcoming books visit www.annlethbridge.com or write to me at ann@annlethbridge.com. I love to hear from my readers.

Haunted by the Earl's Touch

ANN LETHBRIDGE

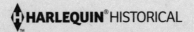

HARLEQUIN® HISTORICAL

Recycling programs
for this product may
not exist in your area.

ISBN-13: 978-0-373-29726-9

HAUNTED BY THE EARL'S TOUCH

Copyright © 2013 by Michèle Ann Young

Printed in U.S.A.

HARLEQUIN®
www.Harlequin.com

ANN LETHBRIDGE

has been reading Regency novels for as long as she can remember. She always imagined herself as Lizzie Bennet, or one of Georgette Heyer's heroines, and would often recreate the stories in her head with different outcomes or scenes. When she sat down to write her own novel it was no wonder that she returned to her first love: the Regency.

Ann grew up roaming Britain with her military father. Her family lived in many towns and villages across the country, from the Outer Hebrides to Hampshire. She spent memorable family holidays in the West Country and in Dover, where her father was born. She now lives in Canada, with her husband, two beautiful daughters and a Maltese terrier named Teaser, who spends his days on a chair beside the computer, making sure she doesn't slack off.

Ann visits Britain every year, to undertake research and also to visit family members who are very understanding about her need to poke around old buildings and visit every antiquity within a hundred miles. If you would like to know more about Ann and her research, or to contact her, visit her website at www.annlethbridge.com. She loves to hear from readers.

Chapter One

The wind keened outside the ancient walls of Beresford Abbey. Bane, following on the heels of the ancient butler along the stone passageway, noticed that only one sconce in five had been lit. Blown out by draughts? Or a sign of his welcome? No matter which, the gloom suited his mood.

'You should have left the dog in the stables,' the butler muttered over his shoulder.

Bane glance down at Ranger, part-lurcher, part-wolfhound, pressed to his left side. 'The dog stays with me.'

The butler tutted. 'And how shall I announce you, sir?' He gestured to the open door a few feet along the gloomy corridor.

A wry smile twisted Bane's lips. Was there a protocol to be followed? If so, he didn't know it. 'I'll announce myself.'

Looking shocked, but also relieved, the doddering old man turned back, shuffling down the dim stone corridor shaking his head. A wise old bird for whom discretion was the better part of valour.

Bane approached the doorway on feet silenced by carpet. He paused at the entrance to the cavernous chamber. The flickering light from ten-foot-high torchères on each side of the heavily carved four-poster bed fell on the features of the shrunken man propped up by pillows. A face lined by dissipation and framed by thin strands of yellowing grey hair straggling out from beneath a blue silken nightcap. Bony shoulders hunched in silk valuable enough to feed a family of four for a year shook with a spasm of coughing.

A dead man breathing his last. Finally. The chill inside Bane spread outwards as he took in the others clustered at the edge of the circle of light. Two women, three men, some of whom he recognised as family. He'd investigated all of his relatives to avoid unnecessary surprises.

The older woman was his aunt, his grandfather's daughter, Mrs Hampton, returned home as a widow. Her gown was the first stare of fashion as befitted her station. Tight curls of grey hair beneath a lace cap framed a middle-aged but still arresting face. As a young woman she'd been lovely, according to his mother, and too proud to make a friend of a lass from Yorkshire. At her side stood her son, Gerald, an almost too-pretty lad of seventeen with a petulant mouth and vivid blue eyes. The other young man was a distant fourth cousin. A Beresford through and through, slight, dapper, with blond hair and light blue eyes and a man his grandfather would have been happy to see as his heir had Bane not stood in the way.

An aspiring tulip of fashion in his early twenties, Bane had seen Jeffrey Beresford in town. They had no friends in common, but they bowed in passing—an acknowledgement of mutual distrust.

The other woman he did not know. Young, with a willowy figure, standing a good head taller than Mrs Hampton, she had inches on both young men. A Beresford also? She had the blonde hair and blue eyes to match the name, though she was dressed simply, in some dark stuff bespeaking modesty rather than style. The desire to see that statuesque body in something more revealing caused his throat to close.

Surprised him.

As a boy he'd had lusty thoughts about anything in skirts. As a man, a businessman, he had more important things on his mind. Women like her wanted home and hearth and a man to protect them. His life was about taking risks. Gambling all, on the chance for profit. No woman should live with such uncertainty. They were too delicate, too easily broken as his mother had been broken. The pain of her death had been unbearable. Not something he ever intended to experience again. Nor was it necessary. He was quite content to avoid the respectable ones while enjoying those who only wanted money in exchange for their favours, the *demi-monde*.

So why couldn't he keep his eyes from this most respectable-looking of females? Who was she? He wasn't aware of a female cousin, close or distant. Not that there couldn't be a whole host of relatives he didn't know about, since he didn't give a damn about any of them. But as his gaze ran over the girl, a prickle of awareness raised the hairs on the back of his neck. A sensation of familiarity so strong, he felt the urge to draw closer and ask for her name.

Yet he was positive they had never met. Perhaps it was the wariness in her expression that had him intrigued.

A blinding flash of lightning beyond the mullioned windows lit the room in a ghostly light. An image seared on Bane's vision. Stark otherworldly faces. Mouths dark pits in pale skin as the air moved with their startled gasps. They looked like the monsters who had peopled his childish nightmares. His enemies. The people who wanted him dead, according to his uncle. His mother's brother.

In truth, he hadn't expected to see family members here. He'd preferred to think of the old man alone and friendless as he gasped his last.

Just like Bane's mother.

If not for this man, his mother might be alive today and the guilt of her death would not weigh so heavily on Bane's shoulders. No matter how often he tried to put the blame where it belonged, on the man in the bed, he could not deny his own part in the events of that day. His thoughtless anger that had put her at risk. Hell, even his very existence, the reason she had run from this house in the first place.

Power and wealth brought invulnerability. His mother had drilled it into him since the day he could understand his place in the world. And that was why he was here. That and to see the old man off to the next world. He simply couldn't pass up the chance to see the dismay in the old earl's gaze.

He could count the number of times he and the old man had met face to face on one hand. But he had always been there, in the shadows, a threatening presence. Forcing his will where it was not wanted. Guiding Bane's education, trying to choose his friends, but his mother's brother had been more than a match for the earl. Bane still remembered his horror as he stood with his uncle on the doorstep of this house and listened to an argument over him, about money, about cruelty and murder. Accusations that had haunted him as a youth. Fed his anger at this man.

But his temper was not the hot flash of his youth, the kind that brought trouble to him and those around him. It was a cold burn in his gut, controlled, and carefully directed. Guilt over his mother's death had taught him that lesson.

Since then, Bane had striven to be the gentleman his mother always wanted him to be. He had battled for the respect of the scions of other noble houses at school and held his head high. But at heart he was the son of a coalminer's daughter. And proud of it. Mining was in his blood and showed in the scars on his knuckles and the muscles in his shoulders developed at the coalface.

He was more Walker than Beresford, whether or not he had any Beresford blood.

The lightning faded. Shadows once more reclaimed all but the man in the bed. As his coughing subsided, the earl's gnarled fingers clawed at the bedsheets, then beckoned.

Resistance stiffened Bane's spine. He wasn't about to be called to heel like some slavering cur. But, no, apparently this particular summons was not for him. The old man must not have seen him yet, since it was the two women who moved towards the bed, Mrs Hampton nudging the younger one ahead of her, making her stumble.

Bane took a half-step, a warning on his lips, but the girl recovered inches from the earl's warding hand, mumbling an apology.

Who was she? Some indigent relative looking for crumbs in the final hours? There would be no crumbs for any one of them. Not if Bane had a say.

'So you are Mary.' The old man's voice sounded like a door creaking in the wind. 'She said you were no great beauty, but not that you were a beanpole. You take after your father.'

'You knew my father?' the girl asked, and Bane sensed how keenly she awaited his answer. Her body seemed to vibrate with the depth of her interest.

The old man grimaced. 'I met him once. Kneel, girl. I'm getting a crick in my neck.'

Like a supplicant, the girl sank down. Anger rose hot and hard in Bane's throat on the girl's behalf, but she seemed unperturbed by the command and gazed calmly into the dying man's face.

She spoke again, but her low voice did not reach all the way to Bane in the shadows beside the door.

The old man glared at her, lifted a clawed hand to twist her chin this way and that. Glimpses of her profile showed strong classical features, a straight aristocratic nose. Lush, full lips. A narrow jaw ending in a decided chin. Not a classical beauty, but a face full of character.

The sight of the old man's hands on her delicate skin caused Bane's hands to fist at his sides, made him want to go to her rescue. An impulse he instantly crushed. A weak old man could do her no harm. And Bane had no interest in her, despite her allure.

She was not his type of woman.

Ranger growled, more a vibration under his hand than a sound. Bane glanced down at the dog and signalled him to settle. By the time he looked back, the old man had re-leased his grip on the young woman. 'No,' the old man said, answering the question Bane had not heard. 'My reasons are my own.'

The girl's shoulders seemed to slump, as if she had hoped for a different response.

Bane remained still in the shadows, content to watch a little longer, content to choose his own moment to re-veal his presence.

The old man peered into the shadows on the other side of the bed. 'She'll do,' he said with a triumphant leer. His smile was a mirthless drawing back of lips over crooked yellow teeth.

The woman, Mary, jerked back. 'I have given my thanks, my lord, I do not need your approval.' Her words rang with defiance. Brave words, but the voice shook.

Bane ruthlessly quelled a tiny surge of pity. He had no room for pity or mercy.

Beresford wheezed a laugh. 'Bold piece, ain't you. No milk-and-water miss. All the better.' He flicked his fingers in dismissal. The girl rose to her feet and turned.

Bane knew the moment she saw him. The widening of her eyes, the hesitation, the flare of recognition in her gaze, not recognition of him as a person, but of his presence. The connection between them was a tangible thing, a twisting invisible thread that kept their gazes locked. And he felt…something. A tightening of his body. The kind that heralded lust. Not something he wanted or needed right now.

He shook his head, a warning to remain silent, and it seemed she understood for she strode back to Mrs Hampton's side as if she hadn't seen him at all. An unwanted trickle of admiration for her quiet calm warmed his veins.

He dragged his gaze back to the man in the bed. It was time to be done with this farce. Bane forced himself not to square his shoulders or take a deep breath. He was no boy worried about his acceptance. He belonged here and he cared not a whit if they thought otherwise. He signalled Ranger to lie down, yet still he hesitated to take the first step.

The earl again looked over into the shadows on the far side of the bed. 'You said he would come,' he quavered.

A man trotted up to the bed. Tight lips. Eyes that darted hither and yon, never resting long enough to be read, bald pate shining. 'He is expected, my lord. I sent word as you ordered.' A dry, officious voice. A clerk of some sort. Solicitor, Bane decided.

'The storm must have delayed him.' The solicitor rubbed his palms together with a papery sound. 'Perhaps tomorrow.'

'Tomorrow will be too late.'

A flash of lightning punctuated his words, the room once more a colourless tableau of frozen players.

Bane stepped into the lamplight in that moment. His shadow loomed black over the bed and up the wall behind the dying man like some portent of evil. 'I am here.'

The old man's gasp was eminently satisfying. No doubt he had carried the hope his elder grandson would miraculously die at the eleventh hour.

Thunder rolled beyond the window, drowning out the old man's muttered words.

Bane's lip curled. It no longer mattered what the old man said. Beresford Abbey was a few short breaths from being passed on to a man who likely had not a drop of Beresford blood.

Oh, the old man had tried to make the best of an heir he despised once he'd discovered Bane had survived to stake his claim. He'd tried to force the twelve-year-old Bane into the appropriate mould. The right sort of school, the right education. As much as his mother's family would permit. And Bane had used what he needed to take back what was rightfully his. His mother had fled the Abbey because she feared for Bane's life. She had lost her own, trying to keep him safe. The powerlessness he'd felt that day still haunted him. He'd fought. How he'd fought. And those men, they had laughed at him. Mocked him. After that day he had sworn he would never let anyone make him feel weak and helpless again. He never had. And never by the man lying in the bed.

He'd used the best of both his worlds. The strength of the coalminers he'd worked alongside in summer holidays and the power of the nobility given by the title he would inherit. He'd taken control of his life.

No one would ever manipulate him again. Not his mother's brother, or the earl.

Bane glanced over at the watchers. If one of them, just one of these relatives, had taken pity on his mother, offered her their support, he might have been able to find a little mercy in his heart. But they hadn't. He bared his teeth in a smile that would do Ranger proud.

The old earl looked him over, his red-rimmed, faded blue eyes watery, his face a picture of scorn. 'So, the scavengers are circling.'

'You sent for me, Grandfather,' he said his tone mocking.

The earl's gaze lingered on Bane's face and he shook his head. 'A curse on your mother for sending my son to an early grave.'

Bitterness roiled in his gut at the vilification. A drunken lord driving his carriage off the road was hardly his mother's fault. His chest tightened until his lungs were starved. Not that he was surprised by the accusation, just by his own visceral reaction, when there was nothing this decayed piece of flesh could do to her any more. 'But for you, my mother would be alive today.'

Yet even as he spoke the words, the old guilt rose up to choke him. The knowledge that he had done nothing to save her. 'But she beat you in the end.'

The old man sneered. 'Did she now?'

The urge to stop the vile tongue edged his vision in red. Involuntarily his fists clenched. His palms tingled with the desire to tighten around the scrawny neck, to feel the flesh and bones crush in on his windpipe. Watch the life fade from those cruel eyes and silence his lips for ever.

He reached for his hard-won iron control over his tem-

per, shocked at how close it was to slipping from his grasp
at this long-awaited moment, grabbed a breath of air and
let the heat dissipate. He would not let his anger overpower his reason. He knew the penalty for doing so. It
would rob him of his victory as it has robbed him of his
mother. There was no need for anger, not now, when he'd
won. He shrugged.

The old devil grinned a death's-head smile. 'Look at
you, apeing the gentleman in your fine clothes, with not
an ounce of nobility in your blood. It is a wonder decent
society tolerates you at all.'

He smiled his own mocking smile. 'They welcome
me with open arms. It is the prospect of a title that does
it, you know.'

Something flashed in the old man's eyes. If Bane hadn't
known better, he might have thought it was admiration. It
was more likely rage at being defeated in his plan to be rid
of his cuckoo in the nest. Thanks to his rough-and-ready
upbringing by his maternal uncle, and later his years of
misery at school and university, Bane had no doubts about
his ability to withstand any torment his grandfather might
devise. He'd spent his life preparing for this moment.

He moved closer to the head of the bed, lowering his
voice. 'You sent for me, old man, and here I am. Speak
your piece. I am a busy man.'

'A coalminer. A labourer for hire.' Scorn dripped from
the old man's thin lips like poison. Spittle spattered his
chin and the lapels of the silken robe bearing the Beresford emblem in gold.

'Aye,' Bane said. 'I know how to earn my keep.' Not
that he laboured with his hands any more, but he could if
need be. He let his gaze drift around the worn bed hang-
ings and worn furniture. 'And I know how to follow your
example, spending money on idle pursuits in town.' He'd

done his share of playing the debauched nobleman since making his bows at court, much to the displeasure of both sides of his family. But he hadn't been wasting his time, no matter what they thought.

The old man raised a hand and pointed a crooked finger at the young men nearby. 'They are real Beresfords.' His whispery voice flicked like a whip at Bane's pride.

He bared his teeth in a hard smile. His was, after all, the final triumph. 'Too bad. There is nothing anyone can do about it.'

'No?' A calculating gleam entered the faded blue eyes and his lips twisted. His gaze darted to the far side of the bed, to the huddle just beyond the lamplight. 'Jeffrey. Gerald. Come to me.'

The two young men came forwards. The dandy, Jeffrey, at a saunter, meeting Bane's gaze surprisingly coolly. The younger cousin, Gerald, known to Bane only as a name, ran to the old man's side and knelt, clutching one of those misshapen hands. 'Grandfather, do not upset yourself.' The boy looked up at Bane. 'Leave him in peace.'

Beresford pulled his hand free and stared at the two young men with a wry expression. 'These are my grandsons. True nobility. Real Beresfords.' He turned his head on the pillow to look at Bane. 'But whose spawn are you?'

Whose bastard, he meant. It wasn't anything Bane hadn't heard before. It barely registered, but the soft gasp coming from somewhere in the shadows cut at him like a whip. The girl. He knew it instinctively. He forced himself not to look her way, despite feeling the intensity of her gaze grazing his skin. 'It doesn't matter,' he said coldly. 'I am your legal heir, so that pair of spoiled ninnyhammers had best crawl at my feet if they want crumbs from my table.' He took pleasure in speaking in the rough tones of his mother's people.

The old man grunted and struggled up on to one elbow, pointing at Bane's face with a crooked finger. 'Think you've bested me, do you? You've got nerve, I'll credit you that. I've watched you. I've got your measure. If you want the wealth and power that goes with the title, then you'll dance to my tune.'

Ranger, by the door, rumbled low in his throat.

'Grandfather!' the young lad at his side said, trying to ease him back down on to the pillows.

His grandfather brushed him aside. 'It takes a clever man to best a Beresford.' His laugh crackled like tearing paper. 'I'm only sorry I won't be here to see it.'

Bane shot him a considering look. The old man seemed just too sure of himself. 'I won't be controlled, old man. You should know that by now.'

As the dying man collapsed against the pillows, his gaze sought out the young woman he'd spoken to earlier. 'Don't be so sure.'

Who the devil was she? Bane sent her a baleful glance. She inched deeper into the shadows, but her blue eyes, her Beresford-blue eyes, never left his face and they held a kind of fascinated horror.

The earl's gaze dropped to his other grandsons and moisture ran down his cheeks, glistening, running into the crevasses on his cheeks. Then he drew in a shuddering breath, his jaw working. He turned his head and his eyes, still wet with tears, fixed on Bane. 'You'll do your duty by the family.'

'I have no family in this house.' Bane let his scorn show on his face. 'You failed to be rid of me when you had the chance and they bear the consequence. The sins of the father will be visited upon these children of your line. And there will be no more.'

The old man chuckled, a grim sound in the quiet room.

'Cocksure, aren't you. And proud. Yet you hold the losing hand.'

The wry amusement gave Bane pause. Intimidation. The old man excelled at terrifying those weaker than himself. Bane was not his or anyone else's victim. He'd made himself too strong to be any man's punching bag. He leaned over, speaking only for the old man to hear. 'You forget, it will all be within my control. My only regret is that you won't see the desecration of your family name.' He flicked a glance at his cousins, the coolly insolent one who hid his true nature from the world and the half-scared boy. 'It would do them good to work at some low honest task for their bread.'

The old man groaned, but there was something odd in his tone, as if he wasn't so much in agony, but stifling amusement. 'You think you are such a cold devil,' he muttered. 'I will be sorry to miss the heat of your anger.'

Bane drew back, searching that vindictive face. 'What have you done?'

'You'll see.'

A resounding crack of thunder split the air at the same time as lightning flickered around the room. The storm's last violent convulsion.

Ranger howled. The old man jerked upright in that wild blue light, the colour draining from his face, from his clothing, from the twisted hand clutching his throat. He sank back with a sigh.

The kneeling boy uttered a cry of despair. Jeffrey leaned over and felt for his pulse. Mrs Hampton rushed forwards. The tall girl remained where she was, a hand flat across her mouth, her eyes wide.

Bane curled his lip as he looked down on the empty shell of what had once been a man who had wielded his power to harm the innocent.

Bane was the earl now. And to hell with the Beresfords.

He spared a last glance for those gathering close around the bed and shrugged. Let them weep and wail at the old man's passing. It was of no import to him.

Weariness swept through him. After travelling hard for three days, he needed a bath and a good night's sleep. He had a great deal to do on the morrow if he was to set his plans in motion. He had debts to pay and a coalmine to purchase.

As he turned to leave, he caught sight of the young woman hanging back, her expression one of distaste. What mischief had the old man planned for her? Nothing his grandfather could do from beyond the grave could harm Bane. But he did not like to think of yet another innocent female destroyed by his machinations.

Unless she wasn't as innocent as she appeared. Was anyone in this family innocent? It was hard to think so. And if she wasn't, then Bane was more than a match for her, too.

He snapped his fingers for Ranger and headed down the corridor, hoping like hell he could find the way back through the maze of passages to his assigned chamber.

While the family members hovered and wept around the body of the old earl, Mary made good her escape. Her brain whirled. Her stomach cramped. And she ran like a cowardly rabbit.

When she'd been invited to meet her benefactor, the man she'd recently learned had paid for her schooling, her every meal, for most of her life, she had wondered—no, truly, she had dreamed that at last some family member, some distant relative, had decided to claim her as their own. A childhood fantasy finally fulfilled.

She'd certainly had no idea that the man was at death's

door until the butler guided her into that room earlier this evening. And when she'd asked her question with breathless hope and seen the surprise in those watery blue eyes and the wry twist to his lips, she'd felt utterly foolish.

Was she a member of his family? The answer had been a flat *no*.

Sally Ladbrook had been right. The man had viewed her as a good work, a charitable impulse, and was looking for recognition before he met his end. Unless he intended to impose the obligation on his heir.

She shivered. Just the thought of the new earl's overwhelmingly menacing presence in that room made her heart race and her knees tremble. She'd been transfixed by the sheer male strength of him, while he had stood in the shadows as still as death.

She halted at the end of the corridor and glanced back. A sliver of light spilling on to the runner revealed the location of that horrid room. Never in her life had she witnessed anything so morbid. She rubbed at her jaw, trying to erase the sensation of cold papery fingers on her skin and shuddered.

To make it worse, once the heir had stepped out of the shadows, the hatred in the room had been palpable. Like hot oil on metal, hissing and spitting first from one direction and then another, scalding wherever it landed.

And the man. The new earl. So dark. So unexpectedly large, even handsome in a brutal way. A powerful man who had overshadowed his dying grandfather like some avenging devil.

He didn't walk, he prowled. He didn't speak, he made utterances in a voice composed of velvet and sandpaper. And his eyes. His eyes were as deep as an abyss when he had stared directly at her. That look owed nothing to the gloom in the room, for it was the same when he stood within the light of the torches. Worse. Because she could see the pinpoints of flickering light reflected in his gaze and still make out nothing in their shadowed depths.

She—who prided herself on being able to stand in front of a class of spoiled daughters and hold her own, at least on the surface, and who, as a charity boarder, had suffered pity and sly comments about her poverty all those years—had managed to stand up to the gloating way the old man had looked at her and crushed any hope that she might have found her place in the world.

But when that piercing gaze looking out from the shadows in the doorway had tangled with hers, it had sapped her courage dry. She'd scuttled ignominiously back to her place without a shred of dignity remaining.

The sooner she left this place, this house with its dark undercurrents, the better. She'd done her duty. Offered her thanks. Surely she was free to go? She would leave first thing in the morning.

She glanced left and right. Which way? The maid who had brought her to the dying man's room had found her way with unerring ease, but Mary no longer had a clue which way they had come, there had been so many twists and turns on their journey from her chamber. Not to mention the odd staircase.

Part-dissolved abbey, part-Tudor mansion, part-renaissance estate, it sprawled and rambled inside and out. She'd glimpsed the house at dusk, perched high on a Cornish cliff, crenulated towers and chimney pots rising to the sky. A complete muddle of a house.

Her room was in one of those square towers. At the north end, the butler had told her when he escorted her there upon her arrival. The tower nearest the abbey ruins. She could see them through her small window. She had also heard the muffled rumble of the ocean somewhere deep below the house, in its very foundations. A very ominous sound. She shuddered as she imagined the house undermined by the force of the sea.

She eyed her two choices and selected the one that seemed to amble north. Picking up her skirts for speed, she hurried on, wishing there was more light, or a servant to show her the way.

Another corridor branched off to her right, going south? Or had that last corner she had turned set her off course? The maid had turned off the main corridor, hadn't she? More than once. She plunged into the new hallway. It looked no more familiar than the last.

She needed help.

She tried the first door she came to. A bedroom, its furniture huddled beneath holland covers. If there ever had been a bell rope, it had been removed.

Blast. She returned to the corridor, heading for another room further along.

Footsteps. Behind her. Thank God. Help at last.

She turned around.

A light flickered and stopped. Whoever held the candle remained masked in shadow.

The wind howled through a nearby crevice, lifting the hair at her nape. Her heart picked up speed. The girls at school had told late-night stories of ghosts and hauntings that started like this. Deliciously wicked in their frightening aspects and heroic deeds. Figments of imagination. She did not believe in ghosts. People like her, practical people, did not have the luxury of such flights of fancy, yet she could not quite quell the fear gripping her chest. 'Who is there?' She was shocked at the tremble in her voice.

The light drew closer. A candle held in a square-fingered hand joined to a brawny figure still in the darkness. Him. The new earl.

How she knew, she wasn't sure, but her skin prickled with the knowledge. Heat flushed up from her belly. 'My lord?' she said. Her voice quavering just a little more than she would have liked. 'Lord Beresford?'

The candle went upwards, lighting his harsh face.

'Great goliaths,' she said, letting go of her breath. 'Do you always creep around hallways in such a fashion?' Oops. That sounded a bit too much like the schoolteacher taking a pupil to task.

The eyes staring down at her were not dark as she had thought in the old earl's bedroom. They were as grey as storm clouds. And watchful.

'Are you lost?' he drawled in that deep mocking voice with its hint of roughness.

'Certainly not,' she replied, discomposed by his obvious indifference. Heat rushed to her cheeks and she was glad the dim light would not reveal her embarrassment. She let her gaze fall away.

'Liar,' he said softly.

She bristled.

'That's better.'

A snuffling sound drew her gaze down. The dog. It sank to its haunches and watched her with its head cocked on one side. It was enormous. 'What is better?' she asked, keeping a wary eye on the dog.

'It is better when you stand up straight, instead of hunching over like a scared schoolgirl.'

As a schoolgirl, she had tried to disguise her ungainly height. It spoke to her discomfort that she had fallen back into that old habit.

She looked up past the wide chest and broad shoulders, past the snowy cravat and strong column of throat, his full mobile mouth at eye level, then up to meet his gaze. Most men were either her height or shorter. This one was taller than her by half a head—he must be inches above six foot tall—and he reeked of danger.

What snatches of conversation she'd heard between him and the dying earl had been positively menacing. And, unless she was badly mistaken, some of the venom shifting back and forth between them had been directed at her.

'If you will excuse me, I must be on my way.'

'On your way where?'

'To my room.'

He shot her a wolfish smile. 'So that was not your room. The one you just left.'

'No,' she muttered, making to step past him.

'What were you doing in that chamber?'

Did he think she was trying to steal? She stiffened her spine, meeting his gaze full on. Such directness usually sent men running for the hills. On this one it apparently had no effect. Or none visible, though she did sense a sharpening of interest in those wintery eyes.

She huffed out a breath of defeat. 'I will admit I am a little turned about. My chamber is in the tower at the north end of the house. I thought I would ring for a servant to guide me, but there was no bell pull in the first room I tried.'

'A clever thought.'

'I am clever.' She bit her lip. That was just the sort of quick retort men did not like. A habit of bravado honed in the schoolroom.

He didn't seem to notice. 'Follow me.' He strode past her down the corridor, the dog following at his heels, leaving her to trot along behind as best she might.

He took a flight of stairs down and then passed along a stone corridor that smelled of must and damp. She was sure she had not come this way.

He hesitated at yet another intersection of passageways. She huffed out a breath. 'Don't tell me, you are lost too.'

He gave her a scornful look. 'I never get lost.'

Doubt filled her mind. 'Have you ever been to this house before?'

'North is this way.' He set off once more with the dog padding beside him.

Hah. Avoidance. He was just as lost as she was. More lost. Because she was quite sure from the increasingly dank feel to the air that they were now in the cellars. The sea growled louder too. Typical. Why would men never admit to being lost?

About to insist they stop, she was surprised when he took off up a circular flight of narrow stairs she hadn't noticed. At the top, he turned left and there they were, at her chamber door. How irritating. And she still had no idea how she got here. It didn't matter. She had no reason to learn her way around, since she would be departing at once.

'Thank you, my lord.' She dipped her best curtsy and prayed he would not hear the wry note in her voice.

He held his candle high and caught her chin in long strong fingers just like the old man had done. But these fingers were warm with youth and strong with vigour and, while firm, they were also gentle. She jerked her head, but he held her fast.

She stared up at his face, at the beautifully moulded lips set in a straight line hovering above hers. His head dipped a fraction. Angled. She could feel his breath, warm on her cheek, inhaled a hint of cologne, something male, mingled with leather and horse and briny air that made her feel dizzy.

She drew in a deep breath as his gaze fell on her mouth, lingering there, until she thought he would kiss her. Longed that he would to break this dreadful tension between them.

Nervous, she licked her lips.

His eyes narrowed and he raised that piercing gaze to meet hers as if he would read her mind. Stroked her chin with his thumb and, she shivered. He leaned closer and for a wild moment, she thought he really did intend to kiss her and her body hummed at the thought.

Instead, he spoke. 'Who are you?' he rasped softly.

'Mary,' she managed to gasp in a breathless whisper, her breathing beyond her control. 'Mary Wilding.'

'Wilding?' A brow went up. 'And what brought you here, Miss Wilding?'

She swallowed. 'I was invited. By the earl.'

'The late earl.'

She nodded.

He stepped back, releasing her face. 'And what is your purpose here, I wonder?'

'It doesn't matter. I will be leaving first thing.'

'I see. Well, Miss Wilding, I bid you goodnight. We will talk before you go.'

She remained frozen as he disappeared back down the twisting stairs and she was left alone, in the silence, not hearing even his footsteps and feeling strangely giddy.

Breathless, from…fear? The fluttering in her belly, the tremble in her hands, could be nothing else. Though what made her fearful, she wasn't sure. Perhaps her reactions? To him? Would she have actually let him kiss her, had he wanted to do so?

Could she have stopped such a powerful man taking whatever he wanted? A little thrill rippled through her. Perverse. Unwanted.

All he had wanted was to question her.

She pressed cold fingers to her hot cheeks and hauled

in a deep breath before stepping inside her small chamber. While thanking her benefactor had been one of the less pleasant experiences of her life, meeting the new earl had been something else entirely. Disturbing and exciting. It might be as well to avoid him before she left.

Coward.

Chapter Two

The maid Betsy, assigned to help Mary dress, arrived at nine the next morning.

Mary didn't needed help dressing. Just as always, she'd been awake and dressed by six, before light touched the grey wintery sky. At school, it was her task to see that the girls were washed and dressed before they came to breakfast. The maid had to content herself with drawing back the curtains and putting coal on the fire. 'This room is always cold,' the girl announced cheerfully. 'Will there be anything else, miss?'

'I would like a carriage to take me to St Ives.'

'You will need to speak to Mr Manners,' the girl said, her Cornish vowels hard to decipher.

Of course. The butler. He would be in charge of such things. 'Where will I find him?'

The small brown-eyed girl raised her brows. 'In the breakfast room. Serving the family.'

The grieving family. She wanted nothing to do with any of them, especially the new earl. But since she needed to order the carriage, she straightened her shoulders and smiled. 'Perhaps you would be good enough to guide me there?'

Betsy bobbed a curtsy. 'Follow me, miss.'

It wasn't long before she was deposited in front of a large oak door off the entrance hall. 'In there, miss.'

'Thank you.' Mary sailed through the door as if she had been making grand entrances all her life. Or at least she hoped she gave that impression.

What a relief. No brooding earl awaited her in the oak-panelled room with its polished furniture and gleaming silver. Only his cousins sat at the table. Blond and handsome, they rose to their feet as she entered.

'Good morning,' she said.

'Good morning, Miss Wilding,' they replied gravely.

The older one, Mr Jeffrey Beresford, gave her a swift perusal. A slightly pained expression entered his vivid-blue eyes. No doubt he thought her dreadfully shabby in her Sunday-best dress, but it was grey and she'd thought it the most appropriate under the circumstances. The younger one nodded morosely.

Both young men wore dark coats and black armbands. Of Mrs Hampton there was no sign. No doubt she preferred to breakfast in her room on such a sorrowful day.

'Miss Wilding,' the butler said, pulling out a chair opposite the Beresford cousins. She sat.

They followed suit.

'Did you sleep well, Miss Wilding?' Mr Beresford asked, assuming the duty of host in the earl's absence.

'Yes, thank you.' She certainly wasn't going to admit to her mind replaying the scene with the earl outside her chamber door over and over as she restlessly tossed and turned.

'Really?' Mr Hampton said, looking up, his face angelic in a shaft of sunlight that at that moment had broken through the clouds and found its way into the dining room to rest on him.

'Is there some reason why I should not?' she asked a little stiffly, surprised by his sudden interest.

He looked at her moodily. 'They do say as how the White Lady's ghost haunts the north tower.'

'You are an idiot, Ger,' the other cousin said. 'Don't listen to him, Miss Wilding. It is an old wives' tale.'

''Tis not,' Gerald said, his lips twisting. 'One of the servants saw her last week.'

'And that is a bouncer,' his cousin replied repressively. 'One servant saw her fifty years ago.'

The younger man scowled.

Mary felt sorry for him. Boys liked their ghost stories as much as foolish young girls did, no doubt. 'It would take more than a ghost to scare me,' she said calmly, 'if I actually believed in them.' It would take a tall dark earl with a sinful mouth to make her quiver in fear. Or quiver with something.

The young man looked a little insulted. 'If you see her, you will tell me, won't you? I've been keeping track of her sightings.' He pushed his food around with his fork. 'They say she appears when there is to be a death in the house.' The utter belief in his voice gave her a strange slithery sensation in her stomach. It also reminded her of last night's events with a pang of guilt.

'Although I had never met your grandfather before last night, I hope you will accept my deepest sympathy for your loss.'

Both young men nodded their acceptance of her condolence.

'Coffee, miss?' the butler asked.

She usually had tea in the morning. And only one cup. But there was another scent floating in the air, making her mouth water and her stomach give little hops of pleasure. 'Chocolate, please, Manners.' She'd had her first taste of chocolate this morning when Betsy had brought her tray and really couldn't resist having it one last time.

The man poured a cup from the silver chocolate pot on the sideboard and added a generous dollop of cream. Such luxury. Wait until she told Sally. Her friend and employer would be so envious. Chocolate was one of those luxuries they dreamt of on a cold winter's night.

The butler brought her toast on a plate and offered her a selection of platters. Deciding to make the most of what was offered—after all, she was an invited guest—she took some shirred eggs and ham and sausage and tucked in with relish. Breakfast at Ladbrook's rarely consisted of more than toast and jam and porridge in the winter months. Ladbrook's School for Young Ladies was rarely full to capacity and the best food always went to the paying pupils. As a charity case, she had managed on leftovers. Since becoming employed as a teacher things had improved, but not by much.

Hope of improving the school was why she had agreed to travel all the way from Wiltshire to meet the late earl. If he had proved to be a distant relation, she had thought to convince him to provide funds for improvements, to make it more fashionable and therefore profitable, as well as enable the taking in of one or two more charity boarders like herself.

She let go of a sigh. The earl's death had put paid to all her hopes, including any hope of some family connection. She ought to speak of the school's needs to the new earl, she supposed, but his behaviour so far had led her to the conclusion that, rather than a man of charitable bent, he was likely to be one of the scandalous rakes one read about in broadsheets and romantic novels.

'What do you think of the Abbey, Miss Wilding?' Mr Hampton asked.

'It's a dreadful pile,' his cousin put in before she could answer. 'Don't you think?'

Tact seemed to be the best course between two extremes. 'I have seen very little, so would find it hard to form an opinion, Mr Hampton.'

'Call me Gerald. Mr Hampton was my father. That pink of the *ton* is Jeffrey.'

His older cousin inclined his head, clearly accepting the description with aplomb. Mary smiled her thanks, not quite sure what lay behind this courtesy for a virtual stranger.

'What shall we call you?' he asked. 'Cousin?'

She stiffened. Had they also formed the mistaken impression they were related, or had they heard the earl's mocking reply to her question and thought to follow suit? Heat rushed to her cheeks. 'You may call me Miss Wilding.'

Gerald frowned. 'You sound like my old governess.'

'I am a schoolteacher.'

Jeffrey leaned back in his chair and cast an impatient glance at Gerald. 'Miss Wilding it is then, ma'am. At least *you* are not claiming to be a Beresford.'

Mary caught her breath at this obvious jibe at his absent older cousin. She had heard some of his conversation with the old earl and gathered there was some doubt about the legitimacy of his birth. She hadn't expected the issue addressed so openly.

Last night she'd had the sense that the old man's barbs had found their mark with the heir. Not that he'd had shown any reaction. But there had been something running beneath the surface. Anger. Perhaps resentment. And a sense of aloneness, as if he too had hoped for acceptance from this family.

She certainly did not approve of sniping at a person

behind their back and their family quarrels were certainly none of her business, so she ignored the comment and buttered her toast. She had more important matters on her mind. Getting back to school. Preparing her lessons. Helping Sally find ways to reduce expenses still further if the earl's munificence was indeed ended.

She smiled at the butler as he added chocolate to her cup. 'Manners, may I request the carriage take me to St Ives after breakfast? I would like to catch the stage back to Wiltshire.'

'I can't do that, miss,' Manners replied stone-faced.

Startled, she stared at him.

Gerald frowned. 'Why not?'

'His lordship's orders. You will have to apply to him, miss.'

The heat in her cheeks turned to fire at the thought of asking his lordship for anything.

'Damn him,' Jeffrey said with more heat than he seemed wont to display. 'He hasn't been here five minutes and already he's acting…' His voice tailed off and he reddened as he realised Gerald's avid gaze was fixed on his face.

'It isn't fair,' Gerald said. 'You should be the heir. He should have the decency to withdraw his claim.'

'He can't,' Jeffrey said. 'The heir is the heir. The proof is irrefutable.'

'It still isn't right,' Gerald muttered.

Jeffrey gave Mary an apologetic smile. 'Gerald takes things too much to heart. And I am sorry about the carriage, Miss Wilding. Would you like me to speak to…to his lordship?' He stumbled on the last word as if he was not quite as sanguine as he made out.

'I would certainly hate to inconvenience anyone,' Mary said. 'Perhaps I shall walk.'

'There's a path along the cliffs,' Gerald said. 'I've walked it often. Take you a good while, though.'

'I advise you not to try it, Miss Wilding,' Jeffrey drawled. 'The Cornish coast is dangerous for those who do not know it.'

Another roadblock. Her spine stiffened. She gave him a tight smile 'Thank you for the warning. Perhaps I should seek the earl's permission to take the carriage, after all.'

Or not. How difficult could it be to walk along the coast? Sea on one side, land on the other and no earthly chance of getting lost. Unlike her experience in this house. And she had absolutely no intention of asking his lordship for anything. The thought of doing so made her heart race.

'Where is the new lordship,' Gerald asked, his lip curling with distaste.

'I believe he rode out, sir,' the butler said. 'More coffee?'

Gerald waved him off.

'I wonder what he is riding?' Jeffrey said. 'A man like him probably has no idea of good horseflesh.'

Like him? Now that was pure snobbery. She wondered what they said about a woman like her, a penniless school-teacher, behind her back. No doubt they had thought she had come to ingratiate herself. How mortifying that they were very nearly right. She felt her shoulders rise in that old defensive posture and forced them to relax, keeping her expression neutral. These young noblemen were nowhere near as vicious as schoolgirls, nothing to fear at all.

'Aye,' Gerald said. 'A man like him will be all show and no go.'

Jeffrey raised a brow. 'As if you would know, cuz. Isn't it time your mother let you have a decent mount of your own?'

Gerald hunched a shoulder. 'I'm to get one on my birthday. And a phaeton.'

'God help us all,' Jeff said *sotto voce*.

The door swung back and the earl strode in. His silver gaze swept the room, taking in the occupants in one swift glance before he made for the empty place at the head of the table.

The new earl was just as impressive in the grey of morning as he had been in the glow of lamplight. Perhaps more so. His black coat hugged his broad shoulders and his cravat was neatly tied. He was not wearing an armband. Perhaps he considered the black coat quite enough, though the rich fabric of his cream waistcoat, embroidered with blue sprigs, suggested he hadn't given mourning a thought when he dressed.

The shadowed jaw of the previous night was gone, his face smooth and recently shaved. He was, as her girls would say when they thought she could not hear, devilishly handsome. Devilish being the most apt word she could think of in respect to the earl, since his face was set in the granite-hard lines of a fallen angel who found his fate grim.

Oh, jumping Jehosophat, did it matter how he looked? After today, she would never see him again.

'Good morning,' he said to the room at large.

The two young men mumbled grudging greetings.

'Good morning, my lord,' Mary said with a polite calm. It wasn't right to treat him like some sort of pariah in his own house. She wouldn't do it. She would be civil. Even if it was hard to breathe now he took up so much of the air in the room.

His eyes widened a fraction. 'Miss Wilding. Up and about so early?'

'As is my usual wont,' she replied, sipping her chocolate, not tasting it at all any more, because all she was aware of was him.

Heat rushed to her cheeks and she hoped he did not notice.

After responding to Manners's enquiries about his preferences for breakfast, he picked up the newspaper beside his plate and disappeared behind it.

A strained silence filled the room. It demanded that someone break it. It was just too obvious that they had stopped talking the moment he entered. He would think they were talking about him. They weren't. At least, not all of the time. It made her feel very uncomfortable, as if her skin was stretched too tight.

She waited until he had eaten most of his breakfast. Sally, widowed by two husbands and therefore an expert, always said men were not worth talking to until they had filled their stomachs. 'My lord?'

He looked up, frowning.

Perhaps he hadn't eaten enough. Well, it was too late to draw back. 'May I request that your coachman drive me to St Ives this morning? It is time I returned home.'

He frowned. 'Not today. Your presence is required in two hours' time for the reading of the will.'

The will? What did that have to do with her? 'That is not necessary, surely?'

He gave her a look that froze her to the spot. 'Would I ask it, if it were not?'

She dragged her gaze from his and put down her cup. A tiny hope unfurled in her chest. Perhaps the earl had left something for the school after all. Had she been too hasty in thinking her quest unsuccessful?

The earl was watching her face with a cynical twist to his lips, as if she was some sort of carrion crow picking over a carcase. Guilt twisted in her stomach. She had no reason to feel guilty. The school was a worthy cause, even if it did also benefit her. And if she had previously hoped the earl's summons had signified something more, something of a familial nature, those expectations had been summarily disabused and were no one's concern but her own. 'If it is required, then I will attend.'

The earl pushed his plate aside and pushed to his feet. 'Eleven o'clock in the library, Miss Wilding. Try not to be late.'

She bristled, but managed to hang on to her aplomb. 'I am never late, my lord.'

He gazed at her for a long moment and she was sure she saw a gleam of amusement in his eyes, but it was gone too fast for her to be certain. 'Unless you become lost, I assume.'

Once more heat flooded her face at the memory of his rescue the previous evening and her shocking responses to his closeness. Her incomprehensible longings, which must not recur. It was ungentlemanly of him to remind her.

He departed without waiting for a reply, no doubt assuming his orders would be carried out. And if they weren't then no doubt the autocratic man would find a way to rectify the matter.

'I'm for the stables,' Jeffrey said. 'I want to take a look at his horseflesh.'

He wanted to mock.

'Can I come?' Gerald asked, his expression pleading.

'If you wish,' his cousin said, kindly, which made Mary think a great deal more of him. He bowed to Mary and the two of them strolled away.

Now what should she do? Go back to her room and risk getting lost? Sally hadn't expected her to spend more than one night here at the Abbey, no matter what hopes Mary had secretly held. What she should do was despatch a let-

ter to Sally telling her what was happening and why her
return might be delayed by another day. She could while
away the two hours before the appointed time in writing and reading more enjoyably than spending the time
wandering the chilly corridors of this rambling mansion
looking for her room.

'Will you direct me to the library, Manners? I assume
there is paper and pen there?'

The butler bowed. 'Yes, miss. It is located further along
this hallway. You cannot miss it.'

If anyone could miss anything when it came to directions, she could and would. But that was her own personal
cross to bear. 'Thank you.'

He gave her a kind smile. 'There is a footman going to
the village this afternoon, if you would like a letter posted,
miss. Ring the bell when you are finished and he'll come
and collect it. You will find sealing wax and paper in the
desk drawer, and ink on the inkstand.'

She smiled her thanks and made her escape.

The library proved to be exactly where the butler had
said and she found it without difficulty.

Nirvana could not have looked any more inviting.
Shelves, packed with leather-bound books in shades of
blue, red and green, rose from floor to ceiling on three
dark-panelled walls. Wooden chairs strategically placed
beside tables of just the right height encouraged a person
to spread books out at will. Deep overstuffed sofas and
chairs upholstered in fabrics faded to soft brown tempted
the reader who liked to curl up with a novel. Cushioned
window seats offered comfort and light on dark winter
days. All was overseen by a large oak desk at one end.

The delights on offer tested her determination to write
to Sally first and read afterwards. But she managed it, sit-

ting at the heavy desk, putting out of her mind what she could not say about the new earl as she wrote of the demise of their donor.

She flicked the feather end of her quill across her chin. Should she mention a possibility of some small sum in the will? It seemed a bit presumptuous. She decided to write only of her delayed return. A mere day or two, she said.

Having rung the bell and sent off her missive, she turned her attention to the feast of books. She selected a book of poems by Wordsworth and settled into one of the window seats.

She didn't have long to indulge because, within the half-hour, Mr Savary, the solicitor who had been at the earl's bedside, arrived with a box full of papers and began fussing with them on the desk.

Mary decided she would remain where she was, at the furthest point in the room from where the family would conduct its business.

At a few minutes past eleven, the family members straggled in. First Gerald with his mother. Mrs Hampton looked very becoming in black. It suited her air of delicacy. She would have been an extraordinarily beautiful woman in her youth. She and her son, who took after her in the beauty department, sat beside the blazing hearth not far from the desk.

Jeffrey, his saunter as pronounced as any Bond Street beau, came next. Not that Mary had ever seen a Bond Street beau, but she'd seen cartoons in the paper, read descriptions of their antics and could use her imagination. He struck a languid pose at the fireplace, one arm resting on the mantel while he gazed pensively into the flames. Regretting being cut out of the title? He didn't seem to care much about anything. Perhaps it was the idea of the earl holding the purse-strings that had him looking so thoughtful.

The upper servants gathered just inside the doorway: the butler, the housekeeper and a gentleman in a sombre suit who could have been anything from a parson to a land steward. They must all have expectations. The old earl had proved generous to her over the past many years, so why not to his servants? Though, in truth, on meeting him, she had not liked him one little bit. There had been an air of maliciousness about him.

She was relieved they were not related. She really was.

But if he left the school a small sum of money, an annuity, or a lump sum, it would be a blessing for which she would be suitably grateful, no matter her personal feelings. She put her book on the table at her elbow and folded her hands in her lap, trying not to look hopeful.

But where was the earl?

Ah, here he came, last but definitely not least. He prowled into the room, looking far more sartorially splendid than the dandified Jeffrey. Perhaps it was his size. Or the sheer starkness of a black coat against the white of his cravat. The room certainly seemed much smaller upon his entrance. And even a little airless.

His hard gaze scanned the room, missing nothing. Indeed, she had the feeling his eyes kept on moving until he discovered her whereabouts. He looked almost relieved, as if he feared she might have *loped off*, as Sally's cockney coachman would have said.

Ignoring the group at the hearth, he swung one of the plain wooden chairs near her window seat around and sat astride it. Arms across the back, he fixed the solicitor with a grim stare. 'Get on with it, then, man.'

The fussy little solicitor tugged at his neckcloth, then

broke the seal on a rolled document. He spread it out on the desk. 'This being the last—'

'No need to read all the curlicues and periods,' the earl interrupted. 'Just give us the details.'

'Yes, my lord.' He took a deep breath. 'Basically, the title goes to you, but all the unentailed income goes to Miss Wilding on condition that she marry within the year.'

The earl's gaze, steel hard beneath lowered brows, cut to her face. A muscle jumped in his jaw.

What had the solicitor said? No, she knew what he had said. But what did it mean? The unentailed income?

'There are ten guineas for Manners, five for Mrs Davis and another ten for Ragwell for his excellent stewardship this past many years.'

The servants mumbled and sounded pleased. They shuffled out of the room at the solicitor's wave of a hand.

Mrs Hampton put a hand to her throat. 'What about my son? And Jeffrey.'

'It is my understanding that the late earl passed on any personal trinkets prior to his…his—'

'His death,' the earl growled.

'I got his ring,' Gerald announced, waving his hand about for everyone to see.

'The seal of the Beresfords belongs to me,' the earl said with almost a snarl.

Gerald thumbed his nose. 'This was my grandmother's ring.'

The earl scowled. 'Then where is the seal?'

Gerald shrugged.

'With the earl's effects,' the lawyer said stiffly.

Mrs Hampton's pallor increased. 'I thought there was to be some—' She caught herself.

The earl stood up and looked down at the little solicitor. 'How much of the income from the estate is unentailed?' His voice was soft, but no one in the room could possibly doubt his ire.

'All of it,' the little man squeaked.

The ensuing pause was charged like air before a storm. The earl's gaze shifted to her and the heat in their depths flared bright before he turned back to the lawyer. 'And you permitted this abomination? This dividing of the money from the land? What man in his right mind does such a thing?'

'The late earl was not always rational when it came to the matter of…' His breathless voice tailed off.

'His heir,' the earl said flatly.

'I followed instructions,' the lawyer pleaded.

The earl's silver gaze found hers again. This time it was colder than ice. 'Very clever indeed, Miss Wilding.'

She stiffened. Outrage flooding her with heat. 'I do not understand what this means.' At least she was hoping that what she understood was not what was really happening.

'You got the fortune,' the earl said. 'And I got the expenses.'

Then she had interpreted the lawyer's words correctly. How was this possible?

Beresford turned on the solicitor. 'It can be overturned.'

The man shook his head. 'If Miss Wilding marries within the year, she gets all income from the estate. If not, the money goes to the Crown.' He glanced down at his papers. 'That is, unless she dies before the year is up.'

'What happens if she dies?' the earl asked harshly.

Mary froze in her seat. A shudder took hold of her body. The hairs on the back of her neck rose. The man spoke about her death without the slightest emotion. He was positively evil.

'In that case, it goes to you, or to your heir, currently Mr Jeffrey Beresford, if you predecease him,' the solicitor said. He smiled apologetically at the young man who was watching the earl with icy blue eyes and a very small smile.

The wretch was enjoying the earl's shock.

The earl said something under his breath. It sounded suspiciously like a curse. 'Clearly the man was disordered. What will the courts think of that?'

'My father was not mad,' Mrs Hampton said haughtily. 'Madness does not run in the Beresford family. But you wouldn't know that, since you have had nothing to do with any of us.'

Mary listened to what they were saying, heard them perfectly well, but it all seemed a great distance off. She didn't think she'd taken a breath since the earl had explained. She worked a little moisture into her dry mouth. 'The will requires that I marry in order to inherit?'

The lawyer nodded gravely. 'Indeed. Within the year.'

'Marry who?' she asked.

The earl's mouth curled in a predatory smile. 'That is the question, isn't it?'

Irritated beyond endurance, she rose to her feet. 'You are hardly helpful, sir.'

Forced to rise also, the earl gave her a mirthless smile. 'I thought you said you were clever, Miss Wilding.'

She looked at him blankly.

'He means you must marry him,' Gerald said, scowling. 'But you could marry Jeffrey or me. That would put a spoke in his wheels.'

The earl glowered, but said nothing.

She strode over to the solicitor, whose forehead was beaded with sweat. He pulled out a kerchief and mopped his brow. 'Well, Mr Savary, is it true?' she asked. 'Does the late earl's will require me to marry…' she waved an arm in the earl's direction '…him?'

'It is silent on the issue, Miss Wilding.' He swallowed. 'Under the law, no one can require your marriage to any particular person. However, if you wish to inherit the money, you must marry someone. Perhaps there is someone….' His words tailed off at a low growl from the earl.

Someone. She wanted to laugh. And then she wanted to cry. Someone. She was a schoolteacher. A charity case. And a beanpole to boot. Suddenly a very rich beanpole. She glanced over at the earl. 'No doubt there will be many someones lining up at my door on the morrow.'

The earl glared at her. 'Over my dead body.'

'Or over mine,' she said as the full enormity of it all solidified in her mind.

'There is that,' he agreed.

'Are you saying you intend us to marry?' she asked.

He looked at her for a long moment and she had the feeling that sympathy lurked somewhere in those flat grey eyes, then they hardened to polished steel and she knew she was mistaken. 'Marry to suit my grandfather?' he rasped. 'Not if I can help it.'

She flinched at the harshness of his reply and was glad that he did not see her reaction as he turned at once to the solicitor.

'There must be some loophole you have not considered. Bring those papers to my study. I will review them in detail.'

He strode from the room.

Mrs Hampton gave Mary an accusatory glare. 'Come, Gerald. Jeffrey. We need to talk.' She departed in what appeared to be high dudgeon for some unknown destination with the two young men in tow.

Unsure what else to do, Mary gathered herself to return to her chamber. She needed time to think about this new development. She could only pray the earl would find a way out of the conundrum. She certainly did not want to, nor would she, marry him. Or anyone else for that matter. She'd put away the hopes for a husband many years before

'Er, miss?' Savary said.

'Yes?'

'There was one thing I forgot to mention to his lordship.'

She gazed at him askance. Forgetting to mention something to his lordship sounded like a serious mistake given the earl's present mood. She had not thought the man so stupid. 'What did you forget?'

'He should have let me read things in order.' He fussed with the papers on the desk. 'You must have his permission. Whoever you choose to marry, he must approve.'

A burst of anger ripped through her at being required to bend to the earl's wishes on this or any matter. Especially one so altogether personal. Proving herself to be suitable to work as a teacher, to gain her independence, had taken years of hard work. She wasn't about to give it up on some stranger's whim. 'I suggest you hurry and tell his lordship the good news. I expect it will make him feel a great deal more sanguine about what has happened here today.'

'Do you think so?'

A laugh bubbled up inside her. Hysteria, no doubt. 'I have not the slightest idea of what goes on in his lordship's mind.' That much was certainly true. 'Please excuse me.'

She stalked out of the room. Whether anger improved her sense of direction, or she was getting used to the Abbey, she found her way back to her room without any problem.

The room was chilly. It was the stone walls, she thought, rubbing her arms with her hands, then wrapping her old woollen shawl around her shoulders. Stone walls needed tapestries and blazing fires. She poked at the glowing embers and added more coal. Then she sat on the edge of the bed and stared through the diamond windowpanes. From here she could see the crumbling walls of what had been the abbey church. And beyond it, the sea pounding on rocks.

Finally, she allowed herself to think about what had happened back there in the library.

Oh, heavens! Marry and inherit a fortune? How could this be?

Not for years had she imagined she would ever be married. She was not the kind of woman men took to wife. They liked little dainty things, simpering girls like the ones she helped train at Ladbrook's School. Years ago, the idea of being a wife and a mother had made her heart miss a number of beats. How it had raced when she thought that Mr Allerdyce who had been so attentive, walking her home from church, treating her like a lady of importance, would come up to scratch, until Sally had discovered it was all a front. He was currying favour with Mary in order to get close to one of her pupils. An heiress. His parting words had made it very clear just what he thought of her as a woman. As hurtful and mortifying an experience as it had been, it had forced her to realise she would never be a wife.

Instead, she'd decided that her true vocation lay with her girls, being a teacher. That they were her family. She only had them for a short while, it was true, and their departures were always a wrench, but they were planned. It was not as though they abandoned her, but rather that she sent them out into the world with her blessing.

Now, this stranger, this deceased earl, had somehow engineered her into a marriage to a man she knew nothing about. She swallowed. What would it be liked to be married to such a man? He'd want an heir. Children. A family, just as she'd always dreamed. Her heart raced. Her chest tightened at the thought of being a mother.

It wouldn't be a marriage born of romantic love. It would be for convenience. A practical arrangement such as people from the nobility entered into all of the time. For mutual gain.

He'd hardly been thrilled at the idea of marrying her to obtain what was rightfully his, now had he? He'd looked positively horrified when he realised what the will intended. As if he faced a fate worse than death.

She gripped her hands in her lap to stop them from shaking. Oh, great heavens, please let this all be a bad dream. Please let her wake up and discover it was a nightmare.

But she was awake. And it was horribly real.

What would Sally advise? Don't trust a man like him an inch. Mary could imagine the hard look in her friend's eye and the knowing edge to her voice. She'd been right about Allerdyce. And look at how easily her father had abandoned her after her mother's death. But she couldn't ask Sally for her opinion. She had to rely on her own judgement. And, so far, nothing the earl had said or done made her want to trust him.

Gradually she became calmer, her breathing less shallow, the trembles less pronounced. One thing she knew, she wasn't going to force any man to the altar. Especially not a man like the new earl.

Her heart gave an odd little kick. The sort of pang that someone less practical might describe as disappointment. Not her, though. Let other women have their romantic notions. There was no room for them in her life.

There had to be some way out of this dilemma. And

no doubt the earl would find it. Once more the uneasy prickles of a ghost walking across her skin rippled across her shoulders.

The earl did not come down for dinner, nor did any of the other members of the family. Mary dined in splendid solitude in the dining room and felt like an idiot. Three footman and a butler wasting their time serving her. If they had told her, she could have taken a tray in her room. She finished as quickly as she could and waved off an offer of tea in the drawing room.

'Do you know where the earl is, Manners?'

'In his study, miss.'

'And where is that?'

'In the south wing, miss.' He bowed and withdrew, leaving her none the wiser, but determined to seek him out and try to come to some agreement with him about the future.

Outside the dining room, she turned right, because left was the direction towards the north tower and her room. It stood to reason the south wing must be in the opposite direction, if the corridors were straight. But they weren't.

After a half an hour of criss-crossing various parts of the house, and once arriving back at the dining room, she was ready to give up.

There was one hallway she hadn't explored yet, because it looked narrow and darker than most of the others. She took a deep breath and gave it a try. It had only one door.

A door that was ajar and throwing a wedge of light into the corridor. She peeped through the crack. Aha. She had found the study and the earl. It was a small room, filled with ledgers on shelves rising to the ceiling behind a battered desk covered in papers. The earl was standing with one foot on the brazier in the hearth and his elbow on the mantel, staring into the flames of a merrily burning log fire. His dog lay prone at his feet.

He wasn't an elegant man, his physique was too muscular, his shoulders too broad, his features too large and square, but there was nothing about him to displease the female eye, especially not now when his expression was pensive rather than hard and uncompromising. He looked not much older than she was. Early thirties, perhaps. And not really so very overpowering from this distance.

Her heartbeat picked up speed and her mouth dried. All right, he was really intimidating. Afraid that if she dallied longer she would flee, she tapped sharply on the door.

Both he and the dog looked up. Thankfully, the dog's head dropped back to its paws and its eyes slid closed.

But his lordship was a whole different matter. His whole attention focused on her. She could feel it like a touch on her face. For a moment, a very brief moment, warmth flickered in his eyes as if he was pleased to see her.

His gaze shuttered. His jaw hardened.

Perhaps not, then. Perhaps he had been expecting someone else, for a moment later his lips formed a flat line and his eyes were icy cold. Almost as if he was angry. And yet she did not feel as if his anger was directed at her. It seemed to be turned inwards.

He left the hearth and strode to the middle of the room. 'Miss Wilding,' he said with a stiff bow.

She quelled the urge to run and dipped a curtsy. 'Lord Beresford.'

'Have you once more lost your way? Did you need an escort back to your chamber? Allow me to ring the bell for Manners.'

The irony in his tone was not lost on her even as his

deep voice made her heart jolt, before continuing its rapid knocking against her ribs. Never in her life had she been so nervous around a man. Not that she met very many men in her line of work. Fathers, mostly. In a hurry to depart. Or men pursuing her girls and needing to be kept at bay.

She decided to ignore his jibe and boldly stepped into the room. 'May I have a word with you, please, your lordship?'

He frowned darkly, but gestured for her to sit in the comfortably stuffed chair in front of the desk. He went around and sat on the other side, clearing a space before him, stacking papers and account books to one side. His face was almost entirely in shadow, while she sat in the full light of the lamp. 'How may I be of service?' he asked, politely enough to almost settle her nerves.

'We must discuss this will.'

She sensed him stiffen, though his hands, linked together on the ink-stained wood, remained completely relaxed. He had strong hands with blunt-tipped fingers. Practical hands, bronzed by wind and weather and scarred across the knuckles. Labourer's hands rather than those of a gentleman.

After a small pause, he sighed, a small exhale of air, as if he had been holding his breath. As if she had caught him by surprise. 'I suppose now is as good a time as any.' His voice was expressionless.

'Was the lawyer able to provide any advice on how the terms might be broken?'

'No. You are perfectly safe on that score.'

He thought her a fortune hunter. The desire to bash him over the head with something rose up in her breast.

But how could he not, given the terms of the will?

The chill in the air was palpable. The suspicion. 'Perhaps you would like to explain why the earl…my grandfather,' he choked out the last word, 'would leave the bulk of his fortune to you?'

'He is the benefactor of the school where I grew up and now work. He supported me there when I was orphaned. That is all I know.'

The earl made a soft sound of derision.

She bridled. 'It is true. I swear it.'

His hands flattened on the table. 'Then he was not your lover?'

She gasped. 'You are jesting.'

The silence said he was not.

'How dare you suggest such a thing?' She shot to her feet.

He followed. 'Sit,' he said coldly. 'You wanted to talk. Let us have this out.'

'Not if you are going to insult me.'

'Sit of your own volition or by my will.' His voice was soft but the menace was unmistakable.

She did not doubt for a moment that the brute could overpower her. 'Touch me and I will scream.'

His face darkened. 'And who will come to your aid, do you think?' he asked softly.

No one. She swallowed.

He let go a displeased sigh. 'Please, Miss Wilding. Take your seat. You are right, we have things we need to discuss.'

For a moment she hesitated, but it was foolish to dash off having worked up the courage to face him. She sat and folded her hands in her lap. 'Very well, but do not cast aspersions on my character.'

His gaze didn't waver from her face. 'Look at this from my perspective. I am trying to understand why my grandfather left you his fortune. Lover is an obvious answer.'

Her hackles rose again. She hung on to her anger. 'Isn't

it more likely I did him some favour? Perhaps rescued him from danger.'

He snorted. 'What sort of danger?'

'He could have ridden past Ladbrook's School where I teach one day and been set upon by footpads. Seeing him from the classroom window, I might have charged out to save him with my pupils at my heels. As you know, there is nothing more daunting to the male species than the high-pitched squeals of a gaggle of females, particularly when armed with parasols.'

Oh dear, now where had all that ridiculousness come from? Her stomach tightened. Rarely did she let her tongue run away with her these days. It seemed she needed to get a firmer grip on her anger.

He picked up a quill and twirled it in those strong fingers. Fascinated, she watched the only sign she'd ever seen that he was not completely in control. 'But it didn't happen that way,' he said drily.

'No. But you must admit it is just as plausible as your scenario. He was a very old man.'

'You think to toy with me, Miss Wilding? I can assure you that is a very dangerous game and not one you are equipped to play.'

'I have no idea why he left his money to me in this fashion.'

'Let us hope you do not. If I discover that you are a willing instrument in this plot of his, things will not go well for you.'

The air left her lungs in a rush at the obvious threat. 'I can assure you…'

'You need assure me of nothing. There will be no marriage.'

'You must have done something to deserve so terrible a fate?'

He didn't seem to notice the irony in her tone. 'I drew breath when I was born.' The quill snapped.

She jumped at the sound.

He tossed the two pieces aside.

A shiver ran down her back. She fought her instinct for sympathy. 'A little melodramatic, isn't it?'

'Much like your tale of rescue.'

She frowned. It was time to play the one and only card in her hand and hope it was a trump. 'Why don't I just sign over the money to you? I need only a very little for myself.'

'The perfect solution.'

She let go a sigh of relief. She really had not expected him to see reason so quickly. 'Then I will leave in the morning, once the papers are signed.'

'No.'

'Why not?'

'It can't be done. The money only comes to you if you marry. I will put the best legal minds to work on finding a solution, and in the meantime you will remain here.'

'I can't stay. I am expected back at the school.'

'Then tell me what connection you are to the earl.' His fingers drummed an impatient tattoo. 'His by-blow, perhaps?' he said flatly.

'I beg your pardon?' She stared into the shadows, trying to see his expression, trying to see if he was jesting, while her mind skittered this way and that. 'You think me the late earl's daughter?'

'You look like a Beresford.'

He thought they were family? Her chest squeezed. Her heart struggled to beat. The air in the room seemed suddenly thick, too dense to breathe. That had been her first thought, also. Her wild hope, but not in the way he was suggesting. Good Lord, did he think the earl was requiring his grandson to marry his aunt? Technically incest, even if he carried not a drop of Beresford blood. 'That is disgusting.'

'Exactly.'

She leaped to her feet and made for the door. 'I will leave first thing in the morning.'

Before she could reach the door, he was there, one hand holding it shut while he gazed down into her face. For a big man, he moved very quickly. And surprisingly quietly.

Judging by the tightness of his mouth and the flash of steel in his eyes, he was not pleased. 'You, Miss Wilding, are not going anywhere until I say you may.'

She shrank back against the door. 'You have no authority over me.'

'Apparently, I do.'

She gasped. 'What are you talking about?'

'According to the solicitor, you are my ward.'

Chapter Three

'Utter nonsense.'

'Savary informed me that he told you that you need my permission to wed.'

'That does not make you my guardian.'

'No, but since I have taken over the responsibilities of the earldom, *that* makes me your guardian.'

'The late earl was not my guardian. I have no need of a guardian, I have lived by my own efforts for years.'

'You have lived off this estate.' He pointed to a ledger on the desk. 'Each quarter a sum of money was paid to a Mrs Sally Ladbrook for your keep and education. A very princely sum, I might add.' His gaze dropped to her chest, which she realised was expanding and contracting at a very rapid rate to accommodate her breathing.

His eyes came back to her face and his jaw hardened. 'And then you show up here in rags hoping for more.'

Damn him and his horrid accusations. Her hand flashed out. He caught her wrist. His fingers were like an iron band around her flesh. 'You'll need to be quicker to catch me off guard.'

'What kind of person do you think I am?'

His expression darkened. 'A Beresford.' He cast her hand aside.

Never had she heard such hatred directed at a single word. It must have tasted like acid on his tongue.

'You are a Beresford.'

His eyes widened. 'I doubt there are many who would agree. Certainly not me.'

'Then you should not be inheriting the title.'

'You are changing the subject again, Miss Wilding.'

The subject was as slippery as a bucket of eels. 'I have had quite enough of your accusations.'

'Are you saying you didn't come here seeking money?'

She coloured. 'No. Well, yes, for the school. It needs a new roof.' Among many other things it needed. 'But I have never met the earl before last night. And there certainly have been no vast sums of money coming to Ladbrook's or to me.'

He glanced across the room at his desk, at the account book, clearly not believing a word.

A rush of tears burned behind her eyes, because she knew it could not be true, unless… No, she would not believe it. 'I need to go back to the school. I need to speak to Mrs Ladbrook.'

He stared into her face, his gaze so intense, she wanted to look away. But she couldn't. Didn't dare, in case he thought she was lying.

Why did it matter what he thought?

Yet she would not stand down. Once more there was heat in that grey gaze, like molten silver, and the warmth seemed to set off a spark in her belly that flashed up to her face. Her cheeks were scalding, her heart pounding against the wall of her chest as if she had run a great race.

Slowly his hand moved from the door to her shoulder, stroked down her arm, his fingers inexorably sliding over muscle and bone as if he would learn the contours of her arm.

His expression was grim, as if this was not something he wanted to do at all, yet he did not stop.

She tipped her face upwards, her lips parted to protest... Only to accept the soft brush of his warm dry velvety lips. Little thrills raced through her stomach. Chased across her skin.

And then his mouth melded to hers, his tongue stroking the seam of her mouth, the sweet sensation melting her bones until she parted her lips on a gasp of sheer bliss and tasted his tongue with her own. Feverishly, their mouths tasted each other while she clung to those wide shoulders for support and his hands at her waist held her tight against his hard body.

She could feel the thunder of his heart where his chest pressed against her breasts, hear the rush of her blood in her veins. It was shocking. And utterly mesmerising.

On an oath, he stepped back, breaking all contact, shock blazing in his eyes.

The thrills faded to little more than echoes of the sensations they had been a moment ago. What on earth was she doing? More to the point, what was he doing? 'How dare you, sir?' she said, pulling her shawl tightly around her.

At that he gave a short laugh. 'How dare I what?'

'Kiss me.'

'You kissed me.'

Had she? She didn't think she had, but she wasn't exactly sure what had happened. Unless... 'Don't think to force me into marrying you by ruining my reputation. You see, that kind of thing doesn't matter to me.'

His eyes widened. 'So that is your plan, is it?'

'Oh, you really are impossible.'

For a long moment his gaze studied her face, searching

for who knew what. 'I will discover what it is my grandfather put you up to, you know. I will stop you any way I can. I have more resources at my disposal than you can possibly imagine.'

She could imagine all right. She could imagine all sorts of things when it came to this man. Resources weren't the only thing chasing through her mind. And those thoughts were the worst of all: the thoughts of his kisses and the heat of his body. 'The best thing you could do is kill me off. Then all your troubles will be over.'

The grey of his eyes turned wintry. His expression hardened. 'Don't think I haven't thought of it.'

Her breath left her in a rush. Her stomach dropped away and she felt cold all over. She ducked under his arm, pulled at the door handle and was out the door in a flash and running down the corridor.

'Miss Wilding, wait,' he called after her.

She didn't dare stop. Her heart was beating far too fast, the blood roaring in her head, for her to think clearly. But now he had shown his hand, she would be on her guard.

After a night filled with dreams Mary couldn't quite recall—though she suspected from how hot she felt that they had something to do with the earl and his kiss—she awoke to find Betsy setting a tray of hot chocolate and freshly baked rolls beside the bed.

'What time is it?'

'Nine o'clock, miss.'

So late? How could she have slept so long and still feel desperately tired? Perhaps because she'd been in such a turmoil when she went to bed. Perhaps because she could not get those dark words out of her mind. *Don't think I haven't thought of it.*

'The weather is set to be fair, miss.' Betsy knelt to rake the coals in the fire. 'Warm for this time of year.'

Mary hopped out of bed and went to the window. 'So it is. I think I will go for a walk.' She dressed with her usual efficiency in her best gown.

Betsy rose to her feet. 'The ruins are very popular with visitors in the summer,' she said, watching Mary reach behind her to button her gown with a frown of disapproval. 'Very old they are. Some say the are haunted by the old friars who were killed by King Henry.'

Mary tucked a plain linen scarf in the neck of her bodice and picked up her brush. 'Superstitious nonsense.' She brushed hard. 'Have you ever seen a ghost?' She glanced past her own reflection at the maid, who looked a little pale.

'No, miss.' She gave a little shiver. 'And I've worked here for three years. But I don't go out there at night.'

Mary coiled her hair around her fingers and reached for her pins. 'The ruins sound fascinating. I will be sure to take a look.' She wished she had used her time in the library the previous day looking at a map of the area instead of reading romantic poetry.

'Would miss like me to fix her hair?' Betsy asked, looking a little askance at the plain knot Mary favoured. 'I can do it up fancy like Mrs Hampton's maid does, if you like. I have been practising on the other girls.'

Mary heard a note of longing in the girl's voice. 'Why, Betsy, do you have ambitions to become a lady's maid?'

Betsy coloured, but her eyes shone. 'Yes, miss. I would like that above all. My brother works down Beresford's tin mine. If I had a better paying job, he could go to school.'

Her mine. Or it would be if she married. 'Is it a bad place to work?'

Betsy looked embarrassed. 'It's hard work, but the manager, Mr Trelawny, is a fair man. Not like some.'

'How old is your brother?'

'Ten, miss. Works alongside my Da, he does. Proud as a peacock.'

The thought of such a small boy working in the mine did not sit well in her stomach. But she knew families needed the income. As the mine owner, if she really was a mine owner, she could make some changes. To do that, she had to marry. And then the mine would belong to her husband and not to her. It was all such a muddle. Being a schoolteacher was one thing, but this…this was quite another. Besides, it was easy to see that if she married the earl, he would rule the roost. He was not the type of man to listen to a woman.

What she needed was some sensible counsel to see her through this mess. While Sally Ladbrook might not be the warmest of people, she had a sensible head on her shoulders. 'Perhaps you can help me with my hair another day. That will be all for now.'

How strange it sounded, giving out orders to another person in such a manner, but Betsy seemed to take it as natural, bobbing her curtsy and leaving right away.

Oh dear, Mary hoped the girl wouldn't be too disappointed that Mary could not offer her a position, but she really couldn't stay. Not when Lord Beresford considered her death a plausible option.

Besides, she desperately needed to speak to Sally about the other matter the earl had raised. The money. There had to be a plausible explanation, other than misappropriation. The earl was wrong to suggest it.

She sat down and drank the chocolate and ate as many of the rolls as she could manage. The last two she wrapped in a napkin and tucked in her reticule to eat on the journey.

She counted out her small horde of coins and was relieved to discover she had enough to get her back to Wiltshire on a stagecoach. After packing her valise and bundling up in her winter cloak and bonnet, she headed for a side door she'd noticed in her wanderings. She just hoped she could find it again in the maze of passageways and stairs.

After a couple of wrong turns, she did indeed find it again. A quick survey assured her no one was around to see her departure. She twisted the black-iron ring attached to the latch and tugged. The heavy door, caught by the wind, yanked the handle out of her hands and slammed against the passage wall with a resounding bang.

Her heart raced in her chest. Had anyone heard? Would they come running? Rather than wait to see, she stepped outside and, after a moment's struggle, closed the door behind her.

She really hadn't expected the wind to be so fierce. She pulled up her hood and tightened the strings, staring around her at crumbling walls and stone arches overgrown with weeds. The jagged walls looked grim and ghostly against the leaden sky, though no doubt it would look charmingly antiquated on a sunny day.

Clutching her valise, she picked her way through the ruins, heading north, she hoped. A green sward opened up before her. Not the cliffs and the sea. In the distance, a rider on a magnificent black horse galloped across the park, a dog loping along behind.

The earl. It could be no one else. Hatless, his open greatcoat flapping in the wind, he looked like the apocalyptic horseman of Death. She shivered.

No, that was giving him far too much in the way of mystical power. He was simply a man who wanted his birthright. And she had somehow managed to get in the way. The thought didn't make her feel any better.

Realising she must have turned south, she swiftly marched in the other direction, around the outside of the ruins, up hill this time, which made more sense if she was headed for cliffs.

The wind increased in strength, buffeting her ears, whipping the ribbons of her bonnet in her face and billowing her cloak around her. She gasped as it tore the very breath from her throat. It would be a vigorous walk to St Ives and no mistake.

She licked her lips and was surprised by the sharp tang of salt on her tongue. From the sea, she supposed. Interesting. She hadn't thought of the salt being carried in the air. Head down, she forged on, looking for a path along the cliff top. The upward climb became steeper, so rocky underfoot she had to watch where she placed each step or risk a tumble. She paused to take stock of her progress.

A few feet in front of her the ground disappeared and all she could see ahead of her was grey surging waves crested with spume. It was lucky she had stopped when she did.

But where was the path mentioned by Gerald? She scanned the ground in both directions and was able to make out a very faint track meandering along the cliff top. It looked more like a track for sheep than for people.

The wind seemed intent of holding her back, but she battled into it, following the track frighteningly close to the edge.

The strings of her hood gave way against a battering gust and her bonnet blew off, bouncing against her back, pulling against her throat. Strands of hair tore free and whipped at her face, stinging her eyes. A roar like thunder rolled up from below.

She leaned out to peer through the spray into the boiling churning water. Hell's kitchen must surely look and sound like this. As each wave drew back with a grumbling growl, she glimpsed the jagged rocks at the base of the cliff and off to her left a rocky cove with a small sandy beach.

Out in the distance, the sky and sea became one vast grey mist. The world had never felt this big in the little Wiltshire village of Sarum. She leaned into the wind and felt its pure natural strength holding her weight. She laughed. She couldn't help it. She had never experienced such wildness.

Something nudged into her back.

She windmilled her arms to regain her balance. Her valise went flying over the cliff. And the ground fell from beneath her feet.

She screamed.

Chapter Four

An iron band of an arm closed around her waist at the same moment her feet left the ground. She hung suspended above the raging sea for what felt like hours, but could only be seconds. That arm twisted her around and plonked her down. Not on the ground, but on a pair of hard muscled thighs gripping a saddle.

Teeth chattering, heart racing, she gazed up into the earl's hard face. With a click of his tongue he backed the horse away from the edge. Was he mad? They could all have gone over the cliff.

Clear of the edge, he halted the horse's backward progress and wheeled around so they were no longer facing the sea. Further along the cliff, a shepherd, crook in hand, was running towards them. The earl waved, an everything-is-fine acknowledgement, which it wasn't, and the shepherd stopped running and waved back.

'Put me down,' she demanded.

A grunt was all the answer he gave.

She felt his thighs move beneath her as he clicked his tongue. The horse headed down hill. Back the way she had come. The urge to protest caused her hands to clench.

'Are you mad?' she yelled over the wind. 'I almost went over the edge.'

His cold gaze flicked over her face. He took a deep shuddering breath as if to control some strong emotion. Fear? More likely anger. His next words confirmed it. 'It would have served you right, my girl. What the devil did you think you were doing?'

She shoved the annoying lengths of hair out of her face. Dash it, she would not lie. 'Walking to St Ives. Now I have lost my bag.'

'You are lucky that was all you lost,' he murmured like a threat in her ear.

He meant she could have lost her life. She swallowed and glanced back towards the headland, where the shepherd, a hand shading his eyes, was still watching them. It would have been the answer to all the earl's problems if she had gone over that cliff. She could have sworn something nudged her in the back. Had he changed his mind at the last moment?

A cold hand clawed at her stomach. She glanced at his grim expression. He'd been angry about that will. She could well imagine him taking matters into his own hands. But murder? A shiver slid down her back.

The further from the cliff they got, the less the sea and the wind roared in her ears. She lifted her chin and met his chilly gaze. 'You have no right to keep me here.'

'I have every right. I am your guardian.'

'Only in your mind,' she muttered.

He stiffened. 'You need a *keeper* if you think it is safe to walk along that cliff top.'

Now he was pretending he minded if she fell. Why? So she wouldn't guess his intentions? It certainly wasn't because he cared about what happened to her. The cold in her stomach spread to her chest. She readied herself to jump down and run for her life.

He hissed in a breath, as if in some sort of pain. 'In heaven's name, stop wriggling.'

'Then put me down.'

'I'll put you down when I am good and ready.'

The big horse pranced and kicked up his back legs. She instinctively grabbed for his lordship's solid shoulders. He tensed and she heard him curse softly under his breath. He pulled the horse to a stop and, putting an arm around her waist, lowered her to the ground. He dismounted beside her.

'No need to interrupt your ride,' she said brightly. 'I can find my own way.'

He grasped her upper arm in an iron grip. Not hard enough to hurt, but there was no mistaking she could not break free. 'How did you get out of the house without anyone seeing you?'

She gasped. 'What are you talking about?'

'I left orders that you were not to leave.'

'Orders you have no right to give?'

'Don't test my patience, Miss Wilding. I will have no hesitation in dealing with you as you deserve.'

She swallowed hard. 'Killing me off, you mean?' Oh, no. She couldn't believe she had just blurted that out.

He released her as if she was hot to the touch. His eyes flashed with an emotion she could not read—pain, perhaps? More likely disgust given the hard set to his jaw. 'I assure you, when I want your death, it will not occur in front of witnesses.'

So he had seen the shepherd and thought better of it. She tried not to shiver at the chill in his voice. 'I will keep that in mind, my lord. Thank you for the forewarning.'

He stared at her, his lips twitching, his eyes gleaming

as if he found something she had said amusing. 'You are welcome, Miss Wilding. Come along, I will escort you back to the house.'

So now they were to pretend nothing had happened? That he hadn't seriously thought about pushing her off a cliff? Perhaps she should pretend she was joking about thinking he wanted her dead. She quelled a shiver. She hated this feeling of fear. Anger at her weakness rose up in her throat, making it hard to breathe or think, when she should be finding a way to beat him at his own game. She gave him a look of disdain. 'Did no one tell you it isn't polite to creep up on a person?'

'I was riding a very large stallion over rocky terrain. That hardly counts as creeping.'

'I didn't hear you over the noise of the sea. Surely you could tell?'

He gave her a look designed to strike terror into the heart of the most intrepid individual. 'I had other things on my mind.'

Such as pushing her over the edge. She began striding down hill. Unlike most men of her acquaintance, he easily kept pace, the horse following docilely, while the dog bounded around them. Surprisingly, his steps matched hers perfectly. On the rare occasion when she'd walked alongside a gentleman—well, back from the village with the young man who delivered the mail—she'd had to shorten her stride considerably because the young man was a good head shorter than she. The earl, on the other hand, towered above her. A rather unnerving sensation.

All her sensations with regard to this man were unnerving. The fluttery ones when he kissed her, the shivery ones when she felt fear and the one she was feeling now, a strange kind of appreciation for his handsome face and athletic build when she should be absolutely terrified. It seemed that whereas her mind was as sharp as a needle, her body was behaving like a fool.

It was this silence between them making her react this way. It needed filling to distract her from these wayward thoughts and feelings.

'The Abbey is an extraordinary house, isn't it?' She gestured towards the sprawling mish-mash of wings and turrets.

His eyes narrowed. 'Highly impractical. Ridiculously expensive to run. It should be torn down.'

Aghast, she stopped, staring up at his implacable face. 'But think of all the history that would be lost.'

'A history of murderous brigands.'

'Rather fitting, don't you think?' The words were out before she could stop them.

He gave her a look askance, as if he found her a puzzle he would like to solve. Well, she had solved his puzzle. She knew exactly what was on his mind. Her murder. A bone-deep shudder trembled in her bones.

They reached the ruins near her tower. He stopped, his gaze fixed on the door through which she had left. 'You came through there.'

It wasn't a question. She shrugged and kept walking.

He caught her arm and halted her. 'Give me your word you will not try to leave again without my permission.'

'You have no authority over my actions. None at all.'

He let go a sigh. 'Very well, that door and all the others will from now on be locked and barred.' One corner of his mouth curled up, and if his voice had not been so harsh, she might have thought it an attempt at a smile. 'You might as well use it to go back inside.'

She pulled her arm free. Anything not to have to spend any more time in his company. Her runaway heart was going to knock right through the wall of her chest. She headed for the door.

'Miss Wilding,' he said, softly.

She turned back.

'Be in the library at eleven o'clock.'

'Why?'

'There is a funeral to arrange.'

Why would she need to be involved in family arrangements? Unless he still thought she was some sort of relation. The very idea made anger ball up in her chest, because while she had longed for it desperately, it wasn't the case. And that was just as foolish as the way her emotions seemed to see-saw around him.

She shot him a glare as he stood there, waiting for her obedience, one hand on a hip, the other gripping the horse's reins, watching her with those unnerving grey eyes as if she was a recalcitrant child.

With no other alternative in sight, she lifted the latch and went in.

As custom dictated, the ladies were not expected to attend the funeral. Mary also refused to attend the reception arranged for afterwards. She wasn't family and there had been quite enough speculation about her relationship to the deceased earl. She had no wish to run the gauntlet of local gossip. Besides, she had nothing suitable to wear now her valise was gone. Reluctantly the earl had agreed.

Heady with triumph at winning the argument, Mary had settled herself in the library with Maria Edgeworth's *Belinda*. Romantic nonsense, Sally would have called it, but it had a depth to it, too, that Mary found fascinating.

'What are you reading?'

Startled at the closeness of the voice, Mary looked up with a gasp. The earl, dark and predatory, loomed over her looking like a dark angel. Much as he had looked at his grandfather's bedside. Perhaps not quite as grim.

'Shouldn't you be at the reception?' she asked sweetly.

'It is over.'

A hot flush travelled up her face as she realised that evening was drawing in rapidly. The afternoon had flown by in unaccustomed idleness. She was already straining to see the words on the page, but she'd been too engrossed to get up and light a candle. She closed the book. 'I didn't realise how late it was.'

He glanced down at the cover. 'A novel. I should have guessed.'

The back of her neck prickled because he was standing so close. Because once more his cologne invaded her nostrils and recalled to mind her disgraceful response to his lips on hers. Her body warmed in the most uncomfortable way at the memory. How could she think about his kiss after he had practically dropped her off the cliff earlier in the day? Her mind must be disordered.

'Was there some reason for your interruption?' She gave him the frosty glance that had new girls quaking in their slippers.

It troubled him not one whit, it seemed. Indeed he didn't seem to notice the chill in her voice at all, since a flicker of amusement passed across his face. Hah! She should be glad he found her entertaining.

He held out a note. 'The post brought you a letter.'

Oh, now she felt bad for being rude.

He moved away to give her privacy and began browsing the shelves on the far side of the room.

She frowned at the handwriting. She had not expected Sally to write after such a short time. Sending mail such a distance was expensive. Now she would owe the earl for the cost of the postage and she had little enough money in her purse. She broke the seal and spread open the paper.

For a moment, she could not quite believe the words she was reading. She read the cold little missive again, more slowly.

Miss Wilding,
Ladbrook School is now closed as ordered by the
Earl of Beresford and the property is sold. I wish
you all success in your new life. Yours, Sally Lad-
brook.

Closed? How could the school be closed? Why would he do such a thing? How could he? Anger trembled through her with the force of an earthquake. The paper shivered like an aspen in her fingers. A band tightened around her chest as the enormity of what had happened became clear. She was homeless.

Abandoned by her only friend in the world. It hurt. Badly.

The earl, who was leaning against the shelves leafing idly through a book, looked up from the pages to meet her gaze. 'Bad news?'

The wretch. 'Bad?' She rose to her feet. 'You take away my livelihood and then ask if it is bad?' She gave a bitter laugh.

He straightened, frowning. 'What are you talking about?'

'You know very well what I am talking about.' Her voice shook with the effect of roiling anger. Everything inside her chest rocked and heaved. Her ribs ached from the force of it. For a moment it seemed she might never breathe again. But she did. And words followed. 'You need not think this will stop me from leaving.' She crumpled the note in her fist and threw it at him. Incredibly, he plucked it out of the air.

She marched for the door, not knowing where she was going, but knowing she could not remain in the same room with him without trying to do him a mischief.

'Wait!' he commanded.

She didn't stop, but once again he beat her to the door, holding it closed with his hand above her head, while she pulled on the handle. She swung around, glaring up at him. 'Open this door.'

He glanced down at the note. 'This school has no relevance now.'

'No relevance?' She wanted to hit him for his stupidity. Instead she dodged around him and went to the window, putting as much distance between them as possible. 'The school was my home.'

She turned to stare out of the window, wanting to bang her fist against the glass, break through it to freedom, like a trapped sparrow in a garden room.

Her stomach fell away. Even if she did, she had nowhere to go. No home. Not even a forwarding address for Sally. Was that his doing, too? Or did Sally blame her for the loss of her school? The selfish, horrid man.

Moisture burned in the back of her throat and pushed its way up behind her eyes. She bowed her head against the pressure and swallowed hard. Tried to regain her composure

The earl drew closer, his gaze puzzled. 'Miss Wilding, surely it is not as bad as all that? You will have enough money to buy a hundred schools when you marry.'

'Marry who?' She whirled around and stared at him. Was that guilt she saw in his face? Guilt because he'd taken away all her options as well as her only friend.

Or guilt because he had decided that marrying her was preferable to her death? Or guilt because he planned…?

A sob pushed its way up her throat. Tears welled up, hovering on her lashes, blurring her vision. She dashed them away, clinging to her anger. 'Ladbrook's is the only home I remember. Everything I owned was there. My books. My mementos from my pupils. Why? Why did you have to interfere?' She struck out at his chest with her fist.

The next moment she found her face pressed to his wide shoulder, her hand gripping his lapel and supressed sobs shaking her body.

'Mary,' he said, his voice achingly soft. A large hand landed warm on her back, tentatively at first and then patting gently. 'I will have your property recovered, if that is what disturbs you.'

The urge to give in to her overwhelming longing for someone who cared battled with her good sense and won. She leaned against that broad chest, felt his heat and his power, and the steady rhythm of his heart as he held her close.

For a moment, she lost all sense of self. Forgot it was his fault things had come to this pass and revelled in the sense of being protected.

'So, this is how it is.' The angry voice came from the doorway. 'What a cur you really are.'

'Gerald,' the earl said, loosening his hold and looking over her shoulder. 'Could you be any more *de trop*?' The sarcasm was back and the raspy drawl.

Apparently oblivious to the threat those soft words contained, Gerald stomped across the room.

Mary pulled away, turning her face to the window while she groped for a handkerchief. The earl planted himself between her and the intruder who was clearly bound and determined to have his say. 'Miss Wilding is distressed. Please leave.'

'Distressed?' Gerald said. 'Aye, I can believe it. And what did you do to bring her to tears?'

'It is none of your business,' the earl replied coldly. 'Go away.'

Mary blew her nose and dabbed at her eyes. A few deep breaths would set her to rights, but she needed to be alone, away from the disturbing presence of the earl, to work out what Sally's letter really meant for her future. 'Please, excuse me, gentlemen.'

The earl put out a hand as if he would stop her, then let it fall. She made for the door and Gerald stepped aside to let her pass as if he barely saw her. His gaze was fixed on the earl. 'You don't belong here, Bane Beresford. We all know what you are. A bloody coalminer stealing a title from the rightful heir.'

Mary felt her mouth drop open in shock. She glanced back at the earl. His body radiated tension. His fists at his sides clenched and released. His dark gaze shifted from Gerald to her and back and then he leaned against the window frame folding his arms over his chest with a cynical curl to his lips. 'And what do you intend to do about it, bantling?'

Colour crept into the younger man's face, still set in an expression of defiance. Did he plan to fight with the earl? He would be badly outmatched.

'Gentlemen, please. This is hardly the way for members of a family to behave to each other,' she said.

Both men threw her angry looks.

Clearly she wasn't helping. But then, what did she know of families? Or friends for that matter? Once more, thoughts of Sally's callous note made her stomach fall away. The hard hot lump she had managed to swallow while wrapped in the earl's arms returned with a vengeance. Tears. A river of them, if the burning behind her eyes was any indication. 'Please excuse me,' she said, ducking her head as she ran for her chamber and privacy.

No one, least of all the earl, was going to see her dissolve into a blob of self-pity.

It took a good four hours before she gained her composure. First there had been tears, then anger at the earl, followed by a new emptiness. It had always been there, the small cold kernel of knowledge that she was unwanted, but as the years had passed, she'd formed an attachment for Sally Ladbrook. First as her pupil and employee, and more recently as a friend. Until today, she hadn't realised how much she relied on Sally's advice and counsel, on that one constant in her life. Now, thanks to the earl, she was completely alone.

It was terrifying.

But why? Why had Sally abandoned her? Was she really so unnecessary to anyone? Or had the earl offered an irresistible lure? If so, then she would never forgive him.

With a final sniff, she rose from the bed and went to the glass on the dressing table. Yes, her eyes were red rimmed and bloodshot. Her cheeks were chapped and sore, and her nose looked like a cherry popped into the middle of her face.

But the storm was over. She was drained of all emotion. Empty.

And that was how she would proceed from here. From now on, she would take no one at face value. Trust no one and rely only on herself.

She straightened her shoulders and went to the basin to bath her face. Her stomach grumbled. She vaguely remembered Betsy knocking on the door, reminding her of dinner and finally going away. She could not have gone to dinner then, hating the thought of anyone seeing her in this state.

There were the rolls she had purloined earlier. She retrieved them from the dresser drawer where she had tucked them after her escapade on the cliff. Hard as rocks, but edible if washed down with water. She munched slowly on the stale bread and considered her options. Find Sally and let her explain what had happened? Or consign her to the devil and set her feet on a new path?

If only she had some money of her own, then she would not need anyone's help. She did have money under this will, but only if she married.

Marriage. A home. A family of her own. How shining and bright the dream had been in her young lonely heart. Mr Allerdyce had shattered those dreams of a knight in shining armour coming to her rescue and falling at her feet. In reality, the best she could ever hope for was a widower with a gaggle of children looking for a cheap housekeeper.

Now, the only candidate seemed to be the earl. Her heart gave an odd little thump, as if it welcomed the idea. But he didn't welcome it. She could not imagine being married to man as cold as ice, who was forced up to the mark. She'd likely find herself dead in a week. Or rather someone else would find her dead. Oh, no. Now that really was the kind of melodrama she discouraged in her pupils.

She mentally shook her head. It was time to move on. The earl might think he'd won by taking away her only sanctuary, but she had more gumption than to give in at the first obstacle. And the fact that he hadn't yet realised it was to her advantage.

Something crashed above her head. She jumped to her feet, looking up. She hadn't known there was a room above hers. Whatever had fallen continued to bang several more times as if it was bouncing and rolling across the floor.

And then it stopped.

How strange.

A servant at work had dropped something, perhaps? She tried to imagine what it might be. Large and heavy and seemingly round.

A low moan echoed through her chamber, then a shriek so piercing she put her hands over her ears. What on earth was going on up there? What on earth would make anyone cry out in such a dreadful way? Were they hurt? There was no other explanation. And if they were in that much pain, they needed help. Urgently.

She wrapped her woollen shawl around her shoulders, then picked up a candlestick to the sound of what now sounded like rattling chains and opened her door.

Then nothing. Silence prevailed. It was over, whatever it was. She went back inside and started to close her door. A bang. Another yell. Something heavy dropped on a toe?

Such a racket, she could not ignore it. She left her room and started up the circular staircase beyond her door. The air out here was strangely cold. As far as she remembered, it was usually the same temperature outside her door as in the rest of the house, now it chilled her cheeks. Had someone opened a window? Her candle was certainly guttering in what must be a draught.

The stairs wound upwards around a central column of fluted grey granite. The way ahead was only visible as far as the next tight curve and the steps were worn into smooth grooves by centuries of feet. They became narrower the higher she went. Clutching her candle in one hand, she put the other on the wall for balance. The stone was ice to the touch.

Now someone was sobbing. Much as she had sobbed earlier. Someone mocking her? Oh, that would be mortifying. She had assumed she was completely alone.

The crying stopped. Footsteps tapped across stone.

A warm breath grazed the back of her neck. Someone following? She whirled around. One foot slipped. She teetered on the step, clutching at the wall, desperately hanging on to her candle. Her heart was thundering like the hooves of a runaway horse. 'Hello?'

There was no one behind her, but she had not imagined that warm rush of air. Indeed, there was no cold draught at all now.

Sweat formed on her brow and upper lip.

Fear.

What did she have to fear?

Then she remembered Gerald's ghoulish tale of a lady in white. She didn't believe in ghosts. She didn't. There had to be a perfectly logical explanation.

She chuckled, laughing at her fears to give herself courage. The sound bounced off the walls and it was several seconds before it died away. The reason the sounds she had heard were so strange: echoes. That must be it. A distortion of normal sounds in the room above.

She rounded the next curve and found a landing much like the one outside her chamber door. Two of the walls had arrow loops high above her head. The source of the cold breeze? If so, there was nothing now. The other two walls had doors set within stone arches, much like the one she had taken to the outside earlier in the day. The first latch she tried didn't budge. The second yielded grudgingly outwards to her pull, requiring all her strength to push it back against the wall. About to step inside, a shadow fell across the floor. A figure surged towards her.

Her heart stopped. She screamed and leaped back.

'Good God, Miss Wilding, what on earth is the matter?'

The earl, looking positively demonic in the flickering light of her candle, was staring at her as if she was mad. She pressed a hand to her breastbone, to quiet her rapid breathing. 'I heard a noise.' She swallowed. 'Why are you here?'

His brows climbed his forehead. 'You may hold the money in thrall, but surely I am entitled to go where I wish in my own home.'

The bitterness in his voice stung. It sounded like righteous indignation, as if he blamed her for this business with the will. He was trying to distract her from the noises she'd heard.

She peered into the room behind him, lifting her candle high. The chamber was completely empty. No sign of anything that could have rolled across the wooden planks. Not even any dust on the floor to show where it had been. 'Is this some sort of cruel game, then? Something to frighten me?' And, if so, to what purpose?

He tilted his head, regarding her intently. 'If you were scared, why did you come up here?'

'I heard a cry for help.'

'Quite the little Samaritan.'

'Hardly little.'

His eyes flashed amusement.

Was he mocking her?

'As you see, there is no one here but me,' he said in reasonable tones. 'Exactly what did you hear?'

If he didn't do it, he must have heard it. Why was he pretending he had not. 'Something rolling. Rattling chains, followed by a shriek. Right above my chamber. And now there is no one here but you.'

His eyes narrowed. 'You sound almost disappointed. Have the servants been telling you ghost stories?'

'Gerald said something about the White Lady at breakfast, but that has nothing to do with it. I know what I heard. You must have heard it, too.'

'I heard a noise,' he admitted grudgingly. 'Someone calling out.'

'It was more than that. Something bounced across the floor.' She gave him a suspicious look.

He gave a shrug. 'Perhaps it was my footsteps you heard.'

'And the chains rattling?'

He pulled a bunch of keys from his pocket. 'I used these to open the door. The stone walls must have magnified the sound.'

'It is not doing it now.'

'You would only hear it from below,' he said in the patient tones of an adult to a foolish child. She knew exactly what it was, because she had used it on many similar occasions. But she was not a child. She knew what she had heard.

Perhaps she had let Gerald's stories colour her imagination, but she had heard something. 'Who was it who called out, then?'

'Again, it might be a trick of the way this place is constructed. Sound travelling through stone from somewhere else.'

He spoke almost as if he was trying to convince himself.

'But if you heard someone call out and came to see, how did you get up here so quickly? Why didn't I see you on the stairs ahead of me?'

'I didn't come up the stairs. I came across the battlements from the other tower. I was going down when…'
He hesitated. 'I decided to take a look in here.'

The outside door opening and closing would account
for the cold wind rushing past her. Perhaps it was only
footsteps and keys echoing off stone walls she had heard.
But it did not explain the shrieks and the moans or what
had made him close himself inside an obviously empty
room.

She bit her tongue. To say more would be to sound hysterical. He was deliberately making her feel like a fool.

'Then in the absence of anyone needing help, I suppose
I should go back down,' she said finally.

He held out his arm. 'Allow me to escort you.' Master-
fully, he took her candle and helped her down the stairs
as if she was made of china. It made her feel strangely
feminine—not something she should be feeling around
him. He was just being polite. But even that seemed out of
character. Perhaps he was trying to allay her suspicions.

Not for a moment did she think his explanations held
water.

At her chamber door he paused, looking down at her.
The air thickened and heated around them. Oh, no! Was
he going to kiss her again? Her heart thudded wildly in
anticipation.

His breathing hitched. His eyes widened as if he was
startled by what was happening. He took a half-step back
from her. 'Until tomorrow, Miss Wilding.'

Her stomach dipped in disappointment. How mortifying.

She sketched the briefest curtsy. 'Indeed.'

His face suddenly hardened into its normal stern lines.
'Do not wander about this house, Miss Wilding. You don't
know what dangers may lurk.'

That sounded very much like a threat. Something inside her trembled at the idea. She stiffened her spine and ignored her racing heart. She reminded herself that she did not respond well to threats.

Chapter Five

To Mary's surprise, the whole family appeared in the drawing room before dinner the next day, although she had seen none of them during daylight hours. The earl looked sartorially splendid this evening in a cream-coloured waistcoat and dark-blue coat, the silver buttons winking in the light of the chandelier.

Whatever the Beresfords said about him not being a gentleman, his linen was impeccably starched and his crisp dark curls artfully disarrayed. The moment she entered, she felt the touch of his steely gaze from where he was standing slightly apart from his relations.

Unwanted colour rose to her cheeks. It had nothing to do with that considering look. It was embarrassment at how poor she looked compared to the rest of them.

With her valise gone, she only had the dress she'd worn yesterday, a fine merino wool decorated with Brussels lace at neckline and cuff. Small pieces of lace, to be sure, but their purchase had been wickedly extravagant for a poor schoolteacher. And hardly worth the investment, once she'd realised Mr Allerdyce's true intention.

Gerald ceased listening to his mother and looked over at her. 'Feeling better, Miss Wilding?'

The boy was as graceless as a puppy to remind her of the scene he'd interrupted the day before. She smiled coolly. 'Quite fine, Gerald.'

His mother's head came up like a hound scenting a fox. 'Not well, Miss Wilding?' She was beautifully dressed, her gown of rose silk and the peacock feather in her turban more suited to a ball than an evening at home. Or were they? What would a country schoolteacher know of the style nobility employed *en famille*, apart from what she read in the fashion magazines?

'She was crying,' Gerald declared with a glare at the earl.

'I received some unwelcome news in the post. The earl had nothing to do with it.'

An expression chased across the earl's face. Surprise? Had he thought she would expose his dastardly plot to his family? Still, she wasn't quite sure why she felt the need to defend him, except that they held him in such disdain, it set up her hackles.

'Dinner is served, my lord,' Manners said.

Mrs Hampton moved smoothly to take the earl's arm. An undeniable flash of annoyance darkened his eyes. He was lucky to have a family. Mary would have loved to have an aunt or two. And as the older and most senior woman present it was only polite that he should escort her into dinner.

He gathered himself quickly, she was pleased to see, walking ahead of the party with all the grace of a courtier. Indeed, his innate elegance continually surprised her.

Jeffrey held out his arm. 'Miss Wilding?'

She took it and instantly became aware of her height. Jeffrey wasn't short for a man, but she was ridiculously tall for a woman, and she looked down on the top of his head. She could see the whorl of hair at his crown. If he noticed the disparity, he didn't show it and seated her opposite his aunt, taking the place at Mary's side. Gerald settled in beside his mother.

The footmen served the first courses and retired. Conversation was desultory. The weather, which was threatening snow. An invitation to be declined because the family was in mourning.

During a lull, Mrs Hampton turned to Mary with a condescending smile. 'You know, there are several Wildings among my acquaintance, my dear. Might you be a relation, perhaps? They are from Norfolk.'

Her heart stilled. Could she indeed have relatives somewhere? How would she ever know? Since soup required careful attention, as she'd always taught her girls, she sipped at her spoonful of leek and potato before she attempted a reply. The delay gave her a smidgeon of time to think how to word an answer that did not make her seem to be asking for sympathy. 'I hale from St John's Parish in Hampshire. I know nothing of my relatives.'

'Perhaps a junior branch, then,' she said. 'Had you belonged to one of the great families, they no doubt would have claimed you.'

'Certainly no family members came forward,' Mary said calmly as if she had never dreamt of an aunt or an uncle searching England for their lost niece.

'I doubt Grandfather would have lifted a hand to help, if there were others with the responsibility,' Jeffrey drawled. 'Can I cut you a piece of this excellent fowl, Miss Wilding?'

'Thank you.'

Jeffrey filled her plate with the chicken and some buttered parsnips.

The earl scowled darkly. 'St John's Parish in Hampshire, you said?'

She met his gaze. 'You have heard of it?'

'No.'

'Nor me,' Mrs Hampton said. 'My brother, now, he is an archdeacon at York Minster.'

'And likely to bore a fellow to death with his sermonising,' Gerald muttered.

His mother appeared not to notice.

Mary had the feeling that Mrs Hampton did a great deal of not noticing when it came to her son. It was one way to avoid unpleasantness, Mary supposed. No wonder he seemed spoilt.

The servants entered to clear the table and added a remove of game pie.

'It must come as a welcome change, Miss Wilding,' Mrs Hampton continued, 'to find yourself visiting such a noble seat as Beresford Abbey. It has been in our family since the Dissolution, you know. The house is quite distinctive, I believe.'

Mary caught herself glancing at the earl for his reaction, but he seemed intent on the wine in his glass, his expression inscrutable. 'It is a very interesting house,' Mary said. 'Full of strange sounds.'

Both Jeffrey and Gerald fixed their gazes on her face, both with expressions of innocence. Gerald more angelic than his older cousin, whose shirt points were so high his neck all but disappeared in the starched white cravat.

'Have you heard strange sounds?' Jeffrey asked. Was his tone a little too innocent?

'What struck me as strange,' she said, 'was how loud the sea sounds in some of the passageways. And sometimes in my chamber.' She had forgotten until this moment that not long before she had heard the racket above her head, the low rumble of the sea had been most distinct.

The earl did look up then. Instead of offering his earlier plausible explanation, he was watching his cousins.

Gerald waved an airy hand. 'Likely the tide was high. Caves run all through these cliffs. Very useful for smuggling or sedition, depending on who holds the crown.'

'The Beresfords are loyal to the House of Hanover,' Mrs Hampton announced.

'They are now,' Jeffrey said with a cynical twist to his lips.

Mary imagined a network of caves beneath the house. 'Is the house likely to collapse?'

'Not likely,' Jeffrey scoffed. 'Or not for centuries.'

Mary didn't like the sound of it at all.

The earl was looking at Jeffrey very intently. 'Do you know the way into these caves?'

'From the sea. I have seen them from the sailboat we use in the summer,' Jeffrey said. 'Never attempted a landing. Too many rocks. The tunnels were blocked up years ago. Isn't that right, Ger?'

Gerald nodded.

The thought of smugglers, or anyone, being able to make their way secretly into the house was downright disturbing.

With a change of tablecloth, the final course appeared. Jeffrey and Gerald descended into an argument about the merits of the local hunt. The earl leaned back in his chair sipping his burgundy and listening with a bored expression. For some odd reason, Mary felt as if he was watching her, but every time she looked his way, his gaze was idly fixed on the two young men.

Which was good. She did not want his attention.

Mrs Hampton gave a little sniff and dabbed at her delicate little nose with a handkerchief and leaned closer to

the earl. 'Now the funeral is over I must think about finding a new home. His lordship was very fond of Gerald
and insisted we stay here after my dear husband's demise.'
She sighed. 'I could go to my brother, naturally. But the
demands of his position—archdeacon, you know.'

The earl grimaced. 'Actually, madam, I was hoping
you would stay. Miss Wilding needs a chaperon.'

Mrs Hampton visibly brightened. 'Miss Wilding is
staying?'

'Naturally,' the earl drawled. 'She has nowhere else
to go.'

Mary felt prickles run across her shoulders and down
her back. Prickles of anger. Prickles of pain at his cool
dismissal of her loss. She opened her mouth to deny his
assertion, then closed it again. He was right. For the moment, she did have nowhere to go. But that didn't mean
she couldn't formulate a plan.

'I suppose I could remain for a while, if I can be of as-
sistance,' Mrs Hampton said, her brightening expression
giving the lie to her begrudging words. 'You would like
that, would you not, Gerald? If we stayed?'

Gerald looked at his mother and his eyes lowered as if
shielding his thoughts. 'I wanted to go to London.'

'Not until we are out of mourning,' his mother said.

'Then it doesn't matter where we go,' her son replied
with a shrug.

His lordship ran a fingertip around the rim of his glass,
his hard gaze fixed on his aunt. 'Miss Wilding needs help
with her wardrobe.'

'My wardrobe is fine,' Mary said quickly.

The earl's grey gaze settled on her and she wanted to
squirm under that intense scrutiny. 'I understood your luggage went astray. We cannot have the Beresford heiress
tramping around the countryside in rags, now can we?'

His glance flicked over her person and heat flushed to her hairline at that critical regard. He must think her such a dowd, but, more to the point, he seemed to have decided he had the right to make decisions on her behalf.

Mrs Hampton smiled at her son. 'Then it is settled. We will stay.'

Her son flushed. His eyes flashed fury. 'I don't see why we want to stay now he is here.'

'A common refrain,' the earl said coolly. He didn't look at Mary, but her stomach dipped all the same. Sympathy in the face of his cousin's rejection, when it really was none of her business.

'I could stay with Jeffrey. At his lodgings,' Gerald said with a defiant look at his mother. 'Couldn't I, cuz?'

Jeffrey almost choked on a mouthful of food.

The earl's lip curled in distaste. 'What about it, cuz?' he asked in silken tones. 'Will you take him in? I for one would be for ever in your debt.'

It seemed the earl didn't need her sympathy.

'Gerald. You would not desert me at such a time,' Mrs Hampton said.

Gerald shot her a sulky glare.

'You could, of course, old chap. Always welcome,' Jeffrey said, recovering his voice. 'But my apartments have only one bed.'

'I could sleep on the floor.'

Mrs Hampton made a sound of horror.

Jeffrey shook his head. 'My man wouldn't like that above half,' he pronounced, as if it trumped all objections.

'Your constitution is far too delicate for such hardship, Gerald,' his mother said. 'I could not permit it.'

'My dear madam,' the earl said clearly tired of the conversation, 'the decision is made. You will chaperon Miss

Wilding and see to her dress. And Gerald will of necessity remain at your side.'

'You cannot do better than my aunt for advice on style,' Jeffrey added, joining the ranks of traitors siding with the earl.

Mrs Hampton simpered.

Mary dipped her head meekly. As a reward she received a suspicious glance from the earl which she met head on with a cool smile.

Gerald, who had subsided into his own thoughts for the previous few moments, raised his head and turned to look at her. 'What of the White Lady, Miss Wilding?' he asked. 'Have you heard any screams or clanking chains?'

Oh, the wretch. It must be he who had made those noises. Though how, when there had been no sign of him, she could not begin to imagine. She couldn't keep her gaze from darting to the earl, to see if he shared her opinion.

He shook his head very slightly. Because he didn't want Gerald to know he was suspected? Perhaps he intended to catch the boy out. She certainly felt better at this proof she had not imagined those unearthly noises, as well as the proof that the earl was finally taking them seriously.

She narrowed her eyes, looking at Gerald's face for signs of guilt, and received a glance of innocent interest.

The butler entered at that moment. 'A gentleman to see you, my lord. Lord Templeton. He says he is expected.'

The earl leapt to his feet. 'Expected, but not this soon.'

'I have taken the liberty of showing him to the library, my lord, since he declined to join the family in the drawing room for tea.'

'Very good. I will join him there immediately.'

It was the first time Mary had seen him looked pleased about anything. His delight made him look decidedly more handsome, but his pleasure only added to her resentment that he still had a friend who would come to visit. Hopefully he would be too busy with the man to notice when she slipped away on the morrow.

'How rude,' Mrs Beresford said, looking at the door that closed behind him. 'I suppose one can't expect manners from a coalminer's son, even if he does have a title.'

'I think he has shown a great deal of forbearance,' Mary muttered.

Gerald grinned at her. 'You did hear the White Lady, didn't you?'

'Certainly not,' she said truthfully, giving him a bland look. It wasn't a lie, because she was now certain it had been Gerald all along.

Jeffrey raised a brow. 'I'm glad to hear it, Miss Wilding. As Gerald said this morning, any sighting of her ghostly form usually heralds a death in the family. And one is enough, don't you think?'

He looked so dashed innocent that perhaps it was him playing cruel jokes and not his younger cousin. Or they were in it together. Her stomach dipped. 'Then we certainly have something to be grateful for,' she replied and put down her knife and fork at the loss of her appetite at what felt like a threat. Another one. 'One is certainly enough for any family.'

'Will you take tea in the drawing room, Miss Wilding?' Mrs Hampton asked with what she must have considered a great deal of condescension to one as so far down the social scale.

Mary gave her a polite smile. 'No, thank you. I find I am quite tired. I think I will retire.'

'Oh, but we should really pull out some fashion plates. Discuss colours, if we are to go shopping tomorrow.'

Discuss fashion plates after all that had been implied? 'Another time.' She hurried from the room.

* * *

Back in her own chamber, she held her hands out to the fire and then rubbed her palms together. Her room seemed even colder than usual. In fact, there was a definite draught. She got up and went to the window to see if it had been left open, although with the curtains so still, it hardly seemed likely.

No. It was closed. She tugged at the latch just to be sure. Put her palms to the edges. Nothing.

Then where was the chill coming from?

Frowning, she toured the perimeter of the room, trying to feel the direction of this strange blast of cold air.

Here. Beside the fireplace.

She ran her palm along the corner beside the chimney-breast and distinctly sensed cold pressure against her skin. Was there something wrong with the chimney? Bricks coming loose, walls falling down? Like those old tunnels?

She probably should report it to the earl. Or his steward. But not now. It was far too late and the earl would be busy with his guest.

She reached out again just to be sure she was not mistaken, running her palm up the wall. The draught stopped at eye level and was forceful enough to send the adjacent candle in the wall sconce flickering and smoking. She pulled her scissors from her reticule and on tiptoes trimmed the wick, grasping the base of the brass sconce for balance.

A grinding noise. Vibration under her fingers. She jumped back, her heart in her throat.

She could have sworn the wall moved towards her. It wasn't moving now and the odd noise had stopped. It had definitely come from inside the wall, not from above like before.

Or at least she was fairly certain it had. And the wall looked odd, out of line.

Once more she put her hand on the base of the sconce. It moved, twisted under her hand. The grinding started again.

The sconce turned upside down as she pushed harder. Quickly she blew out the candle. The last thing she needed was to start a fire.

A section of wall slowly swung inwards, stopping at right angles. Cold air rushed past her. She wrinkled her nose at the musty smell. In the distance she could hear the sea, much as she had done when the earl had led her to her room by way of the basement. And again before those strange noises above her head. Pulling her shawl tight against the sudden chill, she stared into pitch blackness.

A priest's hole? It would make sense for a house with a connection with the Roman Catholic Church to have such a thing. She'd heard about them countless times when reading history books. She also read about such things in Gothic novels. They always led to something bad for the heroine. Only this wasn't a Gothic novel and she wasn't a heroine. She was a sensible schoolteacher.

Hopefully, whoever had used the priest's hole had managed to get out, though, and it didn't contain their wasted bones. She shuddered at the thought of someone trapped inside the darkness behind that wall. Nonsense. Anyone who went in must have known how to get out when the coast was clear.

She peered in. The space appeared larger than one would expect. How odd. She went to the bedside table for her candlestick and marched back to the gaping hole. She held the candle out in front of her and revealed what looked like a passage into a tunnel that branched left and right. A tunnel? One of those that led to the caves described at dinner tonight? It didn't look in the least like a ruin. And why did it lead straight to her chamber? Her stomach gave a sickening lurch.

Who else knew about this? And exactly where did it go? Down to the sea? To the outside? Could she use it to escape the earl's high-handed edict that she might not leave? Her heart beating loud in her ears as she held her breath, she stepped over the threshold.

The hairs on the back of her neck stood to attention.

What if the door closed behind her, leaving her trapped? She backed out into her room, set her candle on the mantel and dragged over the chair from beside the hearth. She stood it in the opening. The door would be unable to close with that in the way. Not completely. She picked up her candle once more and plunged into the dark.

The candle's flickering light illuminated rough-stone walls glistening with damp. Creeping along one step at a time, she wondered what on earth she would find. The passage took a turn and came to a set of stairs leading up. Stairs that seemed to mirror those just beyond her chamber door, only narrower and the steps rougher-hewn. She climbed upwards carefully and came to a blank wall. She raised her candle high and saw a sconce much like the one in her bedroom. She twisted the base and started back as the wall shifted inwards, revealing the chamber above her room and in the corner, against the passage wall, a length of chain and a rusty cannonball.

In that instant she was sure the earl had lied. This was how he had got into that room. He was the one making the unearthly noises. But why? Did he plan to drive her to madness and have her locked away, thereby taking control of the money? Or did he want to frighten her into his arms? Into marriage? Or did he think to blame a ghost for her death?

Her mouth dried. The air wouldn't seem to fill her lungs. She swallowed hard. Inside she was trembling. Weak. Wishing she knew just what he was up to.

Surely Gerald and Jeffrey knew about this passageway? It was the sort of thing no self-respecting boy would miss. Unless they truly believed that the tunnels had collapsed long ago. If their grandfather had told them it was so, would they not have believed him?

Whoever knew about this had ready access into her chamber. Suddenly her skin felt too tight and her scalp tingled. That person could come and go into her room at will.

Hastily, she closed the secret door and hurried back down the steps, pausing outside the entrance to her room to make sure everything was just as she had left it.

She let go a breath she hadn't realised she was holding. Should she explore further, or simply face the earl with her findings in the morning? It would be good to know if it led outside to freedom. She took a quick breath and continued on past her room. Darkness closed in around her, apart from the small circle of light cast by her candle.

At the sound of a deep low rumble of male voices she froze. Was someone else in the passageway? There was no glimmer of light ahead. No footsteps accompanying the voices. She continued on more slowly and came to a fork in the tunnel. By heavens, it seemed there was a veritable rabbit warren inside the walls. And they looked in good working order, too. Was there something else going on here? Was the old earl involved in smuggling? French brandy was smuggled all along the coast of Cornwall at great profit.

The voices were louder now, though still indistinct. If she could hear them, they would be able to hear her if she called out. But that would give her discovery away and she wasn't ready to do so. Not yet.

With one hand on the clammy wall and the candle held out in front of her, she pressed on, slowly, one step at a time. This part of the tunnel was not quite high enough for her to stand upright, but as long as she kept her neck bent, she managed not to give the top of her head more than the odd scrape.

She turned another corner. Now the voices were as clear as if she was standing in the room with the earl and, she supposed, his visitor, Lord Templeton.

'To speedy success. Hopefully it won't take too much time away from your duties,' the earl said. A chinking of glasses ensued.

What on earth could they be talking about? Whatever it was, it was not her business.

'What more do you know about her?' Lord Templeton asked.

'Nothing, except he left her a fortune.'

They were talking about her. Then it was her business.

'What is she like?'

Her breath caught in her throat. She winced. She did not want to hear this, but for some reason she could not move.

There was a long pause, as if the earl was taking his time considering the question. Oh, she really should go.

'Tall. Stubborn to a fault,' he said quite softly, sounding almost bemused. 'Certainly not my type,' he added more forcefully.

Nor was he hers.

'I suppose you have thought about the other solution,' Templeton said.

She stilled. Another solution would be a very good thing, wouldn't it? Some way out of their predicament?

The earl made a sound like a bitter laugh and said

something indistinct. Then continued more clearly. 'I want know what I am dealing with before taking drastic action.'

Drastic? What did he mean by drastic? She recalled the push that had almost sent her over the cliff. Her mouth dried. Her heart knocked against her ribs. She leaned against the wall for support. A sick feeling churned in her stomach. Fear.

An overreaction? Drastic could mean anything. The fact he stood to inherit by her death didn't mean he would actually plan it.

Surely he couldn't be that evil.

'I'll do anything you want,' Templeton said. His next words were too low for her to hear.

If they were plotting against her it would help to know what they had in mind. She put her ear to the wall.

A piece of rock crumbled against her fingers and rattled to the floor.

'What was that?' Templeton asked.

She held her breath, frozen to the spot. If the earl knew about the passageway, would he guess someone was inside, listening?

'Ranger heard it, too,' the earl said. His voice drew closer. 'What is it, old fellow?'

The dog whined, then she heard a snuffling sound as if he had his nose pressed against the stonework.

'It's either a mouse or a rat,' the earl said, so close to her ear that she recoiled. 'I wouldn't be surprised if the inside of the walls weren't crawling with vermin. Something else to eliminate when I have the money situation resolved.'

Something else to eliminate? The tunnels and her? Her stomach pitched. She had to get away from this place. As soon as possible. Sooner.

'Another brandy, Gabe?' The earl's voice moved further away.

'Thank you. That had better be the last though, if I am to leave at first light.'

She didn't dare wait to hear more in case she made more noise and he decided to investigate. And besides, she'd heard all she needed to know.

Terror blocking her throat, her legs almost too weak to hold her up, she walked through the dark and the damp holding on to the rough stone for support. At the sight of the light streaming into the tunnel from her chamber, she ran the last few steps. Panting with the effort of not collapsing in a heap, she sent the wall back to its proper place.

Her heart knocking hard against her ribs, her stomach in a knot, she leaned her back against the wall. She squeezed her hands tightly together as the words went round and round in her head. *Drastic action. When I have the money. Another thing to eliminate.* There was only one conclusion she could draw from his words.

Her mind refused to focus. *Think, Mary. Think.* She took a deep breath. And another. The trembling eased. Her breathing slowed. She looked around at the bed, the door, the window. Stepped away from a wall anyone could open from the other side.

Anyone. The earl or his friend could walk in on her as she slept and take drastic action. Panic clawed its way back into her throat. Then she must not sleep.

It would not work. No one could remain awake all day and all night. She had to find a way to block off the entrance.

She tried putting a chair in front of it, then the dresser, but nothing seemed substantial enough to hold back a chunk of stone wall.

Perhaps she needed a different tack. Something that would warn her the moment the door started to open. Give her time to hide. Or run. Something loud. The crash of a set of brass fire irons like the ones standing on the hearth, perhaps. She gave them a push and they went over with a satisfying clang and a clatter.

Perfect. She stood listening, waiting to see if anyone had heard. Would the sound carry down that tunnel to the earl? Would he come to investigate?

Not by the secret tunnel, surely? She glared at the now-perfectly positioned wall. Oh, no. He would not come that way. He would not want her to learn he had easy access to her room. She strode to the chamber door and turned the large iron key.

Her panic started to fade and her mind cleared. She looked at the fire irons from several angles. They needed to fall at the very first movement, but they had a wide base and needed a good push at the top to make them topple. Something more precarious was required.

The slender vase on the dressing table, perhaps. She stood it beside the crack in the wall and carefully balanced the fire irons on top. It took a few tries to get it to stay in place. She nodded grimly. One push and it would topple.

She flopped down on the edge of the bed and stared at her odd structure. Now what?

Now she needed to plan her escape. Where she would go, she wasn't quite sure, but anywhere was better than here. Anywhere was better than the house of a man who talked of drastic action and getting his money, when the only way the money would go to him was if she died.

An ache filled her heart. Everything she'd ever known was gone. Sally. The school. Her girls. She would have to start all over again.

For a moment, she'd let herself hope she might belong here. That she might actually have found a family. The old longing clutched at her heart. Such a childish thing, to want what could never be.

She must have bats in her belfry. Her father hadn't wanted her—why would anyone else? Certainly not Beresford. All he wanted was his rightful inheritance. And who would blame him? She really wished there was a way she could give it to him before he resorted to drastic action.

She climbed beneath the sheets, fully clothed, ready to run at a moment's notice, and lay concocting a plan of her own. A way to turn the trip to St Ives to her advantage.

Chapter Six

The visit to St Ives had turned into a family outing. The earl had ridden ahead with his cousins, while Mary and Mrs Hampton had travelled by carriage. Mary spent most of the journey parrying the older woman's questions about her past and she could not have been more glad when they arrived at their destination.

The carriage pulled into the courtyard of a small hostelry. 'We always walk from here,' Mrs Hampton announced.

The footman let down the steps and Mary followed her companion out of the carriage into a bustling courtyard. The air smelled of the sea and fish. At any other time, she would have been eager to explore the town, but finding a way to depart claimed her immediate attention, since on the other side of the inn courtyard a sign proclaimed 'Ticket Office'.

While the men saw to their horses and Mrs Hampton chatted with an acquaintance who had rushed over to offer condolences, Mary wandered casually over to the wicket below the sign and, with her heart picking up speed, smiled at the man inside.

'Can I help you, ma'am?' he asked.

A quick glance told her the earl was busy seeing to the horses. He looked every bit the Earl of Beresford today, in his close-fitting riding coat and muscle-defining doeskin breeches. She was positive, if she tried, she could see her face in the highly polished Hessians. To the manor born. Though it was the intensity of his expression as he dealt with the head groom, the square jaw and firm mouth, that drew her attention. It was too bad that such an attractive exterior hid a villainous heart. 'Does the stage leave from here for London?' she asked the clerk in a low voice.

'Not London miss, Exeter, every day, at six in the morning. You can pick up the stage to London from there.'

'But is there nothing that leaves later in the day? Say this afternoon?'

'There's a coach to Plymouth at two this afternoon. You'd have to stay overnight there and pick up the mail coach to London.'

Plymouth. 'How much does it cost?'

'One shilling and six pence.'

She had that much and a little more. And the earl would never think to look for her in Plymouth. She raked around in her reticule and put the required amount down on the counter. 'One, please. For this afternoon.'

'Planning a journey, Miss Wilding?' The deep voice from behind her held amusement and an edge of steel.

She gasped.

'The young lady bought a ticket to Plymouth,' the clerk said.

'No,' the earl replied, scooping up her money. 'She did not.'

The ticket man shook his head. 'Young women today…'

The earl gave him a tight smile. 'Precisely.'

Heat rushing to her face, Mary glared up at him. 'You have no right to say where I may or may not go.'

The earl gave her a bored look. 'I thought we had already discussed this,' he drawled. He took her arm and gently and firmly drew her away from the wicket.

She pulled her arm free. 'You cannot force me to stay. Please return my money.' She held out her hand.

'Until the matter of the will is settled,' he said in a low murmur, 'I require your presence here.' He took her hand in his and his fingers closed around hers in an unbreakable grip. Not hard, or painful, but firm. 'Now let us to our purpose for coming here today, shall we?' He gave her a pleasant smile so that anyone watching would see a most kindly expression. Looking at him now, at his large frame blocking her way, his cold eyes making his point, she could not help but remember his words from the night before. *Drastic action*. A shiver ran down her spine.

And if she screamed? Called attention to her plight? What then? Would anyone come to her aid? The only person left in the yard was Mrs Hampton, who was looking at her impatiently. No, it would be better not to make a scene where the earl would have the upper hand. She would find a chance to slip away quietly.

She inhaled a deep breath. 'Very well. Let us go shopping.'

If she hadn't known better, she might have thought the earl gave a sigh of relief.

'You do not seem like the sort of man who would enjoy a visit to a mantua-maker, my lord.'

'Oh?' He looked at her with one brow cocked in question. He gave her such a heart-stopping smile, her jaw dropped in wonder. 'And what sort of man do I seem to be?'

A dangerous one, if the way her heart was beating in her chest was to be believed. And a scoundrel who kissed unsuspecting maidens, too. 'I suspect you are interested in more manly pursuits. Shooting at things and riding roughshod over people.'

He laughed. In that moment his face changed and her heart tumbled over at how attractive he looked with those silver eyes alight and a genuine smile curving his lips. 'I see you do not hold me in any high regard, Miss Wilding,' he said.

Oh heavens, was that regret she heard in his tone? Or was it her own longing colouring her judgement? She could not afford to let him charm her. To weaken her resolve.

'I just assume you are like most men, for whom a trip to the dressmaker would be torture.'

'It seems you don't know me at all, Miss Wilding.'

'Are you ready, Miss Wilding?' Mrs Hampton asked at their approach.

Mary nodded her assent.

'Then let us be off.' The widow strode briskly out of the courtyard with Mary and the earl following behind. The streets were so crowded, they were soon forced to go single file, like a crocodile of schoolchildren, Mary thought wryly, very aware of the earl hard on her heels. She also noticed that other pedestrians moved out of their way the moment they saw the three of them coming towards them. She suspected it was the earl's looming presence behind them causing the wide berth given to their party.

Mrs Hampton stopped outside one of the shops lining the street and turned back to speak to Mary. 'Mrs Wharton is not of the same calibre as a London dressmaker, you understand, but she is not bad and her prices are reasonable.'

As the earl ushered them inside, a bell above the door tinkled.

A thin-faced woman, with her hair pulled back beneath

her cap and bonnet, curtsied. 'Why, Mrs Hampton, how good to see you and after such a long time, too. Come for your mourning clothes, have you?'

'Certainly not. The ones from last year are perfectly adequate. No. It is Miss Wilding who requires your services.'

The woman's surprised gaze swivelled to Mary and then up to the earl. She frowned. 'A family member, miss? Needing black?'

'Goodness me, Wharton, you do jump to conclusions. Miss Wilding is…' her face took on an expression of dismay '…a family friend.'

The woman's eyebrows rose. 'What can I do for you, miss?'

'A complete wardrobe, if you please,' the earl said. 'To be charged to the Earl of Beresford.' He removed his gloves and toured the shop, touching the bolts of silks and muslins displayed on the shelves.

What on earth must the woman think of a man purchasing a wardrobe for a woman not a relative? Mary knew what she was thinking from the knowing gleam in the other woman's eyes.

Mary felt the heat crawl up her face. This was too much. And it didn't make sense. Why would he be purchasing clothes for her, if he was planning her demise, unless it was to draw people off the scent?

Whatever his purpose, she would not put herself under such an obligation. 'Two morning gowns are all I require,' she said firmly. They would replace what the earl had caused her to lose. That was fair.

Mrs Hampton glared at her. 'Nonsense. Every young lady needs walking dresses. A dress for the opera. A ball gown. A riding habit. At the very least. Not to mention gloves, bonnets, and—' she shot a wary look at the earl '—other items of apparel.'

Mrs Wharton's jaw hung open.

Mary understood exactly how she felt. 'I would prefer to see what you have already made up,' she said with a feeling of desperation at the silken trap closing around her.

'Something we can take with us today,' the earl agreed, bestowing so charming a smile on Mrs Wharton, she simpered. 'The rest can follow along later.'

The seamstress rubbed her hands together, a dry raspy sound like snakeskin over rock. 'A complete wardrobe it is then, your lordship.' She ran a critical eye over Mary. 'No frills or bows.'

Tall girls couldn't wear frills or bows. It made them look like mountains. It seemed Mrs Wharton and Sally agreed on that score. 'Come this way, miss, so I can take your measurements. A glass of wine for you, sir? Tea for you, Mrs Hampton?'

The earl nodded his agreement. The woman scurried behind a curtain, no doubt to relay her instructions.

'Surely there is no reason for you to stay, my lord,' Mary said as he settled himself in one of the visitors' chairs and stretched out his long legs. He looked altogether too comfortable. Too much at home, as if this wasn't the first time he had participated in the dressing of a female.

An idea that gave her a nasty little wrench.

'Ah, Miss Wilding, but there is. I wish to see you attired in the first stare of fashion.' The hard look in his eyes warned her not to argue.

'But surely Mrs Hampton—'

'It is a long time since I was in town,' the widow said. 'I am sure his lordship has a much better idea of what is all the crack these days than I. My dear Miss Wilding, everyone knows that gentlemen have discerning taste when it comes to ladies' fashion.' She blinked rapidly, as if she realised just what she'd said.

Mrs Wharton reappeared. 'This way, miss.' She gestured to a door at the back of the room.

With a glare at the earl, Mary stepped through the door into a small dressing room containing a looking glass, a low stool and a young woman standing ready with measuring strings.

'Daisy, while I take miss's measurements, run and fetch the blue dimity and the yellow silk. With a little alteration, I think they will fit perfectly.'

The girl scurried off.

Gritting her teeth, Mary let the seamstress strip her down to her stays and chemise, and held still while the woman measured and tied her knots in the string. And all the time Mary stood there practically naked, she kept thinking about the earl sprawled in the chair only a few feet away.

Daisy returned with the gowns requested over her arms. They looked far too expensive and not at all practical.

'They do not seem to be what I had in mind,' she said. 'I prefer something more…similar to the gown I wore in here.'

The seamstress made a little moue of disgust. 'Perhaps we should let his lordship be the judge.'

Mary gasped. 'Certainly not.' She wasn't going to parade herself in front of him.

'Help her into the blue one, Daisy,' the seamstress said. 'I am going to look and see if we have anything more akin to miss's taste.' She disappeared out of the door.

The young woman unlaced the blue gown and held it ready. 'If miss would bend a little…'

The usual problem of her height was what the girl meant. With a sigh, Mary ducked and the dress was slipped over her head. It went on with a whisper. Such light airy fabric. So silky to the touch.

The girl made a couple of adjustments to the bodice with pins and glanced down. 'We will have to add some trim to the hem.'

Mary glanced in the mirror and recoiled. The figure in the mirror wasn't her, surely. This woman wore a gown cut shockingly low across the bosom and edged in vandyke lace. So much skin. And the tops of her breasts were clearly visible. She tugged the fabric higher to no avail, not to mention that the sleeves did not reach her wrists and the skirts were well above her ankles. She looked ridiculous.

Daisy opened the door. 'All ready, Mrs Wharton.'

'There is something missing, surely,' Mary said, staring at her chest. 'A fichu. Or a shawl. You need to find something else. This one will not do at all.'

'I think it looks perfect,' a dark male voice said. She swung around, startled to see his eyes roving her body from her head to her heels. Heat flared in that silver gaze.

Answering heat rushed through her blood. Her insides fluttered alarmingly. A blush rose up her chest to her face. 'You can't come in here.'

Mrs Wharton swept in with swathes of lace. 'Why ever not? You are fully dressed. Let us see, now. Up on the stool, now, please, miss.'

The earl's charming smile was directed fully at her. He looked utterly gorgeous and was clearly enjoying himself. 'Allow me.' He held out his hand.

A large hand and as steady as a rock, when she was trembling inside like an aspen and her knees had the consistency of butter.

She glanced up at his face and saw his jaw tighten as he realised she intended to refuse his aid. Why she did it, she wasn't sure, but she gave him her hand, felt the warmth of his fingers around her cold ones.

He raised her hand to his lips, all the while keeping his gaze locked with hers. A startlingly warm brush of his mouth against her skin felt far too familiar, and terribly unnerving. A shiver ran down her spine, a special little thrill.

'I am glad to see we have come to an understanding,' he said in a murmur meant only for her.

She almost moaned at the way that deep rasping voice made her insides clench. The impression of strength when he supported her as she stepped up left her feeling weak.

Now their eyes were on a level, their gazes locked in a breathless awareness. Her skin tingled all over. Her heartbeat unsteady, out of rhythm, made her breathing unnaturally fast.

His gaze drifted downwards from her eyes, to her parted lips, down her throat to her chest and, God help her, what she saw in his expression was a powerful hunger. Her breasts tightened under his scrutiny.

A sensation of being utterly feminine swept over her, warming her from the inside out, making her limbs feel suddenly languid.

'Let me take a look at that hem,' Mrs Wharton said, dropping to her knees.

And the spell, or whatever it was that had occurred between them, broke. The earl stepped back, his face in its usual taut lines, his gaze guarded.

Did he fear she'd seen too much?

Mary closed her eyes. She was imagining things. He was here to make sure his money didn't slip out of his grasp. That was all there was to it.

While the dressmaker pinned lace to the bottom of

the gown and added matching fabric to the sleeves, Mary avoided looking at his lordship.

After a few minutes he said, 'Alter the other one the same way.'

'I would prefer a higher neckline,' Mary said.

'No,' his lordship said and walked out.

'It is perfect the way it is, miss,' the seamstress said, handing her down. She twitched at the skirts, checked the bodice and nodded. 'Perfect. Let us see to the rest of your order now, shall we?'

Daisy returned to help her into her own gown.

By the time Mary was dressed and back out in the shop, his lordship was nowhere to be seen.

'He bethought himself of an urgent errand,' Mrs Hampton said at her look of enquiry. 'He left orders as to the rest of the items to be purchased, however.' She pointed to a pile of fine linens and gloves on the counter.

Mary tried not to feel disappointed he had left. She should be pleased, because while she was being buttoned into her gown, she'd had another idea.

'I'll have the two gowns sent up to the livery before the hour is up,' Mrs Wharton finally said, when all the choices had been made. 'I'll parcel these up to go home with you now.'

'I still think you should have that military-style riding habit made,' Mrs Hampton said, sounding quite weary, but there was a sparkle in her eye, likely because Mrs Wharton had thrown in a gown for her as commission for bringing Mary to her shop.

'I don't ride,' Mary said quickly. Her only experience on a horse had been sitting on the earl's lap and, while the thought of it made her blush, it certainly didn't count as riding.

Mrs Hampton glared. 'You don't play the pianoforte either, I'll be bound, but that is no reason not to visit the music room.'

As a metaphor it didn't really work. And Mary did play. Very well. It was one of her few ladylike accomplishments. But Mrs Hampton didn't need to know that. She smiled sweetly. 'If I decide to visit the stables, I shall be sure to order a riding habit ahead of time.'

The widow sniffed. 'I will speak to the earl about it.'

'It is none of the earl's business,' Mary said resolutely and prayed Mrs Hampton would leave it there.

Outside the shop, the street was bathed in the light of a sun that had barely lifted itself above the horizon and was already on a downward path. It hung so low that facing into it caused everyone to squint.

'Do we return to the carriage now,' Mary asked, 'or is there time to explore a little? I would love to walk down to the quay.'

'Certainly not. It reeks of fish. Next we go to the haberdasher. I am in need of some ribbon and a paper of pins.'

They walked a few yards down the hill to the next shop Mrs Hampton wanted to visit.

Mary glanced longingly down the hill where boats lay off shore. Boats carried passengers. It would take but a moment to slip aboard one of those waiting for the tide to turn.

'I have never visited a seaside town before. It will take but a moment to walk down to the shore and back while you complete your purchases.'

Mrs Hampton looked doubtful. 'If only one of the males of our party were on hand, I would be less concerned. The men on the wharf are dreadfully rough and ill mannered.'

'I will just go as far as the next bend in the road, look at the harbour and walk back.'

Her companion let out a sigh. 'You are a very determined young woman, Miss Wilding. I really do not have the energy to argue. If the earl does not like what I cannot stop, then let him take you to task.'

She disappeared inside the shop.

So, the earl had instructed Mrs Hampton to act as not only her chaperon, but as her guard. How annoying. In that case, she did not feel so bad about not telling her the truth.

She walked down to the corner and the harbour spread out below her. Fishing boats drawn up on the beach; nets drying in the sun; men and women plying their trade along the waterside. Just like the landscapes she had seen in books. Out on the sea, waves rippled, catching sunbeams and tossing them back with a glitter that would outdo a diamond necklace.

Breathtaking. Enchanting.

Nothing like the wild sea she had seen the other day from the top of the cliff near the Abbey. This sea looked friendly and enticing. After a quick glance over her shoulder, she hurried down to the wharf. A young man in uniform stepped in front of her. 'Can I help you, miss?'

Surprised she stared at him. 'I don't think so.'

'Lieutenant South, miss. Revenue officer. May I know your name?'

'Miss Wilding,' she replied, surprised. 'I thought I might hire a boat.'

The young man winced. 'His lordship said you might find your way down here. I regret that there are no boats for hire today.'

Mary gaped at him. 'His lordship?'

'The Earl of Beresford, miss.' He coloured. 'You really should go back to your family. The earl said he was sorry for your disagreement and that he would buy you the bonnet you wanted.'

'Bonnet?' She almost spluttered the word, but she could also see there was no sense in arguing with the young man. The earl had been before her. How could he have guessed her intention, when she'd had no idea of coming down here until but a few moments ago? And this young lieutenant was looking at her as if she was some spoiled miss sulking over a bonnet. It was really too much. She was going to have strong words with his lordship. Very strong words indeed.

'Good day, Lieutenant,' she managed through gritted teeth. He bowed and she turned and marched back up the hill to her…to her gaoler. This was intolerable and so she would tell him.

The hill seemed a great deal steeper on the way up. She was required to lean into the slope and watch where she put her feet on the uneven pavement, not to mention dodging people headed downhill.

She glanced up to catch her bearings. Ahead of her, a brewer's dray blocked half the road. Pedestrians were manoeuvring their way around it.

'Careful, miss,' a man with a handcart said when she almost ran into him.

'I beg your pardon,' she said, sidestepping out into the road to avoid him.

'Look out!' a male voice cried.

She looked up, expecting to see yet another cart heading down the hill. She gasped. Not so. A barrel hit the cobbles and bounced. Behind it stood a tall broad-shouldered familiar-looking figure, hand outstretched. A slighter figure darted into the alley, barely avoiding the barrel when it landed.

A woman screamed. A man shouted and leapt clear.

The barrel was rolling right for her, rumbling and banging over the stones. She picked up her skirts and ran for safety against the wall of the nearest building. She slipped, falling to her knees. Pain shot through her foot and up her shin. Sickening.

The barrel was upon her.

She struggled to get to her feet. A hand grabbed her under the arms and pulled her clear.

The barrel slammed into the wall two feet from her with a resounding bang—into the very spot she had thought to take refuge. Splinters flew. Beer showered the cobbles and nearby pedestrians. One of its iron hoops bowled on down the street, clanging and bouncing wildly, scattering people in its path, disappearing around the bend, terrified shouts marking its passage.

'Are you all right?'

A youngish man, decently dressed but hatless, was holding her against his chest, looking thoroughly discomposed, his hair ruffled and his cheeks pink. 'Are you all right, miss?' he asked again.

'I'm fine,' she croaked, trying to ignore the throb of pain in her ankle.

A hand grabbed her and pulled her away. 'Miss Wilding,' the earl said, his voice full of anger, his chest rising and falling as he fought to catch his breath. His gaze raked her person, his eyes wide with anxiety. He blinked and then all she could see in his expression was the usual stern disapproval. 'I see you are like a cat, Miss Wilding. You have nine lives.' He turned to her rescuer with a frown. The man stepped back and put a respectful distance between them.

She stood on one foot, not daring to test her weight on the other. 'This gentleman saved my life. Thank you, sir.'

Her rescuer bowed. 'It was nothing.'

The earl frowned. 'Then I owe you my thanks also.' He didn't sound terribly grateful. He sounded annoyed.

The young man took another step back. 'I was glad to be of help.'

'Did you see what happened?' the earl questioned, looking at him intently.

'I saw nothing until I saw the barrel bowling down hill and the young lady falling. I acted without thought.' He glanced up the hill. 'Jack Bridges should be whipped at the cart tail for letting a barrel go like that.'

Mrs Hampton puffed up to their small group. She glared at the crowd gathered around the smashed barrel, some on their hands and knees sopping up beer with whatever came to hand. ''Pon rep, what a dreadful hullaballoo.'

'Free beer will do that,' the young man said.

'Why,' Mrs Hampton said, smiling, 'it is Mr Trelawny, is it not?'

He bowed. 'My condolences on your loss, madam.'

'Thank you. Let me introduce you to the new Earl of Beresford,' she said, gesturing to the earl. 'And his ward, Miss Wilding. My lord, this is Mr Trelawny, manager of the Beresford mine.'

The earl's expression eased a fraction. 'Well met, Trelawny, even if the circumstances are not ideal. I had planned to visit the mine later in the week.'

The young man shook his hand. 'I would be delighted to show you around, my lord.'

'And me, too,' Mary said. 'After all, I am the owner.'

The earl's face darkened.

Trelawny's cheeks reddened. 'It is not really a suitable place for a lady,' he said. 'It is much too dangerous.'

'I will view it on your behalf,' the earl said.

Mary smiled sweetly at the foundry manager. 'Do you employ children, Mr Trelawny?'

He swallowed. 'A few.'

'Then I will definitely want to see for myself.'

The earl looked as if he was biting back the urge to argue. 'We will discuss this later,' he said finally. 'Right now I am more concerned with getting you ladies off this street before a riot breaks out.'

Indeed, the men and women crawling around in the road looked ready to come to blows over the rivulets of beer running down the hill, as they jostled and pushed each other.

A burly individual joined the fray. 'Get back from there,' he yelled. 'That's my beer.'

'Let 'em be, Jack,' a man shouted. 'You can't pick it up. Don't be a dog in the manger.'

The man swore.

'Bridges, you fool,' Trelawny called out. 'That barrel could have killed someone. It knocked this lady down.'

'No,' Mary said. 'It didn't. But it would have if you hadn't acted so swiftly.'

Trelawny coloured. The earl glowered.

The publican, an apron tied around a belly as round as the barrel, wandered down to join the milling scene. 'I ain't paying for that 'un, Bridges,' he shouted. 'It were still on your cart.'

Bridges rounded on him. 'A barrel can't just fall off. One of your men dropped it.'

'Did not.'

'Did.'

'My men weren't nowhere near it. They were rolling old barrels out. Someone give it a push.'

Mary recoiled. Had that outstretched hand been pushing, rather than trying to hold the barrel back? She glanced up at the earl to find him watching her face, his eyes narrow, his jaw tight. A band seemed to tighten around her chest. Was he worried about what she had seen? Was that the cause of his earlier anxiety?

'Who is to pay for it, then?' the carter asked, putting his fists on his hips. He glared at the thinning crowd, snatched his hat off his head and waved it at the people still sopping up the last dregs. 'If I finds out one of you did it on purpose, I'll have you in front of the beak, so I will.'

The crowd jeered and then melted away.

Jeffrey sauntered up to them, his hat at a rakish angle. 'What is going on?'

'Never mind,' Mrs Hampton said. 'Where is Gerald? It is time we headed home.'

'I don't know where he is,' Jeffrey said. 'He decided not to come with me to the gunsmith's shop.'

Gerald emerged from a nearby alley. 'Here you all are.' He gave them an angelic smile.

It seemed the whole party was now back together and the earl was still glowering. At her. 'Why were you out in the street alone?'

She felt her face heat as she remembered her mortification at the quay. 'I went to look at the harbour and was making my way back to meet Mrs Hampton.'

'She was never out of my sight,' Mrs Hampton declared.

Mary had no intention of giving her the lie. Indeed, she felt grateful that the widow had decided to support her story even if it was only to protect herself.

'If you will excuse me,' Mr Trelawny said, 'I have an appointment. I will look forward to your lordship's visit,' he said to the earl. 'And Miss Wilding. Please send word to the mine as to when I should expect you.' On that he bowed and strode off.

'Good man, Trelawny,' Mrs Hampton said. 'According to the earl.' She bit her lip. 'The late earl, that is.'

The current earl said nothing. He was still looking at Mary with suspicion in those slate-grey eyes. But the throbbing in her ankle was growing worse.

'Miss Wilding, you have had quite a shock, I think,' Mrs Hampton said. 'You are looking quite pale.'

She was also feeling dizzy. 'Yes, I would like to return to the Abbey.'

She took a step. Pain lanced up her leg. Nausea pushed up her throat. The world did a cartwheel. She clutched at the nearest solid object. The earl's arm. He caught her, held her up, the warmth of his body permeating her clothes, the scent of his cologne, something dark and musky, making her senses swim even worse.

She leaned against his strength.

'You are hurt,' Jeffrey said accusingly.

'It is nothing,' she said, flushing hot, pulling away from the earl. 'I twisted my ankle when I fell.'

The earl's eyes widened—something hot flared in their depths. Shock? Or annoyance that her injuries were so minor? 'Jeffrey,' he barked out, 'do something useful. Ride for the doctor and have him come to the Abbey right away.'

Jeffrey's blue eyes flashed resentment. His lips compressed. Then he gave a stiff nod. 'I will see you there.' He marched off up the hill.

'Are you able to walk, Miss Wilding?' the earl asked in an unexpectedly gentle tone of voice. 'If I support you?' He offered his forearm. His large well-muscled forearm. It looked like a lifeline from where she stood with all her weight on one foot. Yet, was it not the same arm that had pushed the barrel at her in the first place? She wished she knew for certain, so she could charge him with his crime.

But she wasn't sure. Had he actually seen his chance and decided to put his drastic plan in action?

'I am sure I can manage.' She took a step and stifled a gasp at the sudden arrow of pain.

'Apparently not,' he said drily.

Before she knew what he was about, he had swept her up in his arms and was striding uphill. Never had she ever been picked up by a man. She could not believe the strength of him. Or how weak the sensation made her feel. And not just because of her injury. It was a strange softness. One from the inside out.

The intensity of it made her gasp. She clutched at his shoulder for balance and he glanced down at her, his gaze a blaze of silver as if he somehow sensed her strange re-action.

Her blood ran hot at the thought.

He lifted his head and looked straight ahead, his mouth tightening, his chest rising as he took a deep breath. 'Not long now, Miss Wilding.'

He sounded relieved. Clearly he couldn't wait to be rid of her. The thought was dreadfully lowering.

There was certainly nothing in his rigid face of the skilled seducer who had kissed her hand in the dressing room. Perhaps he had been merely toying with her, as a cat toys with a mouse. Seeking to put her off guard.

It had almost worked. Her stomach dipped. 'I am sure I could walk, given time,' she said stiffly.

'You would only make matters worse,' he said grimly. 'And who knows what would befall you next?'

'It wasn't my fault the barrel broke free.'

'You should have remained with your chaperon and nothing would have happened. Next time, perhaps, you will listen.' His voice was silky soft with menace.

He'd known she wouldn't stay with Mrs Hampton, otherwise why he had warned the Revenue man down at the dock? And then he'd been right there, at the top of the hill, waiting beside the cart. She had recognised him, even though she'd only caught a quick glimpse. And he was the only one who would profit by her death.

A shudder rippled deep in her bones. And her heart ached as if it had received a blow.

Chapter Seven

'Well, doctor? Is it broken?' The earl stood in the doorway of her chamber, watching the doctor's every move while Mary lay supine on her bed. His voice was unnecessarily harsh, Mary thought, trying not to wince as the doctor poked and prodded at the swollen flesh of her ankle, then gently rotated her foot.

Pain. She hissed in a breath and closed her eyes.

'Be careful, man,' the earl said, his voice sounding strained.

Mary opened her eyes and saw his fist clenched on the doorframe, his face filled with concern.

Sympathy. Something she had not expected from him. And for a moment it warmed her, until reason prevailed. While her heart might be fooled into thinking he cared, she was far too realistic to be taken in. The only person he cared about was himself and the stupid inheritance. Now he would have to think of some other way to be rid of her.

Once more that painful squeeze in her chest. Foolish hurt.

Mentally, she gave herself a shake. At least she knew the truth. At least she was now thoroughly on her guard. But it seemed as though her plans to leave would have to be put off until her ankle was better. It seemed she was well and truly trapped. And at the earl's mercy.

He must have sensed her scrutiny, because his glance flicked to her face. He tensed, his expression becoming guarded, as if he feared she might read his thoughts.

'I am sorry to be such a nuisance,' she said bitterly.

Beresford folded his arms over his wide chest with an implacable glare. 'You should have thought of that before wandering off alone.'

'Not broken,' the doctor announced, apparently oblivious to the animosity. 'Badly sprained. I recommend binding it up and plenty of rest.' The doctor smiled at Mary. 'No dancing for a while, I am afraid, Miss Wilding.'

Dancing was another thing she didn't do. Or at least not well. What man wanted to dance with a woman who could look right over his head and who had a tendency to want to lead? She smiled, albeit a little wanly. 'Thank you, Doctor.'

With quick efficient movements, he bandaged her ankle and foot.

Jeffrey peered around the earl. 'How are you feeling, Miss Wilding?'

The doctor flicked her skirts over her lower limb. 'She is well enough.' He smiled down at her. 'I will give you some laudanum for the pain.'

She shook her head. 'Laudanum makes me feel sick.'

'Then I'll have the housekeeper make you some willow-bark tea.'

'You will take the laudanum as the doctor ordered,' his lordship snarled.

'Cuz, if she doesn't want it, she doesn't,' Jeffrey said in placating terms.

Not placating at all apparently, for the earl bared his teeth. 'Thinking to rule the roost, are you, bantam?'

Good Lord, were they fighting over her? Nothing like an injured woman to bring out the protective side in men, she supposed. She'd heard of it, but never experienced it for herself. Being the target of such discord created a very odd feeling in her breast, to be sure. A sort of warm glow. How irrational.

Unless the earl was hoping to have her drugged and helpless. The warm glow seeped away, replaced by ice in her veins.

'Willow-bark tea will do just as well,' the doctor said absently, packing up his bag. 'Not everyone responds well to laudanum, my lord.'

A triumphant gleam lit Jeffrey's eyes, but she didn't think the earl could see it since Jeffrey stood behind him.

'Let me show you out, Doctor,' the earl said. 'I have some questions for you.'

Mary glowered at his back as he left. No doubt he was planning to get a more detailed prognosis. Or to convince the doctor to leave the laudanum.

'Is there something I can get for you, Miss Wilding?' Jeffrey asked. 'Tea? Something to read?'

Oh dear. He was also going to treat her like an invalid, when she would really rather just hop around and do for herself. Still, she would go mad sitting here staring into space if they insisted she remain lying on her bed. 'A book, if you please. I was reading one in the library. It might still be on the table where I left it.'

'At your service, madam.' He flourished a bow and sauntered off with a jaunty whistle. He'd forgotten he was a man about town, at least for the moment. It was nice to see him with a little less cynicism.

She relaxed against the pillows, resigned to wait for his return. From where she reclined, she could see blue sky and clouds out her window. This was the closest she was going to get to the outdoors for a while. There would be no escape for several days. Provided she survived that long.

Her mouth dried.

A prickle of awareness at her nape made her glance up. She expected to see Jeffrey with her book. It was the earl, his expression far from happy.

'There is no need to fuss over me, Lord Beresford. Please, do continue about your business. I am sure you have many important matters requiring your attention.'

He recoiled slightly. And she had the strangest sense she had hurt his feelings. A pang of guilt made her regret her sharp words.

'What happened back there in St Ives, Miss Wilding?' He didn't sound hurt, he sounded as if he thought she was lying.

She frowned. Was he worried that he had aroused her suspicions? She decided to play innocent. 'I don't know what else you expect me to say.'

'So you did not see what caused the barrel to break loose?'

Again the flash of memory of his hand outstretched as the barrel left its mooring. And a slender man darting away. A man who could have been anyone. She recalled the conversation she had overheard from behind his wall. Perhaps Beresford's friend, Lord Templeton, had not left for Hampshire and the earl was worried that she might have seen his friend. That she was on to his plan to be rid of her?

She shook her head. 'I was too far away.' She tried not to wince at the lie.

His jaw flexed. 'Why do I have the impression you are not telling me everything, Miss Wilding? Don't you trust me?'

At that she couldn't help but chuckle under her breath.

'I scarcely know you, Lord Beresford, and so far you have done nothing but issue commands and edicts.' And talk about drastic measures in private. 'Where might trust be found in that? Please, believe me, there is nothing more to add to what I have already told you.'

An odd expression passed across his face. A mix of frustration and disappointment, as if he actually hoped she would believe he deserved her trust.

Guilt stabbed her. He had rescued her from the edge of the cliff. He had carried her most tenderly up to the carriage. And sometimes she had the feeling, when she looked at him, that he was dreadfully lonely. Like now. A painful pang squeezed her heart.

A small sneaking sensation inside her said she should trust him. A small fragile feeling that would be easily bruised if he proved her wrong. She would have trusted Sally with her life. It seemed that trust had been completely misplaced. What reason did she have to trust the earl?

No, trust was not something she needed to hand out willy-nilly at the moment. Not if she was using her head instead of her emotions.

'Here are some books, Miss Wilding,' Jeffrey said, breezing past his lordship and setting the pile down on the bedside table. 'You here again, Beresford?'

The earl glared at him. 'Not for long. Miss Wilding needs her rest.' He looked pointedly at the younger man and raised a brow.

Jeffrey curled his lip as he bowed. 'I will see you later, Miss Wilding,' he drawled. The cynic was back.

But she did not see the earl at dinner, nor anyone else, because she took a tray in her room. She had no wish to be carried about by his lordship or a footman. She told

Manners she would stay in her room until she felt able to walk with a cane. Jeffrey had provided her with a mountain of books to read and she had managed to hop across her room after Betsy finished preparing her for bed, to set up her makeshift alarm. As a further means of defence, she kept one of the heavy iron pokers alongside her beneath the counterpane.

For all her worries, nothing disturbed her sleep, except dreams of the earl's strong arms around her, which annoyed her considerably.

By the next afternoon she was able to dress and sit in the chair by her bedroom window, reading until the light began to fade.

Betsy bustled in with some packages. 'Two gowns arrived from Mrs Wharton and his lordship says you are to join the family at dinner.'

Mary frowned at the parcels, wishing she could refuse them outright, but she'd been wearing the same dress for three days and it didn't make any sense to get on her high horse after they'd been altered to fit. The earl had refused to wait for their delivery to the carriage after yesterday's accident, so Mrs Wharton must have sent them by carter today. 'I prefer to take a tray in my room.'

Betsy looked anxious. 'He said he would come for you in an hour and, dressed or not, he would carry you to the dining room.'

A little thrill fluttered through her at this masterful statement. A thrill she should not be feeling. Heat crawled up her face. 'How dare he—?' She pressed her lips together. One did not shoot the messenger. If she had words to say, she would say them to his lordship.

Betsy held up the blue muslin, the one with the dreadfully low neckline. 'This one, miss?' Betsy asked. 'Or this. Such a pretty shade of yellow. And silk, too. Much more suitable for dinner. There's a feather dyed to match for your hair.' She held up an ostrich plume, then glanced at the clock. 'We should hurry, miss. His lordship will be here in no time.'

Ready to carry her to the dining room, dressed or not. He wouldn't dare. Or would he? She had the distinct impression his lordship would dare anything at all, if it suited him.

'Very well, the yellow.'

Betsy made short work of getting her into the shift and stays that had accompanied the gowns. They were beautiful garments, much nicer than anything Mary had ever bought for herself. They felt wonderful against her skin.

'And now for the gown,' Betsy said, gently bunching up the fabric in her arms so she could slip the dress over Mary's head.

It went on with a whisper. So light and silky and a perfect length. Betsy fastened it at the back, handed her a pair of lacy gloves and gestured to the chair in front of the mirror. 'If miss will sit down, I will do your hair.'

Mary could see from the girl's face that she was dying to be given free rein. She shook her head with a smile. 'Do what you can, then.'

Her hair was too straight and to heavy for anything fancy.

She sat down and glanced at her reflection. She winced. This gown was worse than the blue one. Never had she felt so exposed. 'Give me my shawl, please.'

Betsy looked scandalised. 'You can't wear that old thing with such a pretty gown, miss.'

She could and she would. 'I will surely freeze otherwise.'

With a sigh Betsy handed her the shawl and picked up the hairbrush. In minutes the maid had artfully twisted

I accept your offer!

Please send me two free
Harlequin® Historical novels and
two mystery gifts (gifts worth
about $10). I understand that
these books are completely
free—even the shipping and
handling will be paid—and I am
under no obligation to purchase
anything, ever, as explained on the
back of this card.

246/349 HDL FNNT

Please Print

FIRST NAME

LAST NAME

ADDRESS

APT.#   CITY

STATE/PROV.   ZIP/POSTAL CODE

Visit us online at
www.ReaderService.com

NO POSTAGE
NECESSARY
IF MAILED
IN THE
UNITED STATES

BUSINESS REPLY MAIL
FIRST-CLASS MAIL   PERMIT NO. 717   BUFFALO, NY

POSTAGE WILL BE PAID BY ADDRESSEE

THE READER SERVICE
PO BOX 1867
BUFFALO NY 14240-9952

Send For
2 FREE BOOKS
Today!

I accept your offer!

Please send me two free
Harlequin® Historical novels and
two mystery gifts (gifts worth
about $10). I understand that
these books are completely
free—even the shipping and
handling will be paid—and I am
under no obligation to purchase
anything, ever, as explained on the
back of this card.

246/349 HDL FNNT

Please Print

FIRST NAME

LAST NAME

ADDRESS

APT.#	CITY

STATE/PROV.	ZIP/POSTAL CODE

Visit us online at
www.ReaderService.com

her hair into clusters of braids on each side of her head and anchored the feather on her crown. She stepped back. 'You look beautiful, miss.'

Beautiful? The girl had stars in her eyes. She looked like a carthorse dressed up as a thoroughbred. Just as Sally always said she would.

A firm rap sounded on the door. It opened without giving her a chance to answer. Blast. She should have had Betsy turn the key.

Lord Beresford stood staring at her for a moment. His hooded gaze ran from her head to her heels and, if she wasn't mistaken, lingered on her bosom for more seconds that was polite. His gaze met hers and his eyes lit with genuine pleasure. Her stomach gave a funny little hop. 'Ah, Miss Wilding. I see you are ready and waiting.'

For a man whose plan to do away with her had failed, he looked remarkably at ease and splendidly handsome. Had her imagination played tricks on her, after all? But as he came towards her, clearly intending to lift her in his arms, it dawned on her that while he might not have succeeded in St Ives, now, unable to walk, she was well and truly at his mercy.

Cold slid down her spine. She opened her mouth to refuse to go to dinner.

His gaze sharpened, his expression tightening as if he had guessed her intent. She could almost see him distancing himself and she felt terribly guilty for letting her prejudices show. 'Yes, I am ready.'

He looked relieved. Did she really have the power to hurt his feelings? It was hard to believe.

In the next moment, he swept her up in his arms and carried her out of the room. Her mind scrambled to catch up with her body's pleasure of once more being in his arms.

He glanced down at her. The earlier gladness had leached from his face, replaced by cool remoteness. 'I won't have poor old Manners dashing from one end of this labyrinth to the other when it is so easy for me to bring you to the dining room.'

So this was all for Manners's benefit. Well, that put her in her place. He was right about the Abbey being a labyrinth. A labyrinth with secrets in its walls. And she ought to be glad of his thoughtfulness for the ancient butler, but perversely she wished it had been the pleasure of her company that made him come to fetch her.

Now that really was illogical.

Just as illogical as the way something in her chest gave a painful squeeze each time she saw him anew. Fear. That was all it could possibly be. They were enemies, fighting over a fortune she had never wanted in the first place.

And still she could not help her admiration for his male beauty as she stared at his freshly shaved jaw and inhaled the scent of rosemary and lemon of his soap. It was a lovely manly smell that went well with all that strength.

Strength enough to push a full barrel of beer off a wagon and into her path. Her stomach tensed, as she realised she'd let him lull her into forgetting.

Why did the man who wanted her death have to cause her heart to flutter? There was obviously something wrong with her. She was turning into one of those desperate spinsters who flung themselves into the arms of any man who showed them the least bit of attention. Good or bad.

Her throat dried. Her insides quaked with the knowledge that, in his case, the attention was all bad.

She stiffened. Held herself as aloof as possible in such an awkward position. And was still aware of the steady rhythm of his heart against her ribs and the warmth of his lithe body.

He glanced down at her briefly, his expression one of regret, heaved a sigh and shifted his grip, holding her a little less close. 'Better, Miss Wilding?'

Clearly he'd sensed her discomfort.

'Much,' she said quietly, because it actually wasn't better at all. Not really.

And when his long rapid stride brought them to the drawing room she could not help her pang of disappointment when he gently put her down on the sofa. She fought the insidious longing to be wrapped in this man's strong arms.

She had learned that such longings led only to misery.

Jeffrey handed her a glass of sherry. 'Feeling better, Miss Wilding?' he asked with a charming smile.

Her heart was fluttering, her stomach in knots, yet she managed a small smile. 'Yes, thank you.'

Mrs Hampton gave her a cool nod. 'I am glad to hear it, Miss Wilding. You gave us quite a scare.'

She had given them a scare? What did the woman think, that she had deliberately sat down in front of the barrel?

'Look what I found,' Gerald crowed, racing into the drawing room. He bowled into the centre of the group surrounding Mary, pushing, of all things, an odd-looking three-wheeled chair. 'Grandfather's bath chair. He bought it the year he went to take the waters for his gout. He never used it. It was kicking about at the back of the stables. It will be perfect for wheeling Miss Wilding about. Come on, Miss Wilding, give it a try.'

Such enthusiasm was hard to squash, Mary thought, warily looking at the contraption.

'She doesn't want to be pushed about in that,' Jeffrey

said with a grimace. 'All she needs is one of us fellows to carry her to the table. I can do it.'

The earl's gaze narrowed.

Gerald's face fell, the triumph of moments before dashed down by disappointment. It was almost painful to watch.

'I think it is a fine idea,' she said. 'Much better than being carried.'

The earl gave her a humourless smile. 'As the one who has so far done the carrying, I suppose I must also express my appreciation.' Far from sounding please, there was a note of disapproval in his voice. Did he think she could use the wheeled chair to escape him? She looked at it with renewed interest.

'It might work in the main part of the house,' Mrs Hampton said with her habitual sniff. 'But many of the passageways are narrow. And who on earth would carry it and Miss Wilding up and down the stairs? That is why my father didn't use it, you know.'

The woman had a point. 'Perhaps it would be better if I stayed in my chamber until I can use a cane,' Mary said. 'I really don't want to put people to all of this trouble.'

'Dinner is served, my lord,' Manners intoned from the doorway.

'No trouble at all,' the earl said and she was airborne again. 'You can use the chair when there are no beefy fellows to cart you about.' He cast a very pointed look at Jeffrey.

Once more she was deposited on a chair. This time the earl placed her beside him at the head of the table where Mrs Hampton usually sat.

The other woman eyed her askance for a moment, then took Mary's usual place.

Mary did her best to eat her dinner, but her ankle had begun to throb abominably. It must be the way she was sitting. Or because the effects of the willow-bark tea had worn off.

During the second remove the earl leaned closer. 'If it is not an insult to say so, Miss Wilding, you are looking quite pulled. You have been moving that piece of fish around on your plate for the past five minutes. Have you had enough?'

'Yes. I find I have eaten my fill.'

'I wasn't talking about food,' he said. 'I meant this.' His glance took in the group around the table. 'Would you feel more comfortable in the library? Sitting with your feet up on the sofa by the fire and reading your book until it is time to retire?'

The way he described it, he made it sound heavenly. The thought of putting up her foot was almost too tempting for words. 'I should probably go to bed.'

'No, I insist.' He raised his voice. 'I am sure Gerald would jump at the chance to push you along to the library.'

Gerald's enthusiastic expression agreed.

The earl gave her a conspiratorial smile. Had he guessed she would not hurt the young man's feelings by refusing? She had the feeling she was somehow playing into the earl's hands by agreeing to his plan. Nonsense. What could happen to her in the library? Besides, she was tired of the four walls of her chamber. A change of scene would do her good. 'Very well.'

Gerald wheeled the chair close. 'Hop in, Miss Wilding.'

Hop being a most appropriate word.

The earl didn't allow it. He stood and lifted her in. Once more that strange languid sensation weakened her limbs and her heart picked up speed. Oh, the man was attractive all right, but what did that matter when he meant her nothing but harm.

No matter how alluring he might be, she must remain on her guard.

As promised, the library was cosy, the fire blazing and the candles all lit.

Gerald came to a halt beside a *chaise longue* that had not been beside the hearth earlier. If she remembered correctly, it had been near the window. It seemed the earl had indeed planned this. But why? Now she wished she had insisted on going straight to her room.

'You should return to your meal,' she said to Gerald, manoeuvring out of the chair and on to the sofa.

He strolled along the bookshelves, his face moody. 'Such dullness. I was supposed to make my bows at court in the spring. We won't be going now that we are in mourning again.' The petulance was back. His moods seemed too volatile for such a young man.

'I know it will seem like for ever, but there is always next season,' she said in a matter-of-fact voice. She did not believe in encouraging the histrionics of young girls and felt the same must apply to boys equally. 'The year will pass before you know it.'

He stopped, pulled out a book and rifled absently through the pages. 'No doubt there will be some other reason not to go. Something concocted by Mama, yet again.'

'Oh, you are in the dumps,' she said, smiling.

He put the book back with a sigh. He didn't look quite so angelic in this mood.

'Do you like to read?' she asked, thinking to turn the conversation to pleasanter topics.

'I used to. I was quite sickly for a time. It was my only company.'

The memories seemed less than happy.

He swung about, his face alight once more. 'I forgot. I promised Jeff I would play billiards after dinner. You don't mind, do you? If I go?'

'Not at all.' She rather thought she'd be glad of it. Keeping up with his mercurial moods wasn't at all entertaining.

He grinned charmingly. 'Miss Wilding, I don't care what the earl says, you really are a brick.'

What the earl says? 'What—?'

Too late, he was already on his way out of the door.

What would the earl have said? That she was an antidote of a schoolmistress. Or that she was here on sufferance? Or he wished her to Jericho? While mortifying to think that he might have said any of those things, it wasn't difficult to imagine him saying them in that biting tone of his. That he would have said them to his cousin, though, that hurt. It hurt behind her ribs in a way she hadn't felt hurt in a very long time.

Because no matter how she tried not to, she had the feeling that, had circumstances been different, she might have liked him.

Oh, now that was pure foolishness. The man was pleasant to look at. He was strong. He was tall. And he was intelligent. He was in all ways…perfect.

For someone else.

He didn't want her any more than she wanted him.

Nice as it would be to live in a house like this, to have a real family, she didn't fit. She belonged with her girls. Educating them about things their families would never teach them: geography, mathematics, philosophy. Let someone else teach them deportment and drawing-room accomplishments. She wanted to expand their minds to the world.

Not that she would ever see much of it. But they might. And she could read about it.

Oh, bother. She had left her book in her chamber. Now this really was torture. Surrounded by the most magnificent selection of books she had ever seen in her life and nothing to read. Could anything else go wrong?

Really? Was she just going to sit here and bemoan her fate? She rose, standing on her uninjured foot and grasping the handles of the bath chair, hopped her way across to the shelves. Where there was a will, there was always a way.

What to choose?

She ran her eye along the titles in gold leaf on the spines of the books at eye level. Sermons. Well, she didn't mind a sermon occasionally, but tonight she needed something lighter, something to sweep her into another world. To help her forget the throbbing in her ankle and the fears lurking at the forefront of her mind. The fears that kept getting tangled up with ridiculous hopes.

The next shelf up held Shakespeare. His tales were wonderful, but difficult to read. Higher up? Novels. Some she had read. *Mysteries of Udolpho. Tom Jones.* A bit *risqué* to be sure, but fun. A slim volume, and much shorter than the others, jammed between them, caught her eye. 'A history of Beresford Abbey'. Now surely that was in the wrong place?

She reached up, but it was beyond her fingertips. She could touch the shelf, but not the book, no matter how she stretched. Ah, here was the answer. A rolling ladder tucked in the corner.

With a clever bit of work with her rolling support, heretofore known as a bath chair, she managed to get the ladder in place. She only needed to go up one step.

Tentatively she put her injured foot on the ground, grip-

ping on to the sides of the ladder for support. Just one
step up.

Her ankle gave a protesting throb. Jehosophat, that still
hurt, but she was up and the book was within her grasp.
It was jammed in tightly. She pulled. The ladder shifted.
She grabbed at the shelf.

'Miss Wilding. What in the devil's name do you think
you are doing?'

She started, then gave a little cry of alarm as the ladder moved sideways.

The next moment, the earl's large capable hands were
around her waist and he was lifting her down as if she
weighed nothing. Again. Making her stomach flutter and
her heart bang against her ribs. Again.

And now he was glaring down at her as he held her at
arm's length, making her feel no bigger than a pea.

'Well?' he said.

'I was trying to reach a book.'

He raised his eyes to the ceiling for a second. A plea
for help, or a plea for patience? 'There are hundreds of
books you can reach without climbing a ladder.'

'Not one I wanted.' Oh dear, she sounded as sullen as
Gerald.

He huffed out a breath. Looked at the shelves. 'Which
one did you want?'

'The one I was just about to take down when you scared
me half to death.' She pointed at the blue leather-bound
book jutting outward from its fellows. 'Stop sneaking up
on me.' Her heart couldn't stand it.

'I was not sneaking.' He reached up and took the book
down. Before she realised what he was about, he put an
arm around her waist. He couldn't possibly...

But he had. With one arm. The man had the strength
of ten. It left her feeling completely in his power. A good

way to let her know she could not win with him. Not a feeling she liked.

He deposited her on the *chaise* with a small grunt. So he didn't find her as quite light as he made out. Showing off, no doubt, though to what purpose she could not imagine. Unless to serve as a warning of his superior strength.

A strong mind was a match for a strong arm any day of the week.

She held out her hand for the book.

He was staring at the words on the cover. 'This is what you wanted? A history book?'

'I like history. I thought I might find out a little more about the house.'

He raised his gaze and his rare smile made an appearance. 'I am glad you are starting to feel at home, Miss Wilding.'

The warmth of that smile sent butterflies dancing in her stomach. She repressed them with a frown. 'There is no sense in going somewhere and leaving again without finding out something about it.' She sighed. 'And besides, it caught my eye because it was out of place, pushed in there with the novels.'

His smile broadened. His grey eyes danced with amusement. 'Did you ever hear the saying, curiosity killed the cat?'

Now he was teasing her. 'Without curiosity we would be no better than the beasts of the field, my lord.'

He laughed out loud. 'Then I hope you find this worth another fall.'

'The first fall was hardly my fault.' Perhaps he was thinking that if she hadn't fallen and been whisked out of the way by Mr Trelawny she might already be out of his way. The lightness she'd been feeling dissipated in a rush.

Sensing the change of mood, he huffed out a sigh. 'The

rest of them went to play billiards. Even Mrs Hampton. I came to see if you wanted to join them. To be truthful, I had thought they would come here after dinner.' He sounded disgruntled, as if they had spoiled his plan. What, had he expected them all to gather in the library, like some sort of close-knit family? The kind of family she had always dreamed of having. Or had dreamed of once, a long time ago. Now, she only wanted her job back. Her classes to teach. Her girls.

He handed her the book and wandered around the room, looking at titles, poking around in cupboards. He looked large and restless, as if he couldn't breathe in the confines of the room. How could she possibly read with him pacing around like a caged lion? To be truthful, with his dark looks, he reminded her more of a panther than a lion. But just as dangerous.

Perhaps he was eager to play billiards and felt obligated to see to her welfare. In which case, it would be easy to set him free. A little stab of disappointment caught her by surprise. What, did she want him to stay? Surely not?

'I am quite happy to sit here and read,' she said, tacitly giving him permission to depart. She glanced down at the little book and flipped through the pages. It was not a printed book. It was handwritten and there were sketches of the abbey looking very different to how it looked today. The paper was old and yellowed. Parchment? At the back of it were what looked like maps. She quickly turned to the middle of the book. She wanted to look at those maps, but not in the presence of the earl.

'Do you consider yourself a blue-stocking, Miss Wilding?' he asked idly, riffling through the pages of a volume he had pulled from the shelves. He held it up. 'A Mary Wollstonecraft acolyte? You have read her work, I am sure.'

'*A Vindication Of The Rights Of Woman*? I think it astonishingly far-sighted.'

He looked at her for a long moment and she had the feeling he was considering his options. 'You agree with her, then?'

'On many counts.' She swung her legs to the floor to face him. Her hands clasped tightly in her lap. 'Why should girls not receive the same education as their brothers? Not everyone is destined to be a wife or a mother. And even in those roles, surely an educated woman is a valuable addition to any family.'

'You are passionate in your beliefs, I see.'

And she had exposed herself to his mockery by the intensity of her response. She stiffened against her desire to back down, to please him. 'Why should I not be, since it is of importance to me as a person?'

'And it is your opinion that a woman need not, by definition of her sex, suffer from an excess of sensibility. You would not consider romantic love as a requirement for a contented marriage?'

Was this a proposal? Her heart gave a painful lurch. 'It is a sound principal from which to begin.' A painful flush rushed to her cheeks, because it was only partly the truth. Whatever she believed in her rationale mind, her heart wanted more than mere friendship or affection.

In her youth, it had yearned for love.

Yet she was not the sort of woman men fell in love with. She had accepted that. And now he was stirring up all those old emotions, those longings. Resentment rose against his probing into old wounds.

'And what of yourself, my lord?' she countered. 'What are your thoughts? You must marry, produce an heir.'

An emotion she could not read flickered across his face. Not a happy one though, of that she was certain.

'My business affairs leave little time for wooing. Besides, I have an heir.'

'Jeffrey.'

He nodded.

She remembered his vow that the Beresford line would end with him. 'So he is, after all, to provide the next generation of Beresfords? Your grandfather would be pleased.' It was an unfair jab, but she could not help but defend herself.

'It won't happen.'

He spoke with such surety, she stared at him in surprise. 'You cannot be sure he will not marry and have children. He is a young man.' Unless he planned to do away with him, too? The idea filled her with sick horror. First that she had even thought of the idea and second that she even thought it plausible. 'It is a rare man who does not marry,' she finished weakly.

He gave her a sharp look. 'You do not then eschew marriage?'

'I do not seek it for myself. But I do not eschew it for others.'

'You believe in choice, then.' A heaviness weighted his words. As if they held an underlying significance.

'Yes. I do.'

'Did you know your father was a vicar?'

She gasped.

Chapter Eight

After a moment of shock, Mary took a deep steadying breath. 'May I know what else you have learned, sir?' How she spoke with such calm, she couldn't be sure, for her pulse was racing so fast that she could feel the thunder of her heart against the press of her stays.

He gave a slight shrug. 'It is of very little help in this bind in which we find ourselves.'

The will was his only concern. Hers ran much deeper. 'My lord, this is my family we are discussing.' How rarely had she used those words, *my family*. It always seemed false to talk about family when one had none. 'I deserve to know all you have learned.'

'As you wish. Lord Templeton has established to his satisfaction that there is little or no chance that you and I are related. On either side of the blanket.'

She stiffened. 'You make it sound as if that is not a good thing.'

'It would have ended this farce immediately.'

She stared at him.

'The laws of consanguinity, Miss Wilding.' He drew up a chair and sat on the opposite side of the hearth. His expression was pensive, but the contrast of flame and shadows on his skin were unnervingly menacing. 'You must be aware of the required degrees of separation for a couple to be permitted to marry.'

Marry. There was that word again. Her face flamed, but he was looking into the fire and fortunately did not see her reaction.

'I—yes, of course I am aware.' She was proud of the way she sounded as if this was purely an academic discussion, even if inside she was as taut as a bowstring. 'Are you thinking you will submit to the terms of your grandfather's will?' Was that the point of his questions? Was he deciding what sort of wife she would make? She held her breath.

He turned away from the fire to look at her, his eyes wide with surprise and silver with intensity. Expressions flickered across his normally impassive face—longing, she thought, and perhaps loneliness. Things that pulled at her too-soft heart. Finally he settled on mockery, which seemed primarily directed at himself. 'Submission. Is that how you see it, Miss Wilding? Without knowing what is behind it all, I'd consider myself a fool to submit.' His voice was a low velvet murmur. A seduction of the senses, when the words, the unspoken criticism, flayed her heart.

She straightened her spine. 'As would I.'

Again something like regret reflected in his eyes as he acknowledged her answer with a sharp nod. 'So you would,' he agreed without inflection.

He rose to his feet. 'May I return you to your chamber? I find I am not inclined for sociability any more this evening.'

Bored with her company, he meant. 'I can ring for a footman.'

'Oh, no, Miss Wilding. Why would I deny myself the pleasure of holding you in my arms?'

Heat bathed her skin. 'Sir, you are impertinent.'

'Yes. I am, am I not?' And without another word he lifted her from the sofa and carried her to her room.

Pleasure. The word rippled through her, leaving her breathless. It was an admission that he, too, felt the attraction between them. And now he was carrying her to her bedroom. Little shivers chased across her skin.

Pleasure indeed. The feel of strong arms cradling her body, the beat of a heart against her chest, for without thinking she had curled her arm over his shoulder. To support herself, naturally. Her fingers itched to test the silkiness of the hair at his nape. Her head longed to lean against that powerful shoulder. Her body yearned to curl into him. All in the name of pleasure.

Little though she knew of it.

Too soon they arrived at her door and he set her down on her feet. Without a word, he reached around her and opened the door to her chamber. She fought the strange sense of disappointment as she turned to enter her room. 'Thank you, my lord.'

He caught her arm, holding her back, and she looked up at him. There was a strange expression on his face. A sort of wry twist to his mouth as he trapped her against the doorframe with one hand above her head and the other resting on the wall beside her cheek.

'My lord,' she gasped.

In the light from the sconce, his face was all hard angles and smooth planes. There was a loneliness about him, she was sure of it this time. An impossible bleakness as he stared into her eyes. His lids lowered a fraction, his mouth softened and curved in a most decadent smile when she nervously licked her lips.

She intended to speak, to warn him off, to push him away, but her fingers curled around his lapel as her knees felt suddenly weak and the tightness in her throat made it impossible to do more than breathe shallow sips of air.

A flash of hunger flared in those storm-grey eyes.

An answering desire roared through her veins. Shocked, heart pounding, she stared into his lovely face, waiting, wondering.

Slowly he bent his head, as if daring her to meet him halfway. Unable to resist the challenge, she closed the distance and brushed her mouth against his. His hand came behind her nape and expertly steadied her as he angled his head and took her lips in a ravenous kiss.

Large warm hands held her steady, one at her waist, the other cradling her head. A storm of sensation swept through her: tingles in her breasts, flutters in her core and the silken slide of his tongue tangling with hers. Delicious. Decadent. Bone melting. Heart stopping.

Thrills chased along her veins, making her tremble and long for more.

A sort of wonder filled her as her fingers finally explored the hair at his nape and wandered the impossible width of those muscled shoulders. Conscious mind disappeared into the hot darkness of desire.

A heavy thigh pressed between her legs, a steady pressure that offered ease to a growing ache. She shifted, parting her thighs to that insistent pressure, only to feel the torture, the aching need for something more. She tilted her hips into him.

On a soft groan, he broke the kiss. His chest was rising and falling as rapidly as her own, his gaze molten. 'Would it really be so bad to be married to me, Miss Wilding?' he asked in a low seductive growl.

Blankly she stared at him, her mind dizzy from his sensual assault.

His short laugh was low and slightly incredulous as

he swept her up and set her on the bed. He stood over her like some pillaging Viking.

Finally, some sense of preservation took control of her mind. 'You must not do this.'

His silver eyes were cold. 'Think about it, Miss Wilding. The alternative is not all that attractive.'

He turned on his heel and the door closed quietly behind him.

She swallowed. The alternative was death.

Shivering, she struggled to sit up, then pressed her fingers to her mouth, where just a few moments ago his kisses had wooed her to the point of insensibility. Had the unthinkable just happened? Had she practically given her virtue to this man? This stranger who to all intents and purposes, would be better off if she died? She gave a small moan as the delight of that moment echoed through her body and her feminine flesh gave a little pulse of pleasure.

Wanton female. Fool, more like.

Was he actually proposing marriage, or had he simply been carried away by the moment, by lust?

According to Sally, men promised many things in the throes of desire, only to go back on their word when they achieved their aim.

And he hadn't asked her to marry him. He'd asked her if marriage to him would be all that bad. She couldn't imagine anything worse, because clearly she could not keep her wits about him when he kissed her. And their marriage wouldn't be about kisses. It was about him getting his hands on his money.

He didn't even want children.

The lawyers in London must have told him there was no other way.

She went hot, then cold. Embarrassment. At him being forced to marry her. At his pretence of desire. Although it had not felt like pretence. Not at all. It had felt deliciously wicked and enticing.

Which was his whole purpose. To entice her into a marriage neither of them wanted.

If only she could get to the bottom of why the old earl had placed them in this ridiculous predicament, perhaps it would help them find a way out of it. Sally Ladbrook was the key. She was sure of it. Should she tell the earl where his friend might look for her, since it seemed unlikely she could go looking for herself any time soon? It was a question she would have to ponder carefully.

It would mean trusting him.

She did not see the earl at all the next day. Likely he was plotting his next move, after her refusal to succumb to seduction. After a night of restlessly tossing and turning, she'd spent most of the day wondering why she had.

He did not join the family for dinner, either. He was closeted with the lawyer, Mr Savary, and his steward, Manners said. He had requested a tray in his study for all three gentlemen. Not something an earl would normally do, Mrs Hampton announced in arctic tones.

Perhaps he was avoiding her. Perhaps he wasn't quite as in control as he made out. Perhaps he regretted last evening's encounter as much as she did.

So much for getting all dressed up for him. Mentally she gave herself a reproving shake. She was glad he had not come for dinner. Imagine the embarrassment of having to converse with a man whose body her hands had roamed the day before. She should be grateful for his consideration. Not that she thought he cared about her feelings.

He was no doubt busy trying to find a way to break the will.

Conversation throughout the meal was desultory, hinging around the visit the two young men had paid to a neighbour that afternoon and catching Mrs Hampton up on local gossip. Since none of it meant anything to Mary, she listened with only half an ear.

The meal was just about done and she was beginning to think she could retire to her chamber unscathed when Gerald turned his angelic-blue eyes in her direction. While he looked utterly angelic, she often had the feeling that the glimmer in his eyes was vaguely malicious. She braced herself for what might come out of his mouth.

'Did you find out anything about our ghost in that history, Miss Wilding?'

She frowned.

'The history of the house. I saw it on your bedside table when I brought you more books.'

She hadn't looked at the book, preferring the novels instead. She had set it aside and forgotten all about it. 'I did not.'

'I can't believe there isn't something in there about her,' he said, sounding disappointed.

'Let me give you the book, so you can look for yourself,' she said calmly.

The sly look was back. 'I would far rather you tell me what it says.'

'I say, old chap,' Jeffrey drawled. 'If Miss Wilding ain't interested in reading about ghosts, then she ain't. It is all speculation and gossip. I've never once seen hide nor hair of a ghost and I've explored every inch of the place.'

Including the tunnels behind the walls? He'd pooh-poohed the idea earlier, but he could have been trying to mislead her. And where had the heir to the title been when the barrel tumbled down that hill?

Could he be the one who wanted her dead? And not the earl?

Or was that her body's wishful thinking, a hope she could absolve the earl, so she could what? Encourage his seduction? Let it sway her common sense? Did she have no shame any more? No intelligence when it came to her thoughts about this man just because he had set fire to longings she had no business thinking about, let alone having?

'Would you care to take tea in the drawing room with me, Miss Wilding?' Mrs Hampton asked.

The woman sounded almost friendly, not the least bit condescending.

'I could fetch your book,' Gerald offered. 'And you could read aloud from it.'

Puzzled at his determination, Mary frowned at him.

His mother gave a little shudder. 'I am not sure it is quite an appropriate topic for the drawing room.'

'Do you believe in this ghost story, Mrs Hampton?' Mary couldn't keep the surprise out of her voice.

'It is a story passed down from generation to generation,' the widow said. 'A warning from our ancestors.'

A chill breeze seemed to pass through the room. Mary glanced up, expecting to see the door open and the curtains lifted by an errant breeze, but there was nothing, only Gerald staring at his mother with an avid expression.

His older cousin looked bored. 'He won't stop until you read it, Miss Wilding,' he said with a weary sigh.

'Very well, fetch the book. We will read it by firelight and scare ourselves to death.'

Gerald gave a whoop of triumph and shot off.

Mary, aided by Jeffrey's arm, limped the few steps to the drawing room. By the time they were settled, Gerald was back with his prize. He turned the pages until he found the chapter he wanted. 'Read from here.'

It was only as he was riffling through the pages that

Mary remembered the maps she had glanced at. The passageways and tunnels, and the caves to which they were connected.

Gerald was clearly familiar with this book, so he must be aware of them, too. But did he know that the tunnel behind her wall was in a state of good repair? Accessible?

She took the book. The handwriting was in the old style, the hand cramped, the letters *f* and *s* almost indistinguishable.

Legend tells us that tales of the ghost of a lady in white go back to the earliest days of the Reformation. Who she is, is lost in the mists of time. That she appears before the death of the Beresford earl is taken as fact by the inhabitants. The predominant tale has her as the wife of the first earl, killed by her lord so he could take another, richer wife. He was hanged when her body was found by his younger brother in the caves below the house.

'She came before Grandfather's death,' Gerald declared,

At his cousin's snort, he glowered. 'I heard her moaning and clanking around on the battlements. Old Ned said he saw her.'

'Old Ned would say your head was shaved and the hair in your pocket, should it lead to a pennyworth of beer,' Jeffrey said.

At Mary's enquiring look, he grinned. 'Old Ned is a gardener. Older than dirt, he is, and twice as thirsty.'

'Ned saw her,' Gerald said, his voice cracking awkwardly, reminding all of his youth. 'I told Grandfather.'

'Not well done,' his mother said.

The hairs on Mary's arms lifted. When she looked up, her gaze found the earl's. He had entered as quietly as a cat and, just as he had the first time she had seen him, he had paused in the shadows beyond the light of the fire and the candles. This time, however, when he caught her gaze, he immediately strode into the light.

'And what did your grandfather say?' the earl asked in such quiet mocking tones everyone in the room strained to hear him.

Gerald flushed. 'He said it was hardly a prediction, when he'd been ill for weeks. But then how do we know it was his death it portended?' He glowered at the earl.

Who ignored him. Instead he crossed to Mary's side and held out his hand. His eyes were the colour of a lake in winter and just as cold. He was back to his normal self. 'What are you are reading from?'

'The history of the Abbey, my lord.' She held it out. 'The book you kindly reached down for me.' She watched his face as he flipped through the pages.

He paused for a moment, frowning, then closed the book with a snap. 'It is hardly a work of erudition if it resorts to ghosts and tales of death.'

'It is a legend, my lord,' Mrs Hampton said, looking up from her embroidery. 'Well known to all Beresford descendants.'

Mary winced at the obvious slight, though the earl seemed oblivious, since he remained looking at her.

'It is foolish nonsense,' Mrs Hampton continued. 'But you have a good voice for reading, Miss Wilding. Clear as a bell. No mumbling, like so many of the misses of today. Read something else.'

'She reads well because she's a schoolteacher,' Gerald said.

He didn't mean it as a compliment.

Mary took a leaf out of the earl's book and ignored him. 'Why, thank you, ma'am. Unfortunately, this is the only book I have to hand, so I fear I must decline.'

Mrs Hampton scrabbled in her reticule. 'I have a book

of sermons written by my brother.' She held it out. 'I haven't had a moment to open it since it arrived. It would be a treat to hear it read.'

The earl stepped between them, ostensibly to save Mary the trouble of rising, and glanced at the title. '*Reflections upon St Paul's Epistle to the Philippians*. It sound most edifying, ma'am.' The wry note to his tone made Mary look at him again. She could have sworn she saw the chilly gaze warm with a spark of amusement. It made him seem more human, somehow, and she barely repressed an answering smile. It wouldn't be polite. She took the book from his hand.

Jeffrey groaned. 'Not more of his ramblings. Forgive me, ma'am but I'd rather blow my head off with a pistol.'

Gerald shot him a glance. 'Target practice? In the old hall?' He looked ecstatic.

Mrs Hampton frowned. 'I don't know what your grandfather was thinking, letting you shoot guns indoors.'

'Every gentleman should know how to fire a weapon accurately,' Gerald said. 'And that requires practice. I should be shooting at Manton's, but since we never go to London…'

His mother pressed her lips together, but Jeffrey nodded his agreement. 'He's right. I'll join you, Cuz. You coming, Beresford?'

'I prefer the pleasure of hearing Miss Wilding read,' he said, his voice a shade more raspy than usual.

That rough sound sent a thrill down Mary's spine. An unwelcome chill. Only it wasn't chill, there was a feverish quality to it that once more sent colour rushing to her face. She didn't have to see it to know her face had turned red, she could feel the prickle of it all the way to her hairline.

'Let them go,' Mrs Hampton said, flapping her embroidery hoop in dismissal. 'They will only laugh and carry on. Foolish boys. But be careful, my son. Pistols are dangerous.'

'I know what I am doing, Mother,' Gerald huffed. He bowed. 'I will see you in the morning. No doubt you will be abed from boredom ere long.'

Jeffrey made a more elegant departure, kissing each lady's hand in turn as he bid them goodnight, then he followed his cousin from the room.

The earl watched him go with narrowed eyes. Mary could not quite tell if he disliked his cousin or merely did not understand him. The two men were very different. It certainly did not appear as if they shared any blood, which might be the reason for their apparent mutual dislike. Perhaps Jeffrey really had hoped that somehow his claim to the title would be recognised.

Mary waited for the earl to sit down, but he did not. Instead he disposed himself with one arm resting along the mantel and his gaze fixed on the fire.

'Begin, child,' Mrs Hampton said. She leaned back against the cushions and closed her eyes.

Mary focused on the words and began reading. Hard as she tried to imbue the words with sense and meaning, the perorations and lengthy admonitions remained dreary and uninspiring. By the time she was done Mary could only pity the members of the archdeacon's congregation.

After only one paragraph a snore emanated from Mrs Hampton's end of the sofa. 'What?' she said, looking around her. Then her eyes cleared. 'Very nice. Wonderful, don't you think, my lord?'

He inclined his head. 'Entirely enlightening, ma'am.'

'Well, yes,' she muttered. 'Of course it would sound so much better in church. He has a wonderful baritone, my brother the archdeacon.'

So much for Mary doing her best.

'Would you like me to read more?' she asked with her heart sinking to her feet at the very thought.

'I think we have more than enough to reflect upon,' his lordship drawled. 'Is that your opinion also, Miss Wilding?'

Now that was really unfair, putting her in such a position, but there was a challenge in his eyes that she could not quite resist. 'I would dare to say one must take sufficient time to absorb such profoundness or it will lose its impact.'

The earl shot her a glance that just might have been tinged with admiration. She felt herself warm in the heat of that gaze.

He took a quick breath and once more his expression was guarded, his eyes cool. Once more he had distanced himself. So confusing and frustrating. Really? Why would she care?

Mrs Hampton beamed at her. 'Quite. Indeed. I shall be sure to relay your sentiments to my brother when next I write.'

'You are too kind, ma'am.'

Mrs Hampton made a great show of tidying up her embroidery, tucking it into the drawer in the table beside her. 'I believe it is time to retire, Miss Wilding.' She rose to her feet and the earl straightened.

Mary held out the book to her. 'Thank you for sharing this fine work with us.'

'Keep it. I am sure you will find it most edifying.' She darted a glance at the earl. 'Shall I write for another copy for you, your lordship? It has a great deal to offer a man in your position.'

Was that an insult? Mary felt a flash of heat on his behalf.

The earl gazed at the widow without expression. 'No

need, ma'am. I am sure Miss Wilding will be more than happy to lend me her copy. Indeed, I am sure I shall enjoy the pleasure of listening to her read on future evenings.'

Mary's jaw dropped.

'Very well, then,' Mrs Hampton said. 'I will say this. I do not as a general rule approve of blue-stockings, or young ladies earning a living, but the pupils at your school were fortunate to have you.' She gave Mary a tight smile.

Mary darted a glance at the earl, who raised a brow. She decided to accept the compliment. 'Thank you.'

Mrs Hampton headed for the door. 'Are you coming, Miss Wilding?'

Mary started to rise.

'Stay,' the earl commanded. An expression of surprise flickered across his face, as if he had not planned his request.

Startled, she stared at him blankly.

'It is early,' he added by way of an afterthought. 'Perhaps you would indulge me in a game of chess, Miss Wilding?'

It sounded like an excuse to get her alone. She swallowed, wondering what she should say.

'I am retiring.' Mrs Hampton gave the earl a pointed glance. 'While Miss Wilding is your ward, my lord, and while in most instances no one should think anything untoward of it, I do think she should follow my example.'

The earl's mouth tightened at what was clearly a suggestion he did not know how to behave like a gentleman— a cruel blow to any man's honour. And a petty triumph for the widow if Mary followed her lead.

He awaited her decision impassively. Clearly his pride would not let him argue his case. Not that he had much of a case after his attempted seductions. She really should go.

'I will stay for a while,' she said impulsively and

flushed. Oh why would she care if she hurt his feelings? If, indeed, he had any feelings.

'Then I bid you both goodnight.' The widow swept out of the room.

Wondering if she had quite lost her senses, Mary watched her go.

'You do play chess, do you not?' the earl asked.

'Indifferently, I am afraid,' she said as calmly as her racing heart would allow. She and Sally had played occasionally, but Mary had the feeling that Sally made up the rules as she went along. Fortunately, it was not something they had been required to teach their pupils. 'I really should retire and leave you to your port.'

'Afraid, Miss Wilding?'

Of course she was afraid. She'd be out of her mind not to be. But it would be a mistake to let him see it. 'I just do not think you will find my chess game much of a challenge.'

He tilted his head. 'Then let us take up where we left off. Will you read for me?'

She glanced down at the book of sermons. 'I'd really rather not.'

The earl pulled a small book from the inside breast pocket of his coat. 'This may be more to your taste.' He held out a small volume bound in worn brown leather and lettered in gold.

She read the cover. 'Spenser's *Faerie Queene*. Not an easy read.'

'But not beyond you, I think.'

There was something in his tone that made her try to read his expression, but as usual his thoughts were shuttered, as he took up his previous stance at the hearth. Once more she was reminded of a dark fallen angel. Or a god cast out from the heavens, much as it seemed he had been cast out by his family. Not unlike her. Something in her chest squeezed. A pang of empathy.

She knew what it felt like to be abandoned.

She lowered her gaze and opened the cover to read: *To Laura, for ever in my heart, LBB.* The B could stand for Bane. If so, it was odd to realise she did not know his first name. And if he had given it to Laura, why was it returned? She glanced up, but he simply nodded encouragement for her to continue. She opened the pages at the beginning. The vellum pages were worn and well-thumbed. 'An oft-read story,' she murmured.

'Yes.'

She coloured at the cold indifference in his voice. He clearly wasn't going to give her any information. And she had too much pride to press him.

She scanned the first few lines, getting a feeling of the flow and the rhythm.

> *Lo I the man, whose Muse whilome did maske,*
> *As time her taught, in lowly Shepheards weeds,*
> *Am now enforst a far unfitter taske,*
> *For trumpets sterne to change mine Oaten reeds,*
> *And sing of Knights and Ladies gentle deeds;*
> *Whose prayses having slept in silence long,*
> *Me, all to meane, the sacred Muse areeds*
> *To blazon broad emongst her learned throng:*
> *Fierce warres and faithfull loves shall moralise my*
> *song.*

Hesitant at first, she struggled with the rhythm and the ancient spelling. But her difficulties were not entirely the fault of the text. She could not help but be aware of the earl's overwhelming presence. The very essence of him pulled at her mind. The intensity of his regard on her face made her tremble inside.

After a time, she lost herself in the lyrical words and the world of warriors. Stanza after stanza rolled off her tongue. Her heartbeat provided the rhythm and her indrawn breath the pauses.

Slowly, she became aware of the low male voice joining hers, at first a murmur and then increasing in volume, until they read together, but he was not reading, he spoke from memory.

She let her voice subside to a whisper, and then die away altogether, watching his face, his gaze fixed on a time and space not of this room. There was sorrow and bleakness in his expression, as if the words did not recall happy memories.

And there was a shade of anger, too, mirroring that of the Knight whose words he spoke.

When he reached the end of the first Canto, he seemed to come to himself and realised she had ceased reading. A faint colour stained his cheekbones.

'You read very well,' he said.

'And you know it by rote.' She let her question go unspoken, but it hung in the small distance between them.

'I heard it read so often I think it is engraved on my brain.'

He reached for the book and tucked it back in a small pocket in the breast of his coat.

She felt a pang in her chest with respect to this Laura, whose book he carried close to his heart. Not jealousy, surely?

'It was my mother's.' His usual rough-edged voice was more raspy than usual, as if it cost him something to speak of it. 'It was the only thing she brought from this house, apart from me.'

She could not quite believe her feeling of relief that it was not something he had given a lover. 'And the giver?' she dared to ask.

'Her husband.'

She noticed that he did not call him his father.

'She read this book over and over,' he continued. 'Long after we heard he had died.' He looked away, clearly not wanting to share his emotions. 'It reminds me of her. Thank you for indulging me.'

There was no sentimentality in his voice and she had the sense the reminder was uncomfortable. She wanted to say more, even to offer comfort, but she had the sense he had said far more than he wished.

'Thank you. I have not read that work in an age.'

'It was not part of the school's curriculum?' he said, his voice sounding normal again.

She sighed. 'There is only so much time in the day and there are other subjects which must be covered.'

'Like chasing off footpads with parasols?'

She glanced just in time to see the faintest quirk to his lips. Was he teasing? Or mocking? She preferred not to know.

'The things people deem it important for women to know,' she said matter-of-factly. 'Needlework, French— with which I agree, by the way—drawing, deportment.'

'All useful attributes, surely?'

'Useful for those seeking a husband, no doubt.' She got up. He rose with her.

'You must excuse me, my lord, I am ready to retire.'

'I notice your ankle is considerably better.'

It was. She had healed far more quickly than the doctor expected. In a day or two she would be walking normally. But she had not intended for him to realise how well she progressed. 'It is well rested. No doubt by the time I reach my room, it will be aching again.'

'Then you must permit me to help you.'

Oh, she had fallen very neatly into that trap, hadn't she? 'Thank you, but I manage fine with my cane.' She bent down and retrieved it from the floor beside her chair.

His mouth was tight when she stood up and the faint warmth of earlier had gone from his eyes. They were as cold as granite. Was he somehow hurt that she had refused his aid?

'It is good for me to walk,' she said, in a feeble attempt to lessen the blow, if indeed she was interpreting his expression correctly. 'I have been sitting too long.'

A muscle jumped in his jaw. He bowed. 'As you wish.'

'Then I bid you goodnight, my lord. Thank you for a pleasant evening.'

'I see good manners were also a part of the curriculum,' he said drily as she passed out of the room.

As she limped back to her chamber, she had the strangest sensation of being followed. A sort of prickling at the back of her neck, but each time she turned around to look, there was no one there. She shivered, thinking of Gerald's tales of hauntings.

Or was it something much simpler—was his lordship following her to make sure she did not stray? Somehow she felt much more comfortable with the first idea.

Chapter Nine

A wisp of light floated above the uneven floor. The nearby rocks lining the tunnel wall and ceiling were shown in glistening relief, the darkness beyond impenetrable. The ground sloped downwards beneath Mary's feet. Steep. Rough. And Mary could hear the sea, a roaring grumbling vibration through the rocks.

The figure ahead beckoned. 'Don't be afraid,' it whispered softly.

Sometimes it was right in front of her, sometimes it disappeared around a corner, leaving only a faint glow in its wake, but as long as Mary kept moving forwards, it was always there, just ahead. The White Lady. It could be no one else.

The chill was unearthly. Mary rubbed her bare arms and realised she was dressed only in her nightrail. Her bare feet were numb. She glanced back down the tunnel. She should get her shawl and slippers. Behind her there was only blackness. How far had she come? It seemed better to go on.

A long low moan echoed around her.

Rattling chains.

The glowing figure headed towards her, twisting like

smoke. Fear caught at her heart. She turned and ran. Into the black. Ahead she could see a small wedge of light. Her chamber. Her stomach dropped away. She was falling. Into the dark.

A shriek split the air.

Mary jolted. Sat up, shaking.

Where was she? The last of the embers in her fire swam into focus. She shivered and looked around.

She was on her bed, her bedclothes on the floor. The only light in the room was a low red glow from the fire. Shadows clung to the walls. The air was freezing. Was that wretched door to the tunnel open? She shot out of bed. Rummaged for the poker among the sheets.

There. The comforting shape of iron. She grabbed it and held it high above her head. 'Who is there?' she quavered.

Her door burst open.

She screamed, backing away, grasping the poker in two hands, staring at the shadowy figure menacing her from the doorway.

'Get out,' she warned, her voice full of panic.

The man, for it was a man and not a ghost, plucked a candle from the sconce outside her door and stepped boldly into the room. The light revealed the earl, dressed in naught but his shirt and breeches.

'You!' she said.

'Miss Wilding. Mary. I heard you scream.' He drew closer, his gaze fixed on her face. 'Give me that.'

He could not possibly have heard her from his room in the south tower. She gripped her weapon tighter. 'Stay away.'

In one swift movement he wrested the poker from her hand and flung it aside.

She pressed her back against the wall.

He stared at her as if shocked, then stepped back, hand held away from his side. 'Take it easy, Miss Wilding.' He replaced the unlit stub in the candlestick on her dressing table with the lit one in his hand.

Her body was shaking. Her heart racing. She put a hand on the bedside table for balance. 'What do you want?'

He recoiled, as if startled by her vehemence, but as he looked at her, his eyes widened, and a sensual longing filled his expression as his gaze drifted down her body. Her insides tightened at the heat of the hunger in his eyes.

She gasped and, glancing down, realised how little she was wearing. She shielded herself with her hands. 'Please. Leave.'

'I think not.' He strode for the chest at the end of her bed and picked up her robe that Betsy had left there, ready for the morning. He threw it at her. 'Put this on.'

She caught it against her, but couldn't seem to move. He huffed out an impatient sigh, came around the bed and threw it around her shoulders, wrapping it around her. "What the devil is going on here?'

He sounded genuinely perplexed. And perhaps even worried.

He had come through the door. Not from the tunnel. She had locked her door. She stared at the fire irons sitting neatly on the hearth. No longer her alarm, but simply fire irons. Someone had moved them since she had fallen asleep. Betsy? The light of the candle also showed the wall was exactly where it should be. How could she explain her fear without giving away her knowledge of what lay behind the wall?

Her breathing slowed. And although her body continued to tremble, she managed to catch her breath. If only she could think. She shuddered.

'Was it a nightmare?' he asked.

A nightmare. That would explain the vision of the ghost. The sensation of falling and yet awaking to find herself on her bed. It didn't explain the freezing temperature.

His eyes shifted to the window, then shot back to her face. His jaw hardened. He crossed the room, closed the casement and spun around to face her. 'What is going on here, Miss Wilding? A midnight visitor?'

She stared at him in astonishment and then at the window. 'Certainly not. Fresh air is healthy.' So healthy her teeth were aching with the urge to chatter—but she did not remember opening it.

'Not in the middle of winter,' he growled. 'Why do I have the sense you are not telling me the truth?'

'What reason do I have to lie?'

'Because you answer a question with a question.'

He was lying, too. There was no earthly way he could have heard her cry out and arrived so quickly unless he was in the tunnel behind the wall.

She tried to keep her gaze away from the chimney. He must not know she was aware of it. He must have entered her room from there, closed it and gone out by the door. That would explain how he had entered when the door was locked. It did not explain the window.

'Why did you cry out?'

'I had a bad dream. I was asleep. Something was chasing me. I fell.' She shook her head. 'I thought I fell. A long way down. But when I opened my eyes, I was here. And you came through the door.'

She started shaking again. It had all seemed so real. Felt real.

'Then it was your scream I heard.'

'I suppose it must have been.' But she'd heard the

scream, too. It had come from somewhere else. Above her head. Hadn't it?

Or had she screamed in her sleep and frightened him off before he could do whatever it was he had intended? Before he could take drastic action. Before she could disappear in the tunnels below the house. Had he then pretended to burst in to allay her suspicions?

She didn't dare give voice to her thoughts, in case she was right. Or in case she was wrong. She was just so confused. She pressed her hands together, staring at his face, trying to read his expression.

'Mary,' he murmured. Then muttered something under his breath. 'Miss Wilding. Sit down before you fall.'

When she didn't move he took her hand and led her to the bed. His large warm hands caught her around the waist and he lifted her easily on to the mattress. He looked down at the tangle of covers at his feet and then back at the window. His mouth tightened.

'Someone was here,' he said. His voice harsh. And it wasn't a question.

She shivered. You, she wanted to say. 'I saw no one,' she forced out. She could not let him know what she suspected. Nor could she accuse him without proof. 'I saw no one. Only…only the White Lady. In my dream.' It had to be a dream. She did not believe in ghosts. Would not.

He cursed softly, then took one of her hands in his, clearly intending to reason with her. His hands curled around her fingers. He frowned. 'You really are freezing.'

He crossed to the fire, stirred up the embers and added a few lumps of coal, then came back to her, taking her hands in his and rubbing them briskly. He rubbed at her upper arms and she could feel the warmth stealing through her body. Not just because his rubbing, but because of his closeness, because of the heat from his body.

He stared into her face. His breathing was also less than steady and there was fear in his eyes, as if she had somehow unnerved him. Fear for her? The very idea of it plucked at her heartstrings, made her want to confide in him. She just didn't dare.

His hands stopped their warm strokes and one came to her chin, tipping her face up, forcing her to either close her eyes or look at him. She chose to be bold, to return stare for stare. She would not show him how much she feared him, or how much she feared her responses to his touch.

'Mary,' he whispered, his rough voice containing a plea, as his warm breath grazed the cold skin on her cheek and his hungry gaze sparked heat low in her belly that seemed to trickle outwards.

'My lord,' she replied, shocked at the husky quality of her voice, at the difficulty she had breathing around the panicked beat of her heart.

A soft groan rumble up from his chest. Then his mouth covered hers. The storm of sensation racing through her body could not possibly be a dream. The way his hands roved her back, the way hers felt the muscle beneath the linen of his shirt. Nothing in her experience could lead her to imagine anything so wildly exciting.

Slowly he sank backwards on to the mattress. And heaven help her, she followed, not willing to break the magic of his wonderful kiss. His strong arms held her close against his body and he rolled her on to her back. He kissed her mouth, plying her lips softly at first, then his hunger grew more demanding, until she parted her lips and allowed him entry. He teased her tongue with little flicks and tastes until she dared taste him back. Such a heavenly silken slide. Deliciously wicked.

When his tongue slowly retreated, she followed with

her own, exploring the warm dark cavern of his mouth, tasting wine and him, mingled in one heady brew.

A sweet ache, trembling inside her with longing, built slowly—a hot, anxious longing.

A low groan rumbled up from his chest and he rolled over her, one knee pressing between her thighs, one hand steadying her at her nape, the other moving to stroke her ribs, to gently cup her breast.

She gasped at the shock of it, at the unfurling pleasure of it that made her breast tingle. As if that light touch was not enough.

She moaned.

He raised his head, looking down into her face. The fire and the candle gave just enough light to see the silver glitter of his eyes, the sensual cast to his mouth as his gaze searched her face, then skimmed down to where his hand rested on the swell of her breast. Slowly he moved his thumb over her nipple. It tightened beneath the fabric of her night rail. And her insides clenched.

Of their own accord her hips arched into him, seeking relief from the tender ache. He closed his eyes briefly, but there was pleasure in the brief wince of pain. And the hunger in his expression intensified.

Again his head lowered and her lips parted in anticipation of his kiss. Only this time his gentle mouth drifted slowly across her cheek in light brushes that made her want more. Until he found her ear and breathed hot moist air that sent shivers sweeping across her breast, down her back, into the very core of her.

She wriggled and moaned.

He laughed softly in her ear, sending another spasm through her body. Then his scorching mouth was moving onwards, to her neck where he licked her and her pulse spiralled out of control, to the hollow of her throat, where he breathed deeply, as if to inhale her essence, across the rise of her breast to the nipple he had stroked with his thumb.

She held her breath.

Then his mouth closed over it. Hot. Wet. His tongue flicking and tormenting while she wriggled and squirmed beneath him, seeking to break the ever-tightening cord inside her.

'No,' she gasped.

He raised his head, looking into her eyes with that penetrating stare as if he could see right into her mind, as if he knew what was happening inside her body. 'No? Shall I stop?'

'Yes,' she whispered, though it took all of her will.

But as he started to move, she couldn't bear it. 'I must not. It isn't right.'

'It feels right,' he said in that deep raspy voice. Seductive. Enticing. 'You feel right.' He cupped her breast. 'Perfect, in fact.' He squeezed his eyes shut. 'But you are right. This must wait until we are married.'

Married. But she hadn't agreed they would be married.

He kissed her mouth. Chastely. Sweetly. Preparing to leave.

Hot with desire and hunger, her lips clung to his. Her hands grasped his shoulders, pulling him down to her, as she lifted her body to press her breasts against his wide chest. It felt so good to be close to him. To feel his strength. To feel connected.

Her thighs parted to press her mons against that beautifully heavy and hard-muscled thigh. She rocked her hips. Sweet pleasure, stole her breath and made her want more.

He broke away.

'You must make up your mind, Mary,' he said, his voice a low growl. 'Marry me and finish this, or…not.'

She stared up at him. He was speaking of lust, not love. He was being forced into this by a grandfather he hated. Once they were wed, would he resent her? How could he not? But what was the alternative?

She turned her face away, trying to think, trying to make sense of it all.

The mattress shifted as he stood. The door clicked shut.

He had left without a word, quietly. Like a ghost. Did he assume she'd given her answer?

If so, what did that mean for her future?

The heat of her body slowly returned to normal and she rose from the bed, feeling the damp chill at her breast where he had suckled. The heat of embarrassment washed through her. How could she be so wanton with a man who—who might well prefer her dead?

She limped across the room and turned the key in the lock. She balanced the fire irons on the vase and stepped back. Had she forgotten to set them there last night? Had Betsy moved them? She couldn't seem to remember.

Could she have moved them herself and wandered down the tunnel? In her sleep? Was she indeed hysterical, her fears getting the better of her once she fell asleep? Could she also have opened the window?

She swallowed the dryness in her throat. Was it her mind playing tricks? Or was she just trying to find an excuse for him, for the earl, because she didn't want to believe he intended her harm?

Was she foolish enough to want to say yes to his offer of marriage?

She crawled back into her bed, her mind going around and around with questions she couldn't seem to answer.

The next morning she felt so listless, so tired, she had asked Betsy to bring her breakfast in bed. She just could not face the Beresford family. Not the earl. Not the cousins. And definitely not Mrs Hampton.

Betsy returned with a tray looking as cheerful as always. 'Eat up, miss,' she said. 'You'll soon feel more the thing.'

'Thank you.' She glanced out of the window at a bright-blue sky. 'The weather looks fine today.'

'Snow's on the way,' Betsy said. 'The calm before the storm.'

Mary laughed, but said nothing. She was used to local predictions of weather. They invariably turned out wrong. There seemed to be this feeling among country folk that good weather heralded bad. She tucked into the tea and toast she had requested while Betsy set out her gown.

'His lordship is off to the mine,' Betsy said, shaking out the creases in the blue muslin. 'I heard him asking for that there black beast of his. Joe says it's a vicious animal. The stable lads are all scared of it.'

Mary frowned. 'The earl never mentioned he was going to the mine.'

'He arranged it with the manager, Mr Trelawny, yesterday.'

And both men knew she wanted to go, too. Did the earl think she wouldn't find out, or had he decided that she would be his wife and therefore the mine would soon be under his control? 'Has his lordship left already?'

'I wouldn't know, miss.'

'Go and find out, would you? And ask him to wait, if he hasn't gone. Ask him to have the carriage readied for me.' And if he had left? Might it be an opportunity for escape? 'Betsy, if I missed him, please ask that the carriage be put to so I can follow on. He must have forgotten I was to go with him.'

Betsy stared at her. 'But your foot, miss.'

'It is well enough. Please hurry.' She'd taken off the bandage before Betsy had come back with the tray and, though her ankle was still discoloured by the bruise, the swelling had quite gone and it only really hurt if she moved carelessly. It was strong enough for a carriage ride and a short walk. She wanted to see the condition of the children at the mine. She'd read a great deal recently by some forward-thinking women about the cruel conditions of such places. She could not bear the thought that those kind of conditions existed at something for which she was responsible.

While Betsy hurried off to do her bidding, Mary dressed. Fortunately for her, she'd been wearing her front-closing stays when the rest of her things had gone over the cliff, so she managed fairly well, and only needed Betsy to fasten the back of her gown when she returned with the news that his lordship was waiting. But not for long.

'I can't say he was pleased, miss, but he ordered up the carriage.'

Mary wrapped her woollen cloak around her, tied on her bonnet and pulled on her gloves. 'And I am ready. Now if you would be so good as to lead me to the front door, I can make sure I am not delaying his lordship any more than necessary.'

She followed Betsy along the corridors and realised she no longer needed a guide. She was becoming quite familiar with the old house's twists and turns. But this morning it was better to be safe than sorry.

Losing her way and arriving late would be all the excuse his lordship needed to leave without her. And this would be a chance to survey the roads around the house. The next time she left, she intended to follow the road across the moors to Helston where his lordship had not warned the inhabitants they must not sell her a ticket for the stagecoach.

As much as she wanted to trust him when he was kissing her senseless, the answer had finally come to her just before she fell asleep. If she agreed to marry him, she would be wholly in his power. He would be able to do anything he wanted and she would not be able to object. A very bad idea while she had no idea why his grandfather had pushed them together.

The first order of business was to find Sally Ladbrook and find out what she knew. Then perhaps she could think about what to do in regard to the earl. Because the last thing she wanted was to be at the mercy of a vengeful husband in a damp and draughty house where ghosts seemed to roam at will and, according to legend, people could disappear without a trace.

Beresford was standing beside the carriage when she exited the house into the sunshine. His face was set in its usual grim lines as he looked up at her approach. There was no sign of his horse. 'Good morning, my lord,' she said brightly.

'Good day, Miss Wilding.'

There was nothing of the passionate man he had been in her room last night in the icy gaze he bestowed on her. She half-wondered if she had imagined the whole thing. But she hadn't. Nor had she imagined the scream that had awoken her from her horrible dream. 'You knew I wished to go with you, my lord. You might have sent word.'

'You weren't at breakfast, Miss Wilding,' he said, with a slight nod of his head, 'or I would have told you of my plans.'

Oh, yes, she really believed that.

His raised a brow. 'I thought you might prefer to wait until your ankle is perfectly well.'

By then it might be too late. By then she might have succumbed to his powers of seduction. 'I prefer to go today. And here I am. Ready to go.'

Something hot flared in his eyes. Anger, no doubt. No man liked a woman with a will of her own. He bowed slightly. 'Your carriage awaits, but time does not.'

One of the grooms leapt forwards to open the carriage door and she climbed inside and settled herself against the squabs. He climbed in after her.

Startled, she edged deeper into the corner. 'I thought you planned to ride?'

'I did.'

'Don't feel you must keep me company.' Oh dear, that sounded rude.

'I never do anything I don't wish to do, Miss Wilding,' he drawled and stretched out his legs, brushing against her skirts in a way that felt all too intimate. But what could she say? He was playing the perfect gentleman, sitting opposite her on the seat, facing backwards.

She winced inwardly. She had intended to make a note of any landmarks she saw as a means of finding her way—she'd brought along a notebook and pencil for the purpose. She could hardly do so with him sitting there watching her. She would just have to try to hold them in her memory.

She stared out of the window, trying to look as if her interest was idle curiosity. Here there was a large barn. There an oddly twisted tree, but they were moving so quickly it was hard to keep track.

'What do you think of Cornwall?' he asked.

Be quiet, I'm trying to follow our route, she wanted to snap. Instead, she pursed her lips as if giving consideration to his question. 'It's very different from the countryside in Wiltshire.'

'How?'

She turned to face him. 'The sea. The moors. The mining. Even the way the people speak. I can barely understand some of their words.'

'It is not so very different from Wales,' he murmured, as if remembering. 'They also have their own language.'

'Did you live in Wales?'

He nodded. 'For a while. When I was young.'

His willingness to talk about the past surprised her. 'Did you like it there?'

His eyes turned the colour of a winter sky. Bleak. Cold. Clearly she'd touched a nerve and she expected him to withdraw into his usual chilly distance.

'No.' He took a deep breath. 'Not true. There were good times as well as bad.' He turned his face to look out of the window as if he preferred to hide his thoughts, but the way the light shone on the window, she could make out his reflection. Not the detail, but enough to see him close his eyes as if shutting a lid on memories their conversation had evoked. 'It was a hard life,' he murmured. 'But I learned about mining and the men who risk their lives below ground.'

'Tin mining?' she asked in the awkward silence.

He turned back, his expression once more under control. 'Coal.'

'Did you work in the mine?'

'As a hewer?' He shook his head. 'I wasn't strong enough, then. I did later. Alongside the men in my uncle's mine. My mother's brother. He believed a man should learn every part of a business he intended to follow. The way he had.'

'Even the heir to an earldom?'

He smiled a little, as if amused by a recollection. The atmosphere in the carriage lightened. His face looked younger, more boyish. 'Especially the heir to an earldom. He is not a great respecter of nobility. He thinks they are all soft and idle.'

'Is that what you think?' she dared to ask.

He gave her question consideration. 'I think there is good and bad in every class of society.'

As did she. Strange how they were in accord on some things and so at odds on others. Like the inheritance, for example, she thought grimly.

He leaned forwards, picked up her gloved hand from her lap and held it his. He massaged her palm with his thumb. The bleakness was entirely gone from his face, and now his expression was pure seduction. 'Have you thought any more about our future?'

The stroke of his thumb was scrambling her thoughts. Her body was vibrating with longing, her pulse jumping. She swallowed. Forced her mind to focus. '*Our* future? I have certainly thought about my own.'

His eyes danced, as if she amused him. 'You cannot think about one and not dwell on the other. Don't take too long to come to a decision.'

'Why?'

The caress ceased, though he did not release her hand. If anything, his fingers closed tighter around it. He fixed her with his inscrutable gaze. 'It's a matter of life and death, isn't it?'

Dumbly she stared at him, taken aback by his frankness.

'What is holding you back?' He moved from his side of the carriage to hers and suddenly the seat felt a great deal smaller. The way his shoulders took up all the space and his thigh pressed against hers. He still had her hand, too. She gave it a gentle tug, but he didn't seem to notice. Instead, he eased down the leather at her wrist. 'You can't deny the spark of attraction between us.' He raised her hand to his mouth and breathed on the sensitive skin where he had pulled the leather apart. She shivered.

He kissed the pulse that now raced beneath her skin. Traced the fine blue veins of her inner wrist with his tongue. 'What can I do to persuade you?'

'You didn't want this marriage,' she managed to gasp.

'The benefits are becoming more and more apparent.' His voice was deep and dangerously seductive. Her eyelids drooped, her limbs felt heavy. She forced herself to straighten.

'I would never be your choice of a wife, if your grandfather hadn't drawn up his will this way. Would I?' Breathlessly she waited for his answer, hope a small fragile thing in her breast.

He raised his gaze from her wrist to her face. His silver eyes glittered. 'If we had met somewhere, you mean—in a ballroom in London?' His mouth quirked downwards. 'I will not do you a disservice and lie. I had no intention of marrying. Not yet. Not until the future was secure. But given the circumstances, it is not such a bad arrangement.'

Cold rippled across her skin. 'And what of love, my lord?'

He chuckled then, deep and low. It was a surprisingly pleasant sound. And his face looked more handsome, less of a devil.

'Miss Wilding. Mary. May I call you Mary?'

Breathless to hear his reply, she nodded her assent.

He tilted his head as if seeing her for the first time, then shook it. 'My dear Mary, you will not convince me that a rational logical woman such as yourself believes in such romantic nonsense.'

Oh, but she did. She did not think she loved this man, though she knew she was attracted to him. Desired him.

But was it enough on which to base a marriage? Others did. But she wasn't others.

She gazed up into his dark features, searching those silver-grey eyes, and realised that this was not the sort of man she had ever imagined in her life. She'd dreamed of a scholarly man. A gentle man, who would listen to her thoughts. Who would respect her ideas. Not this dark dangerous man who set her pulse fluttering and her body longing for wicked things.

Her insides gave a tiny little pulse of pleasure at the thought of those wicked things.

But she should think with her mind. Her rational mind. Just as a man would.

'What if at some time in the future you meet a woman you really wished to marry? Will not your resentment be great?'

He cupped her face in his hands, his large warm hands, and she felt the tremble in his fingers, as if he was struggling under some emotion as his gaze searched her face.

She could not help but look at his finely drawn lips before she raised her gaze to look at his face where she found the heat of desire in his eyes. 'My lord,' she whispered.

'Bane,' he rasped. 'Call me Bane.'

But she couldn't speak, because his mouth had taken hers in a ravening kiss and, lord help her, she was kissing him back, running her hands over his shoulders, tangling her fingers with his hair. He lifted her on to his lap and she felt his strong thighs beneath her bottom. The way he rocked lightly into her, and the deep groan from his throat, stirred her blood and made her heart beat too fast.

It felt as if his hot mouth was all over her and her skin was on fire from its touch.

'Marry me, Mary,' he whispered against her throat.

'Marry me,' he said, undoing the buttons of her coat and pressing his lips to her clavicle.

The carriage jolted, swaying over to one side, and he grabbed her around the shoulders to prevent her from falling. Then it came to a halt.

Bane cursed softly. 'We will continue this conversation later.' He lifted her off his lap and set her back on the seat.

The hard cold man was back. The man she recognised. And as she did up her buttons and straightened her hair, she could not help but wonder how much the passionate man was really him.

The groom opened the door. Bane picked up his gloves and his hat and stepped out. He reached up to help her down. His glance was swift and assessing. His brief nod assured her that she did not look as if she'd been ravished, though her lips still tingled from his kiss and her cheeks glowed from the scratch of his jaw.

And then the noises assaulted her ears.

A constant thumping she could feel vibrating under her feet and pounding through her head.

His lordship shook hands with Mr Trelawny, who was standing waiting for them. The poor man's eyes widened when they rested on her, but he smiled manfully. 'Miss Wilding,' he said, shouting to be heard above the noise of the great machine some distance away. 'I was not expecting you today, but welcome to Old Men's Wheal, as it was called once. I hope your...' He glanced down at her feet, then coloured. 'I hope you are quite recovered from your unfortunate accident.'

She smiled at the young man. 'But for you, Mr Trelawny, I doubt I would be here to tell the tale,' she said, leaning close to his ear to make herself heard.

The young man's colour deepened.

Bane surprised her by swiftly catching her hand, pull-

ing her close and putting it on his arm. 'Show us the workings, Trelawny.' He did not raise his voice, but clearly the
manager heard for he nodded and gestured for them to
follow. He led them to the machine making all the noise.

'Stampers,' he yelled.

Bane's gaze swept over the monstrous structure, a
beam supported on legs. Heavy metal tubes hanging from
the beam on chains, rising up and down alternately, each
one crashing down to crush the rocks shoved beneath it
by a couple of men.

Driving the whole was an enormous waterwheel that
clanked and creaked, adding to the cacophony. Beyond it
three large pools were being stirred by women with long
rakes and shovels.

Compared to the beauty of the countryside through
which they had passed, it was ugly and dirty. And the
noise was horrendous. She could not imagine working
with that sound all day.

As far as she could see there were no children.

She put her hands over her ears, but it did nothing to
lessen the noise. 'From here, the black tin is taken to the
foundry at Hayle. You should visit it some time,' Mr Trelawny shouted.

Bane nodded. 'Where do they get the coal?' This time
even he had to raise his voice.

'Wales.'

He grimaced.

'The mine is this way,' Mr Trelawny said. 'Up the hill.
The carriage will take you up to the entrance, Miss Wilding.'

'We will all go in the carriage,' Bane said when they
reached it.

How strange. She let him help her back in. Mr Trelawny climbed up with the driver, citing the dust and

dirt he had gathered from his visit to the workings earlier that morning. Getting ready for the new owner's visit,
no doubt.

Bane dropped the window and the noise of the stamper
continued to assault their ears. 'Imagine living with that
din day after day,' she said. 'Those poor men. They must
go home with a headache.'

He cast her a sharp glance. 'They are paid well enough.'

She pressed her lips together. She had no wish to start
an argument, but she had to be glad there had been no
children working near that noisy machine.

As the carriage wound its way to the other side of the
hill, the thumping faded to a bearable level. It was more
like the sound of a heart beating loudly from this distance.

The carriage once more halted and they stepped down.
The view of the surrounding countryside was breathtaking—open common, trees in the valley, sheep on the
moor—but right here, on the side of the hill, industry was
an ugly scar. Bare rock. Gravel. A horse walking steadily
round and round a revolving drum. Every now and again,
a bucket full of rocks would appear at the surface to be
emptied into the back of a cart by a couple of workers. No
doubt those rocks would end up at the stamper.

Another horse went round and round, pulling a chain,
and beside it a strange-looking object spurted water into
a ditch.

'A rag-and-chain pump,' Mr Trelawny explained, 'to
remove water from the shafts. Let us go down. The men
are expecting us. Please be careful where you walk, Miss
Wilding. The ground is rough and there are some disused
shafts here and there from the ancient workings.'

At her nervous glance, he smiled. 'If you stay close to
me at all times, you will be fine.'

Bane shot him a glare and Trelawny flinched.

'This way,' he said, hustling them towards a stone structure. It looked a bit like a square Norman tower, without crenellations or arrow loops. He ducked inside and, after glancing around, Bane urged her to follow with his hand at the small of her back. The stone chamber was lit by candles.

Mary immediately recognised the greasy smell of melting tallow. They'd been forced to use tallow in the kitchens and working areas at the school when money was in short supply—or apparently in short supply. She felt a little trickle of resentment at the thought, but had no time to think about it, because Mr Trelawny was directing her to a wooden trestle around the wall. 'You'll need boots,' he said, sorting through a small pile. 'It is muddy down there.'

As she sat down and her eyes adjusted to the smoky light, she noticed the large gaping hole before her and the flimsy-looking rope ladder leading down into the depths.

'You will need a hat, my lord,' Trelawny said, handing him a battered-looking felt object with a candle stuck in a lump of something nasty-looking on the front of it. 'You, too, Miss Wilding.' He frowned. 'You will have to remove your bonnet.'

She looked at him and looked at the ladder and looked back at him. 'How far down does it go?'

'The first adit is about twenty feet down. Not far at all, miss. Old Jem is waiting at the bottom for us. There's other parts of the mine where the depth is close to one-hundred-and-eighty feet.'

She felt a little faint at the thought of going into the bowels of the earth a mere twenty feet. 'Why don't I wait up here for your return? I am not really dressed for climbing down ladders.'

'I should have loaned you a pair of my breeches,' Bane said and there was a teasing note to his voice.

When she looked at him, he was smiling. And looking quite at home. 'Come now, Miss Wilding, I thought you had more gumption. It was your idea to come.' He actually looked as if he was enjoying himself. And he seemed to want to include her. It was quite a revelation.

'I didn't know about the ladder,' she said weakly. 'I don't think my ankle is up to it.' It was the first thing that came into her mind.

'You haven't let that stop you in the past. I will carry you down.'

Why was he being so insistent? 'You couldn't possibly.' She shuddered.

'You are no heavier than a hod of coal and I have carried a few of them in my time. Come on, Miss Wilding. Buck up.' Before she knew what he was about, he had lifted her off her feet and tossed her over his shoulder. 'Don't move now, Miss Wilding, or we will both fall.' He heaved one leg over the side of the hole, grasping on to the railing. He paused. 'Light my candle for me, would you, Trelawny?' he said with great good cheer.

Never had she felt so undignified. Or so foolish. Oh lord, that was his hand on her posterior. Holding her steady? Was he going to climb down using only one hand? 'Really, my lord. I would be quite happy to wait up here for your return.'

'You must think I am a complete fool, Miss Wilding, if you think I am letting you out of my sight for more than a minute so far from the Abbey.'

Oh, drat. He thought she intended to run away. He began to descend and she pressed her teeth into her lip to stop herself from crying out in fear and clutched on to the tails of his coat. The walls of the shaft glowed softly in the light of the tallow candle on his hat and after a while she began to relax. His movements were lithe and sure and his body in perfect balance. She trusted him. In this, at least.

After what seemed like a very long time with his shoulder pressing beneath her ribs and making it hard to breathe, but was probably only a minute or so, another light appeared. Several, in fact, dotted here and there on ledges around a wide cave.

Her ears were filled with the sound of rushing water. It echoed off the walls, yet sounded far off.

Bane set her carefully on her feet, held her for a moment while she found her balance, then stepped back.

Mr Trelawny jumped down beside her.

A bent and bowed figure appeared out of the dark. He had a clay pipe in one hand and a disapproving expression. 'For what brought 'ee a woman down here? Bad luck it is.'

Mary stared back up the ladder and was able to see a faint glimmer way above them. The candles.

'Don't be foolish, man,' Bane said. 'Miss Wilding is the owner of this mine. If she wishes to look at her property, she has every right. Besides, women are only unlucky on ships.'

Mary's jaw dropped at his quick defence and at his announcement of her ownership.

The old man grumbled under his breath. 'She ain't got a light.'

'She does,' Mr Trelawny said, producing another of the hats. 'If you would just slip your bonnet off, Miss Wilding, let it hang by the strings, if you will, and you can put this on.'

She did as he suggested and he tied on the stiff felt hat, pushing it down hard, then lighting the candle. She was surprised at how much better she could see around her. 'Thank you.'

'Try to keep you head down as we go through the tunnels. They are low in places and while the hat will protect you somewhat, you can still get a nasty bruise if you are not careful. Follow Old Jem there and I will bring up the rear. Not too fast, now, Jem. I don't want anyone getting lost.'

'No indeed,' Bane said. 'Miss Wilding, hold on to my coat-tails if you please. I shall feel better if I know where you are at all times.'

The strange little cavalcade set off, stopping now and then when Mr Trelawny called out to Jem to stop so he could point out items of interest. Bane seemed greatly interested in each tiny detail.

'Where are the men working?' she asked on the third-such stop.

'Further along, Miss Wilding. They are hewing and hauling today. I thought it best we didn't use any black powder during your visit. We will find them near the horse-whim stope.'

When she looked at him blankly, he smiled. 'Whim means the drum turned by the horse to bring the buckets up. Stope refers to where we dig it out. There is a significant lode of ore in that part of the mine.' He pointed to a dark seam of rock running along the tunnel. 'This is also ore. Blue peach, we call it. But it is pretty well worked out and what is left is of poor quality. Further on, the lode is heavy with tin.'

'Then let us go there, since it is what Miss Wilding wishes to see,' Bane said.

And they set off again. In places the tunnel was narrow and low and both she and Bane had to duck to avoid the sharp rocks in the roof. Once her bonnet got hooked up on a promontory and Mr Trelawny had to set her free. They laughed about it, while his lordship, unable to help from where he stood, simply glowered at them. And what a glower it was with the flickering light of their candles bouncing off the rough granite walls and the brim of his hat throwing his eyes into deep shadow. Why, he looked almost jealous.

She shivered. And it wasn't an entirely unpleasant sensation. It seemed that his seductive words in the carriage had infected her body.

To prevent getting hooked up again, she untied the ribbons of her bonnet, retied them and hung it over her arm. 'I'm ready,' she said at his lordship's impatient sigh.

A short while later, the tunnel opened out and all around her were moving pinpoints of light and the sounds of shovelling overpowering the background noise of running water. It was a bit like watching Oberon's fairies, until you realised that the sparkling lights were attached to rough felt hats worn by men shovelling rocks into iron buckets. And lads running from smaller tunnels and crevasses with wooden wheelbarrows. Small boys of eight or nine.

Work stopped as they realised that their visitors had arrived. There were some startled looks between the miners as they realised they had a woman in their midst and then some touching of forelocks and awkward bobbing of heads at her and Bane.

'This is the shift foreman, Michael Trethewy,' Mr Trelawny said. 'Lord Beresford. Miss Wilding.'

Another very Cornish name. These people had lived in this isolated part of the country for centuries. The man himself was big and brawny. He bowed to Mary and looked surprised when Bane held out his hand, but shook it anyway with a ham of a hand. The two men stared into each other's eyes for a moment with a measuring look and then released the shake. Both looked satisfied with what they had discovered from that brief contact.

A meeting of like minds. Mary inwardly shrugged. Men had their own secret codes, Sally had said. This must be one of them. She was more interested in the condition of the boys pushing those heavy barrows. While the foreman introduced Bane to the other men and they talked about lodes and weights and percentages and even black powder, Mary followed one of the boys into a side tunnel. It came to a dead end. A man lying on his back picked away at the roof. Rock fell around him and the boy shovelled it into his barrow.

They looked up at the appearance of Mary's light. The man struggled to stand. 'Please,' she said. 'Don't let me interrupt, but the rest of the men are back there, meeting his lordship. The new earl.'

'Aye. I ought to have come.' He wiped his face on his sleeve. 'Me and the boy had a bet on that we could finish out this stope by day's end. I forgot about the visit.' To her surprise, he sounded a little resentful.

'Are we interrupting?'

'The lad is paid by the barrowful. He's the only one in his family working after his da's accident.'

The boy ducked his head. He looked healthy enough, if a little pale. So why was he anxious?

She crouched down to meet his gaze full on and to ease the ache in her back from stooping over. 'Do you find it hard, pushing that barrow?'

'I'm stronger than I look,' he said defensively. 'I don't need Peter to break the rocks, not really.' He looked anxiously at his companion.

'I do my share.' The man's face looked sullen.

'I am sure you do. Both of you.' She couldn't quite grasp why she was ruffling their feathers. 'Is it good working here at this wheal?' She was proud that she had remembered the correct word. 'Are you treated well?'

If anything the man looked even more sullen, perhaps even suspicious. Perhaps because she was a woman. Perhaps he was worried about bad luck.

'We haven't had our pay this month,' the boy blurted out. 'The men aren't happy.'

The man hushed him with a look.

'Why is that?'

'We hear the old earl's will is all tied up,' the man said.

Oh, Lord, did that mean there was no money to pay these men until she was married? She couldn't believe that was so. She would have to tackle Bane about it. No, not Bane, his lordship.

'I am sure Lord Beresford will sort something out as quickly as possible,' she said. Was this the reason for his emphatic proposal?

The man shrugged. 'We best be going to pay our respects, lad, or be found lacking.' He sounded a little bitter. 'After you, miss.'

She could do no more than make her way back to the cavern, where she found Bane and Trelawny deep in conversation with a couple of men as they stared at yet another of those blue veins in the rock. There were pink veins, too, she noticed, and white ones. The veins did not run straight along the walls but at an angle. She followed one of the pink ones with her gaze, it glistened in the light of her candle as it disappeared into another, even smaller tunnel. She decided to see where it led.

A short way along was another of those horrid shafts, with a ladder disappearing into the darkness above her head. No candles glimmering up there from this one. An old disused entrance, perhaps.

With her fingertips running along the rough rock, she

turned a sharp corner. Here the tunnel divided. Something about this configuration seemed familiar, as if she had been here before. Was that a light she saw in the distance? Another man working, unaware that the new earl had arrived and wishful to meet him?

Should she let him know? Would he be equally unfriendly? She decided to take the other fork.

This tunnel was much darker, the air stuffy, yet cold. The sound of running water drowned out any noises from the cavern behind her. The tunnel was getting lower and narrower and the terrain rougher under her feet. Time to go back. This must be a disused part of the mine.

As she halted, she saw the lip of yet another shaft. This one right in front of her feet, going down. Only a small ledge on one side allowed for passage. Ugh. She was not going to think about going around it.

The air stirred behind her. The hair on her nape rose. She started to swing around. 'Who—?'

'You little fool,' a harsh voice whispered in her ear. A hand shoved her in the middle of her back and she was falling.

Chapter Ten

She grabbed for the edge of the hole and managed to catch it. Heart in her throat, blood rushing in her ears, she dug with her toes, seeking purchase.

'Help me,' she croaked.

There was a soft laugh and then silence. Somehow she knew she was alone. And she could not hold on. Slowly, her weight was dragging her down. Where was the ladder? She could feel nothing but the smooth sides of the shaft. There. Her knee hit something jutting out from the wall. Her arms trembled with the effort of holding her weight. They weakened. Then gave out. Her fingernails scrabbled to hold on. She was slipping. Falling.

Only to stop with a jerk. She was caught. By her elbow. Not her elbow, the bonnet strings hooked over her arm. She was dangling from her bonnet. She grabbed on to the strings with her other hand.

Gasping for breath, sobs forced their way up into her throat. *No. Don't panic. Think.* Those ribbons were not going to hold her for very long. Carefully she turned her head, letting the light from her candle show her what her feet had missed. The ladder. Just off to her right. The ropes looked frayed and rotten. Not strong at all, but it was her only chance.

Carefully she inched one foot over to the closest rung. She got her foot into it. Then her other foot. She had to let go of the ribbons, her only lifeline, and reach for the ladder.

What if it wouldn't hold her weight?

Don't be afraid, a soft female voice said in her head. *Do it.*

It was the same voice she had heard in her dream.

She let go of the ribbons and grabbed for the rope with her right hand. Got it. Shifted her weight on to the ladder, then let go of the ribbons and grabbed on with her left hand. With a whisper, the strings, lightened of their burden, slid off the spike. Her bonnet fluttered into the darkness below.

The ladder gave an ominous creak.

She gasped and clung on for dear life, frozen in place. *Do not panic. Climb. Slowly. Three rungs.* That was all she needed to climb. Gritting her teeth, swallowing her sobbing breaths, she made the painful ascent.

And then her head was above the lip of the shaft.

Oh, God, what if the person who had pushed her was still there? There was nothing she could do. She had to get up and out. She forced herself up the next rung and then threw her body over the edge. The next moment she was rolling away from that dreadful hole and lying gasping on the floor of the tunnel. Rocks were digging in her stomach. Her hands were burning. But she was alive. She dragged herself to the tunnel wall and sat leaning against it, gasping for breath.

And then she realised the way back was on the other side of that horrible hole. She gazed at the ledge and her body shook. She could not cross. She could not.

Slowly her pulse returned to normal and her breathing eased. She felt the chill of sweat cooling on her face and down the centre of her back. She could not stay here. She had to do something. Call for help? But she kept hearing that voice in her ear. The triumph. *You little fool.* That deep, dark whisper. It could have been anyone. Her heart clenched.

He wouldn't.

But he had. *Mary, stop being such a trusting idiot.* There was no other explanation. She hadn't agreed to marry him, hadn't fallen for his seduction, so he'd decided to take his drastic action.

She'd walked right into his trap. No wonder he had seemed so willing to bring her along to the mine, when previously he had seemed opposed to the idea. She should have known a man like him wouldn't really want her, a spinsterish schoolmistress. It had been all a ruse to get his own way.

And for some stupid reason, there was a terrible ache in her chest. It felt as if a hole had opened up and she wanted to cry.

The candle spluttered, then died.

Her misery was complete. Now she was alone and in the dark, with a murderer lurking somewhere about. She leaned back against the rough wall and closed her eyes, holding back the tears that wanted to run down her face. Why, oh, why had she given in to her longings for a home, a husband of her own, given in to the hope that somewhere in the world there might be a smidgeon of love just for her?

She swiped at her face with the heel of her hand. She'd shed enough tears over what she could not have. She would not shed any more.

She opened her eyes. To her surprise a light glimmered off in the distance, a soft sort of glow. Like the one in her dream. She pushed to her feet and, bent double at times, followed the source of the light.

It wasn't long before she realised that it wasn't men working and it wasn't the ghost of the White Lady leading her astray. It was daylight.

Wonderful daylight.

On her hands and knees now, splashing through freezing water that trickled down the walls and turned into a rivulet, she crawled out on to the hillside. She was out.

She collapsed and lifted her face to the sky, inhaled deep breaths of cold air and thanked God. Slowly her brain started to function. First, she took an inventory of her person.

Her knees were scraped, her skirts torn and soaking wet, her hands hurting. Her cotton gloves had been shredded by the rocks and her fingertips were raw and a couple of them were bleeding. She was still trembling inside, still shaken to her very core. But she was alive.

What had happened made no sense. Why had he been so seductive, talking of marriage on the carriage ride here, if he had intended to kill her? Or had he meant only to allay her fears?

Did she go back to the mine and face him? Or did she get as far away from here as possible? Wasn't now her chance to leave, when they would have discovered her missing and be busy searching in the dark?

You little fool. She'd be a fool to stay.

Hot moisture trickled down her face. She dashed the tears away. She didn't even know why she was crying, why she felt so betrayed. She'd known all along he hated the idea of their marriage.

The pretty words, the hot gazes, the kisses—they'd all been designed to allay her suspicions. And she'd let female sensibility overcome good sense, just as he'd no doubt planned.

She struggled to her feet, tossed her miner's hat aside and made for the nearest stone wall. For once, luck led her in the right direction. It was the wall that lined each side of the road up to the mine. After a while, she found a farmer's gate into the road. Now if she was really lucky a farmer would come along in a cart and offer her a ride.

She half-walked, half-ran along the rutted lane. How long would he search for her underground? How long would he keep up the pretence of looking for someone he already knew to be at the bottom of a deep hole?

At the sound of bridles jingling and the grind of wheels, she spun about. It wasn't the hoped-for farmer's cart, it was a carriage. His carriage. He wasn't searching the mine, he was sitting beside the coachman, driving his team straight towards her. He wasn't searching for her, at all. Why would he waste his time, when he had thought he knew where she was?

Dizziness washed through her, the world seemed to spin around her head, the grey clouds, the distant thumping of machines pounding in her ears. She should never have followed the road. She should have cut across country. And then she was falling. Falling into darkness.

When she came to her senses, she was in the carriage. It was rocking on its springs, tearing along at breakneck speed. And she was alone, lying on the seat with a blanket over her and a cushion beneath her head.

Where were they going? Where was Beresford?

She sat up, her head spun and she put a hand to temples that ached. A glance out of the carriage window told her they were pulling into the Abbey's drive.

Her stomach sank to her shoes. She was back in his power. Back where he could do with her as he willed.

The carriage pulled up outside the great door to the Abbey. The driver leapt down in a crunch of gravel and wrenched open the door.

Beresford.

She covered her mouth with a shaking hand at the look of fury he cast her. Anger flashed in his eyes. 'You little fool.'

The words were like a knife piercing her heart.

She should have gone across the fields when she had the chance.

'You are right,' she said in a low voice. 'I am a fool.' Because she hadn't wanted to believe he wished her dead. She looked at him. 'I was a fool to trust you.'

She ignored his hand and stepped down from the coach and, head held high, marched in through the front door held open by Manners.

The butler's eyes widened in shock at the sight of her. 'I'll send Betsy to your room, miss,' he said, sounding concerned.

'Thank you.' She didn't look back. Didn't care to. If she did, she might cry, and she wasn't going to do that. Not over him.

Nor would she go to dinner. Sit there being pleasant to a man who had tried to drop her down a deep hole in the ground? Certainly not.

But would he suspect that she realised that it was him? As it was, she should not have said that about not trusting him.

Very well, she would tell him she'd been angry because she thought he was leaving without her instead of searching. Again the bitterness rose like bile in her throat. And the fear. Of course, he wouldn't search when he assumed he'd succeeded.

She wouldn't let him get away with trying to kill her, now she was sure. She was going to find a constable. Or a magistrate.

What if they wouldn't believe her? What if they brought his supposed ward right back here? Then she wouldn't go to the authorities. She would just disappear. Tonight. It might be her last chance.

Betsy popped her head around the door. 'I brought some salve for your poor hands, miss.'

Betsy had been horrified at the sight of her hands and knees when she'd help Mary bathe. It was that soaking in the tub that had got Mary's brain working again. Returned her power of logic.

She smiled. 'Thank you.'

Betsy smiled back. 'A parcel came from Mrs Wharton while you were out today. A new gown. It is a lovely deep rose.'

Mary stared at her. 'I didn't order another gown.'

'His lordship did. He was tired of seeing you in the same gown for dinner, Mrs Wharton's girl said.'

His lordship was tired of seeing her. Full stop. She turned away, worried that her expression might give away the welling feeling of sadness. So his lordship had ordered her a gown. Then she would wear it. And let him make of that what he would.

After dressing in the low-necked, high-waisted gown with its pretty velvet ribbons, she gave Betsy free rein with her hair, as she planned her departure for after midnight.

'It has started snowing, miss,' Betsy said between teeth full of pins. 'We don't get snow very often in these parts. The children will be out playing in it tomorrow.'

'You sound as if you would like to join them,' Mary said looking up. She gasped at the sight of herself in the mirror. Betsy had turned her straight hair into a confection of ringlets and curls. 'Oh, Betsy, that is amazing.'

'Thank you, miss.'

'You really should be a lady's maid.'

Betsy beamed. 'Yours, I hope, miss?'

'We'll have to see,' she said, hating knowing she must disappoint the girl.

She got up from the stool in front of the dresser and gazed at the wall. How on earth could she escape, knowing that at any moment his lordship could walk through that wall and catch her out?

Her glance fell on the little history book on her side table. It had drawings of the old Abbey. And maps. She had forgotten about the maps. Perhaps they held the key.

She picked the book up and looked at the last few pages. There were plans of the house. Each floor in detail. And odd little markings, little dotted lines running along beside some of the walls. Along the walls of her room and the one above. Those dotted lines connected each of the towers, and then carried on to where the cliffs and the sea were marked.

The caves under the house.

It also showed a passage from the cellars to the old ruins.

Had the earl seen these maps, when he had glanced at this book? She hoped not.

'Gloves, miss,' Betsy said. 'It is a good thing you bought more than one pair. The ones from this afternoon were ruined.'

'Thank you, Betsy. Thank you for all you have done for me since I have been here.'

Betsy beamed. 'Do you need me to walk you down to the drawing room, miss?'

Mary smiled. 'No. Do you know, I think I have finally got the hang of it.' Right when she was ready to leave.

When she arrived at the drawing room, the Hamptons were there and Jeffrey, but there was no sign of the earl.

Manners entered shortly after she did. 'His lordship sent his regrets,' he said. 'He will not be dining tonight.'

A rush of relief shot through Mary.

Jeffrey held his arm out for his aunt and Gerald escorted Mary. 'How was your visit to the mine?' her dinner companion asked when they were seated.

'Very interesting.'

'Dangerous place, mines,' Mrs Hampton said. 'I am surprised his lordship let you go. You did not actually go inside, did you, Miss Wilding?'

The irony struck a nerve and she had to force herself not to laugh. 'I did.'

'I say,' Jeffrey said. 'Good for you. I shall have to ask old Trelawny for a tour myself. I didn't think they allowed people to walk around down there. Gerald and I used to sneak in there as lads, but the old manager wasn't nearly as particular as Trelawny.'

'I am a part-owner,' she pointed out.

Mrs Hampton gave a disapproving sniff.

'I heard you got lost down there,' Gerald said.

Mary stared at him. 'How did you hear such a thing?'

'Some of the men were talking in the inn. They said his lordship was in a proper temper that you had wandered off.' His gaze held speculation.

Anger rose hot inside her, but she filled her mouth with meat and let the act of chewing and swallowing before she answered cool her temper. 'I got lost.'

'There are a lot of old workings,' he said, looking at her rather strangely. 'Some of them go very deep. They are quite dangerous.'

'You were lucky you didn't fall down one of the old shafts,' Jeffrey remarked. 'I hear some of them date back to the dark ages. A couple of men from the village have lost their lives in them over the years.'

'Next you will be telling me the place is haunted,' she said with a sugary smile and a pretended shiver.

'Oh, no,' Gerald said blithely. 'I've never heard tales of ghosts in the mine.'

'Then perhaps it was a guardian angel who helped me find my way out.'

'I expect you just followed your nose,' Jeffrey said dismissively.

The door crashed open. The earl stood on the threshold.

Her heart gave a familiar jolt, then dipped as she recalled his perfidy.

'I hope I am not interrupting,' he said smoothly, looking at Mary.

'Not at all.' She gave him the benefit of that sugary smile and was pleased when his eyes widened. 'I thought you weren't joining us for dinner.'

His lordship gave her a piercing stare. 'I'm not.' He sat down at the head of the table. Mary was glad she was at the other end, opposite Gerald, for the earl had a glitter about his eyes and a set look to his jaw that did not bode well. He was looking at her with angry suspicion, no doubt frustrated at the failure of his plan. She focused on the food on her plate. If she looked at him, she might give away her anger. Her rage.

He waved off the plate that Manners offered him and poured himself a glass of the burgundy from the decanter near his elbow. He leaned back in his chair and, against her will, Mary found her gaze drawn to him, to the form of the man. The solid strength. The way his coat hugged his manly shoulders.

She forced her gaze back to her plate.

No one said a word.

It was as if his presence had dampened any pretence of civilised conversation.

Mrs Hampton signalled to Manners to clear the table. 'Will you take tea in the drawing room with me, Miss Wilding?' she asked as she rose and the gentlemen followed suit.

'Miss Wilding is otherwise engaged,' Beresford said. He glowered at the two younger men. 'Why don't you two fellows go off for your usual game of billiards and leave me and Miss Wilding to our conversation?'

The chairs went back and the cousins followed Gerald's mother out of the room.

Cowards.

But she didn't really blame them. She wished she could follow them, but she seemed to be pinned to her chair by that bright steely gaze fixed on her face. He gestured for the servants to leave.

Her mouth dried. She could hear her heart beating faster than she would like. He looked different tonight, less controlled. He sipped at his wine, watching her over the rim. A muscle ticked in the side of his face. 'What the devil did you think you were doing?'

She sat bolt upright in her chair. 'I beg your pardon?'

'Running off like that when my back was turned.'

It took a moment for her to understand. And then the answer came to her. He was making out that he thought she had tried to run away. How very clever of him. Did he think she would play along with his pretence? She pressed her lips together and lifted her chin.

He glared at her. 'Why go to such trouble, when you knew I would fetch you back?'

It would have been a miracle if he could have brought her back from the dead. She bit her tongue. She must not arouse his suspicions. Not let him know that she understood full well what he was up to. 'I got lost.' She watched his face for a reaction. All she got was a sound of derision.

'Believe what you will,' she said calmly, keeping her gaze steady with his.

'Then it seems I owe you an apology, Miss Wilding,' he drawled.

She could not imagine he was apologising for pushing her down a hole in the ground. 'Why?'

'Why what?'

'Why do you owe me an apology?'

He pushed his chair back and in a few lithe strides came to stand by her chair, looming, dark, still angry. He made her feel very small indeed. And that was quite a feat.

'I apologise for assuming you had broken your word and left without informing me.' He sounded as if he didn't believe what he was saying.

Because he knew it wasn't true. He knew she'd only wandered a little way down one of the tunnels. 'Apology accepted,' she said with remarkable calm. 'What made you seek me on the road?'

'One of the men said he glimpsed someone climbing the ladder. I was surprised not to find you in the courtyard.'

'Did he now?' She could not keep the sarcasm from her voice.

He gave her a puzzled look. 'He did.'

'All is well that ends well, then.'

He glowered. 'From now on, I will be keeping a very close eye on you, madam.'

She almost groaned out loud. 'If it will stop me from getting lost, I would much appreciate it.'

His eyes narrowed. 'Don't think to play your tricks off on me.'

'My tricks. What tricks would those be?'

'You know very well what I am talking about.'

'Was there anything else you wanted to say to me?'

He looked as if he wanted to throttle her. 'Not at this moment.'

'Then if you will excuse me, I will retire.'

'No.'

'I beg your pardon?'

'No I will not excuse you. We will go to the drawing room, take tea like sensible people, and enjoy some civilised conversation.'

'I don't believe you know how to have a civilised conversation. How to give orders, yes. How to impose your will on others, yes. But conversation? Sadly not.'

A pained look flashed across his face as if her words had the power to wound. Hardly. Annoyance was what she was seeing, nothing else. Annoyance that she wasn't just falling willy-nilly in with his wishes.

'You will excuse me, my lord. It has been a long and tiring day. I have no wish for conversation, civilised or otherwise.'

She rose to her feet. He stood up. As always, she was taken aback by the sheer size of him. The width of him. The height. She had to lift her chin to gaze into his eyes, to show him her determination. And he did not give, not one inch.

He gazed back, his eyes cold. 'You speak as if I am the one at fault for your weariness, Miss Wilding.' His mouth tightened. 'If you had stayed with your party—' He closed his eyes briefly. Took a breath as if mustering all of his patience. 'What is done is done. But understand, I will not have you wandering off again.'

'More commands? And where do you think I will go, my lord? I have no home, no relatives, no position of employment.'

'You do have one position.' His voice softened. 'Mary, after our conversation in the carriage I thought…I had the impression…'

She lifted her chin and allowed a chill to creep into her voice. 'What impression, my lord? That I had succumbed to your very obvious attempt at seduction?'

Pain filled his eyes. For once she had no trouble recognising his emotion and something horrid twisted inside her, like the blade of a knife slicing its way into her heart. Was she mad? She did not care if her words caused him pain. Could not.

She turned her face away, so she did not have to look into those fascinating silver-grey eyes, or to gaze on his handsome face. She was all too easily swayed by his wiles.

She was like a rabbit fascinated by the snake whose only intention was to make it the next meal. *Little fool.*

'If you will excuse me, my lord? I find myself exhausted by the day's events.'

He stepped back, frowning. 'Then I must bid you goodnight, Miss Wilding.'

He held out his hand for hers.

Reluctantly she accepted his courtesy, intending to rest her fingers lightly in his, but when his hand curled around it and he brought it up to his lips, she winced at the pain of it.

He tensed and glanced down. Before she could stop him he had gently peeled off her cotton glove and revealed the grazed skin and broken nails. His face hardened. 'These are the lengths to which you would go?'

The anger in his voice was unmistakable. He released her hand. Strode to the door, opening it. He paused. 'Miss Wilding, if there was any other way, believe me, I would not do this.'

Do what? Kill her? Was that supposed to make her feel better?

Her chest squeezed painfully.

Chapter Eleven

Back in her chamber, Mary picked up the little history book and turned to the maps. It clearly showed the tunnel to the old ruins. Hopefully it was in as good condition as the one running beside her chamber.

She put on her warmest gown, the last of the ones she had brought with her from Wiltshire, and donned her practical half-boots. She lay down on her bed to rest before it was time to leave, unable to stop herself from pondering Beresford's last words.

The bleakness in his voice had touched a chord deep inside her, started an ache. A feeling she was missing something important. Sometimes she felt as if he was speaking in riddles.

She shook the feeling off. He was playing her again, like a fish on a line. Turning her on her head. But each time she heard those whispered words in her head and what he had said when he jumped down from the carriage: *You little fool.* For some reason she could not match them up. It was as if the words were spoken by two different people, for two very different reasons.

Or was it simply his seductive kisses turning her upside down, making her want to believe he was not the cause of her fall? Her long, deliberately forgotten dreams of a home, a husband, children playing at her feet, a real family, conspiring to make her yearn to believe in his innocence, to believe the seduction and not the facts.

Why did she want to believe? Had her foolish heart done something she had sworn she would never do again—could it be possible she had fallen for him?

Despite everything she knew.

If so, she really deserved all that had happened.

A numbness crept into her chest. The sort of emptiness she'd felt after she'd learned the truth about Allerdyce, only deeper. Colder. It was the only way not to feel the pain of knowing he'd sooner kill her than marry her.

And so she must leave. Without regrets. Without feeling anything. She got up and carried her candle to the clock on the mantel. Two in the morning. The household would be asleep by now. She wrapped her cloak around her and pulled up the hood. She had no valise. Nothing to carry except her reticule and that she had tied around her waist under her skirts for safekeeping.

Quietly she opened her chamber door.

It creaked.

She held still, waiting, wondering if the alarm would be raised. Nothing. She opened it a little more. And then she saw him. Beresford. Sitting on the bottom of the circular stairs leading up to the room above.

She froze, waiting for him to leap up and force her back into her room.

His chest rose and fell in deep even breaths. She raised her candle higher and saw that his eyes were closed. He was sleeping, his head resting against the rough stone wall, his large body sprawled across the steps, in a sleep of utter exhaustion.

In sleep he looked so much younger, as if all the hard

lessons of life had been washed away and he was a boy again, with high hopes and sweet dreams. Her heart ached for that unsullied boy she had never met.

What was he doing here outside her door? Making sure she could not leave, obviously. Was that how he had arrived at her room so quickly the other night? No wonder he looked so weary if he had taken to sleeping here. One wrong sound and he would awaken and no doubt lock her up in her room.

She had to hurry, before he awoke and caught her. But somehow she could not drag herself away. She would never see him again and the sense of loss was almost more than she could bear.

Because, in spite of everything, in spite of the coldness he wore like armour against the world, she had glimpsed a softer and kinder side. And, yes, a vulnerable side that called to her in ways she did not understand, as well as a seductive side she found almost irresistible. Which she should not be thinking about now, but somehow she could not help it as she gazed at his face, at the small frown between his brows. He looked troubled and she wanted to smooth those cares away. She longed to press her lips to his lovely mouth and lose herself in his wonderful kiss.

She loved him.

The realisation filled her chest in the region of her heart with a sweet kind of ache.

Why not stay? Why not accept his offer of marriage? Perhaps in time, there would even be children despite what he had said. Had it not always been her dearest wish? A home. A family of her own.

And live her life knowing he would never return her love.

The thought sliced her heart to ribbons. She pressed a hand to her ribs to ease the terrible pain.

He stirred, shifting position, looking for ease he wouldn't find on the cold hard stone. If he awoke now, she would surely be lost. The next time he assaulted her with kisses and sweet seduction, she would be unable to resist.

To love and not be loved, it was all she had known. But with him it would be a disaster. She could feel it in her bones.

The was no other choice. She had to go.

Heavy-hearted, she crept over the threshold and closed the door behind her. Once more she glanced down at his sleeping form and had the wild urge to press her lips to his mouth. To bid him farewell. But she couldn't.

Instead she crept away, like a thief in the night, and took the stairs down to the cellar, the stairs he had brought her up that very first night, before either of them knew about the will. The first time he had kissed her.

She would never forget his kisses as long as she lived. When he was kissing her, she felt alive, like a different person, strong, sure and, heavens help her, beloved.

It was all a lie. A figment of her foolish longings. He didn't want her. He'd made it perfectly clear he didn't. He was being forced into this by a man he hated. And in time indifference might well turn to hate.

At the bottom of the stairs she turned left, away from the sound of the sea. Halfway along the wall, there was another sconce. Another entrance to yet another secret passage, if the map was correct. And this one would lead her outside to the old Abbey ruins.

She twisted the sconce.

Nothing happened.

Her heart rose in her throat. She'd got it wrong. Blast. She'd left the book in her room. She couldn't check the map. She'd been so sure she had memorised it correctly.

She glanced up and down the hallway, lifting her candle. There were no other sconces. She tried again. Twisting hard. She felt it shift. A little. It was stiff from disuse, perhaps.

She put the candle down and used both hands. The sconce turned painfully slowly. And the grinding noise echoed down the hallway. Heaven help her, Beresford would hear it. She had to hurry.

She wrenched it hard. The wall moved a little, then a little more, and then it opened fully. She picked up her candle and darted inside, found the mechanism on the other side and closed it behind her.

Now all she had to do was make it out to the ruins and run as fast as she could. And never look back.

The cold seeped into her bones. She felt as if she had been walking for hours, but she knew it was far less than that. Betsy had been right about the impending snow. It was up over her ankles and made walking difficult. And the wind seemed determined to impede her, too. It gusted this way and that, tearing at her cloak, blowing flurries of snow in her face so she couldn't see where she was going. Not that she could see much at all, it was so dark.

But if it was too dark to see her way, then it was too dark for anyone to find her. She clung to that hope and forged on. Going east. Keeping the wind on her right, as best as she could tell, because it constantly changed direction.

And she had to be correct, because the sound of the sea had faded away. She was heading into the countryside. Towards Halstead. Soon she should come across a road, with signposts and milestones and then she would be able to take her bearings.

She stopped to catch her breath, to look behind her for signs of pursuit. Nothing. Just the wind and the blowing snow. Hopefully his lordship was still sleeping outside her chamber door. He was going to be very angry when he awoke and found her gone. Hopefully that would not occur until later in the morning. She'd asked Betsy not to wake her too early, complaining of being tired.

It was all she could do.

She struggled on. The snow was drifting now. Getting deeper in some places and leaving the ground bare in others. And it also seemed to be lessening. She looked up at the sky and saw the glimmer of the moon through scudding clouds. Then a patch of stars.

The storm was over.

Her heart picked up speed. Even more reason to hurry. But now, with the moon casting light and shadow over the landscape at irregular intervals, she could see her way. See the line of a hedge that marked the edge of a field. See the moors rising in their white blanket off to her left. If she could just see the road. She looked around for a landmark. Something to tell her where she was. How far from the Abbey she had come.

Not far enough yet. She knew that. Not if his lordship was determined to find her. She would have to find a place to hide, somewhere he wouldn't look for her.

Again she glanced back over her shoulder. And gazed in horror. Oh, dear lord, what had she been thinking? That the snow would hide her? There, tracking across the field, was the dark imprint of where she had walked. She'd left the easiest trail for him to follow.

Wildly she glanced around her. She needed to find the road. Somewhere where other people walked and drove. Somewhere where her footsteps could not be identified.

She took careful stock of her surroundings and headed for the hedge where the snow was piling up on one side and clinging to the top and leaving the ground bare on her side.

Once in the lea of the hedge, with her footsteps no longer clearly visible to the most casual observer, she retraced her steps, going back on herself, hoping that he would not realise she would dare take such a risk.

She pulled her cloak around her, tried to ignore that her hands were freezing and her feet turning to blocks of ice and hurried on, taking the hedgerows, zigzagging in different directions, until she was dizzy, with no clue where she was. And still she did not find a single lane or road.

Yet there had to be one.

Had to be. She sank down to the ground to catch her breath, to think. She was exhausted. Tired. It would be just so easy to sleep for a while. To gain her strength.

Not a good idea, to sleep out here in the open. People froze to death under such circumstances. She had to find a place out of the wind. An inn. A barn. Any kind of structure. A flurry of snow stung her face. She frowned. Why was she panicking? The snow had been falling when she left the Abbey. It would have covered all traces of her footprints, and if these flurries kept up, then by morning there would be no sign for Bane to follow. Bane. She must not think of him as Bane. He was the Earl of Beresford. And a man who wished her at Jericho. Or worse.

She pushed herself to rise and took stock of her surroundings again. There. A barn. She could spend the rest of the night there and travel on in the morning. In daylight. She must have travelled five miles at least. Hopefully it was far enough for dawn would soon be upon her. Then she would get her bearings and move on. It would not be long before she was questioning Sally Ladbrook.

Filled with new purpose, she skirted the field, keeping to the hedges since they offered protection from the wind, and she was still concerned about leaving too easy a trail for the earl to follow.

The snow stopped again. The wind dropped, proving her caution correct. She inhaled deeply. There was something about the smell of the air. Cold. Crisp. Sparkling clean as it filled her lungs. She'd never inhaled anything quite like it. She rubbed her hands together to warm them as she walked.

Somewhere in the distance a dog barked. It sounded excited, as if it had been disturbed by an intruder. There must be a farmhouse or a village nearby. That was good news. Somewhere to aim for in the morning. Right now she just wanted to rest. To sleep. She shook her head to clear it. A few more yards and she would be able to lie down.

Another sound cut across the deep quiet. Hoofbeats. Travelling fast. She swallowed. Perhaps a traveller on a nearby road? In her heart, she knew it was not. She huddled deep against the hedge and looked back. A dark horse with its dark rider was cutting across the neighbouring field, heading straight for her, a dog bounding along at the horse's heels.

It couldn't be.

It was. It could be no one else. Hatless, his coat flying in the wind, it was Beresford. He hadn't seen her. He could not have. She picked up her skirts and ran for the barn, praying the door would be open. Praying he would not see her. Praying she could make it there before he cleared the hedge into this field.

And then she was there at the barn, huddled against the wall. The door was on her side. And closed.

She glanced over her shoulder. Beresford was coming up on the hedge. For the next moment or two he would be blind to her as he took the jump. She dashed to the door. To her great relief it opened and she slipped inside, closing the great door behind her. She scampered up the ladder to the loft, threw it down behind her and collapsed into the straw, breathing hard. Now all she had to do was remain as quiet as a mouse and pretend she wasn't here. She shivered. Despite her run, she was still freezing.

She took great gulping breaths of air in an attempt to fill her lungs and get her breathing back to normal as she listened to the sound of hoofbeats closing in on the barn. If she was lucky, he would keep on going, thinking she would have continued on without stopping.

The horse slowed and stopped.

Dash it. How had he guessed?

The dog whined, then barked.

The dog. He was using the dog to follow her. Inwardly she groaned. She had never considered the dog. That he would use it to hunt her like a wild animal had never occurred to her. And it should have. But she didn't know much about dogs and hunting. She had thought of Ranger as a pet, if she had thought of him at all. Since that first night the dog had not been seen anywhere in the house except his lordship's chamber.

Perhaps her disappearance up the ladder would fool the animal.

She lay still, jaw clamped, trying to stop her shivers, and listened to the barn door open, to the sound of a horse being led inside, to the excited barking of the dog.

'Mary,' Beresford called out in commanding tones, 'I know you are in here. Give up. Don't make me come and find you.'

She remained still, trying hard not to breathe. Trying not to let the sobs of fear welling in her throat and the cold seizing her limbs overcome her will to remain utterly silent.

'Down, Ranger,' he said.

The dog whined and was quiet.

She could imagine them down there, him in his great-coat glowering around the barn, listening, the dog at his feet. She strained to hear what he was doing over the sound of her banging heart.

Nothing. Not nothing—she could hear breathing. A laboured sort of panting. The horse. She held herself rigid, breathing in small sips of air, wondering if he could hear the pounding of her heart, while she knew he could not.

A click of metal against rock. An all-too-familiar sound of a tinder being struck. Light glowed through the floor-boards. He must have found a lantern. She buried herself deeper in the straw, knowing in her heart it was hopeless.

She wanted to weep with frustration.

A thump.

She turned her head and saw, in the light cast by his lantern from below, the top of the ladder appear in the hole she had climbed through. If she pushed it away from the edge, it would pitch him to the ground.

She imagined his lifeless body sprawled on the paved floor beneath. It would be a fitting end. Except she could not make herself do it. She wasn't the murderer here.

His head appeared above the floor. He raised his lantern and she saw his dark ruffled hair, a face reddened by the wind, eyes filled with fury as he took her in. He leaped over the edge and stood before her. He set down the lantern, peeled off his gloves and stuffed them in his pocket.

Trapped. She backed up into the shadows, the blood rushing in her ears. They were all alone. What had he said that first day? *If I wanted to do away with you, I would not do it in front of witnesses.* There were no witnesses now.

She'd played right into his hands by running.

His expression softened. His mouth turning sultry as

he shook his head. 'You didn't think I would let you leave me, did you, sweetling?'

Bewildered by his words, she stared at him.

'You little fool,' he whispered tenderly. 'Why won't you trust me?'

She trembled at the sound of his voice. Shuddered from the cold in her bones. 'Say it again.'

He raised a brow. 'Trust me?'

'No.' Her voice shook. She could not imagine why she felt so desperate. So hopeful. 'Say "you little fool". Say it the way you did just now.'

A small smile curved his lips. 'You little fool,' he said softly.

It sounded nothing like the voice in the mine. His voice had its own special raspy quality she would recognise anywhere. He could not have been the one who had pushed her into the mineshaft. Could he? Her heart felt so certain, even if her logical mind refused to believe.

Which did she trust most?

There was a light in those pale-grey eyes, gladness mingled with the shadows of concern and something softer, more heartwarming. If she hadn't felt so cold, she might have been better able to understand what it was, but she was freezing, her body shaking, her teeth ready to chatter if she said one word.

She was too cold to feel fear.

'I—I'm s-s-sorry...' she got out.

'There will be time enough for sorry later,' he said, moving towards her.

Backing up, she tried a scornful laugh through her shivers. Pure bravado. 'I mean, I'm s-sorry you found me.'

His answering smile was so bright, steel-edged and glittering, her heart lurched. 'Not sorry enough, my dear. I can promise you that.'

He yanked her close, holding her tight with one arm around her shoulders, his mouth coming down hard on her lips. His tongue plundering the depths of her mouth. A punishing kiss. Searing. Possessive?

She certainly felt possessed, mind and body. Wild. Feverish as she responded to the hot pleasure of his kiss with a moan in the back of her throat. She didn't want to respond to him, to yield to the strength and his heat. Her mind knew it was a mistake, but he'd found her, and there was nothing she could do about it. It seemed she was helpless in the face of his seduction.

She couldn't fight the feelings inside her any longer. The traitorous longings. She twined her hands around his neck, felt his heat wash over her and breathed in the scent of snow among the essence of him. She loved the way he smelled. She let herself sink into the darkness of so many sensations she felt overwhelmed. Excitement. Longing. Desire.

His large hands roamed her shoulders, her back. It felt so good to be held. To feel the connection that strengthened with each passing moment. More especially delightful was his warmth. He pushed back her hood and cradled her face in his wonderfully warm hands. He pulled back from her, breathing hard. 'My God, you are freezing.' He touched her shoulders. 'And soaking wet.'

'It was snowing,' she said.

'I ought to put you over my knee and spank you,' he said through gritted teeth. 'Do you have any idea how dangerous it can be wandering the moors in weather like this?'

'It is safer than staying at the Abbey.'

His dark brows lowered in a frown. 'Are you saying I can't protect you?' He sounded furious. And frustrated.

She stiffened. 'Protect me from whom?'

'From yourself.'

Without another word he picked her up in his arms and made for the ladder. 'Put me down,' she gasped. 'You will fall.'

'Let us hope not,' he said through gritted teeth. 'Hold on.'

He let go of her with one hand, reached for the ladder and stepped on to it. There was not help for it, she put her hands around his neck and clung on. It was either that or fall ten or more feet to the floor.

Ranger wagged his tail in greeting when they hit the ground. Mary gave him a glare. 'But for your dog, you would never have found me.'

He gave a grunt in answer and put her down next to the stallion who was contentedly munching on hay. He pulled the horse away and mounted him with fluid ease. 'Give me your hands.'

She hadn't liked riding the horse the last time and she was sure she wouldn't like it any better now. She shook her head.

'It is either that or be tied on behind the saddle like luggage.'

That sounded worse. She approached the horse gingerly.

'Don't worry, he's calm after such a good run.'

She winced and held up her hands to him.

'Put your foot on top of mine,' he commanded.

She did so, with some difficulty, and then flew upwards. He somehow caught her under the arms and set her on his lap.

'Ready, Miss Wilding?' His voice wasn't offering an option.

She sighed. 'I suppose so.'

He urged the horse out into the night, setting it into a steady canter.

* * *

She couldn't believe how little time it took them to reach the drive up to the Abbey. Minutes. Not the hour or two she had been walking. 'How did we get here so fast?'

'You were walking in circles,' he said grimly.

Something hot rose in her throat. A hard lump of disappointment at her own inadequacy. She should have been miles from the Abbey. She sniffed the tears away.

She heard him mutter something under his breath that sounded like 'God save me', but she couldn't be sure with the wind rushing in her ears and the sound of hoofbeats. What she was sure of was the band of iron around her waist holding her firmly in place and the hard wall of chest at her back.

If she hadn't felt quite so cold, she might have enjoyed the wild ride in the wind and the dark. He rode the horse right into the barn where a sleepy-eyed groom was waiting with a lantern.

His eyes widened when he saw Mary, but he took the reins the earl threw at him and turned his back while Beresford helped her down.

'See him well rubbed down, if you please, Sol,' his lordship said. 'Some warm bran and not too much water. Ranger, with me.' He grabbed Mary around the shoulders and marched her into the house by the side door. The one by which she had left that very first day. Tonight it was unbarred and unlocked.

He walked her past the corridor leading to her chamber in the north tower.

She dug in her heels. 'Where are we going?'

'You'll see, soon enough.'

But she knew where they were going. He was heading for his rooms. 'You can't…'

'I can do whatever I please in my own home, as you will soon discover.'

He flung open a door to a chamber and pushed her inside. A room where a large four-poster bed took up most of the room. A fire blazed merrily in the hearth where a pot hung from the crane, and gave off a faint aromatic aroma. In front of a comfortable-looking sofa was a table. The two glasses said he was expecting company.

Startled, she turned to face him.

He kicked the door closed with his heel, took off his coat and flung it on a chair. He gave her a tight smile and began attacking the fastenings of her cloak.

She pushed his hand away. 'What are you doing?'

'Getting you out of these clothes before you are chilled to the bone.'

'I can undress in my own room.'

'You are not going anywhere before you and I talk.' He finally untied the knot at her throat and pulled off her cloak. He spun her around and started on the buttons of her gown.

'I can't undress in here.'

'You can and you will. Either you do it, or I will do it for you.'

A shiver ran down her back at the dark notes in his voice, the seductive promise laced with the heat of his anger. He might be completely in control, but she could still sense his anger running hot beneath the surface.

She folded her arms across her chest. 'I can't. Not with you watching.'

He walked around her, picked up a robe from across the foot of the bed and handed it to her. 'Put this on.' He locked the door and pocketed the key. 'I'll be right next door.'

He disappeared into what must be his dressing room.

'Close the door,' she said.

'My back is turned. I am not some errant schoolboy who needs to peek, Miss Wilding. I can assure you I have seen my share of women in various stages of undress.'

That was supposed to make her feel better?

She let her sodden gown slip to the floor, and stripped off her stays. She put her arms in his silk robe, so smooth and slightly cool against her skin. It was embroidered with dragons. It seemed very fanciful for such a dark man.

'Are you done?' he asked.

She picked up her gown and looked around for somewhere to hang it. He strode in without waiting for an answer. He took the garment from her hand and tossed it over a wooden chair.

'Now,' he said, with a hard smile. 'Sit there, Miss Wilding, on that sofa beside the hearth, and tell me what the devil you think you were doing tonight. Perhaps you can give me one reason why I should not punish you for setting the house in an uproar?'

Chapter Twelve

He was unbelievable. One minute he was kissing her with a passion that curled her toes inside her boots. The next he was treating her as if she was a child.

'I do not appreciate your tone of voice, my lord,' she said stiffly. 'Or your threats. Indeed, I find myself heartily irritated by them. And by you. I am not your ward. I am not anyone's ward. And what I do is my own concern. Now, if you will excuse me, I will return to my room.' She held out her hand for the key.

It was somewhat difficult to be haughty in a red robe covered in green and yellow dragons, but she thought she'd pulled it off tolerably well.

'Sit!' he snarled.

She jumped.

He spun away, raking his fingers through the hair at his temples. Clearly he was very close to losing his temper. It was the first time she'd seen him so close to losing control of his emotions. She eyed him just as warily as she had eyed his stallion earlier that evening, but she wasn't going to let him scare her. She was finished with being terrified.

'The key, if you please, my lord.'

Slowly he turned to face her. His eyes blazed fury. His fists opened and closed at his sides and he took a deep shuddering breath.

'We cannot go on like this,' he said with soft menace. 'I learned young that losing my temper only makes a bad situation worse, but you drive me to the brink of madness, to the point where I have no control.' He took another deep breath. 'So here it is, one last time. Please, Miss Wilding. Would you do me the very great honour of sitting down so we can talk like reasonable adults?'

What woman could resist a plea like that from such a man? Not Mary, even if she ought to. While his words were cool, his eyes were hot. The same heat she felt in her belly.

Slowly she sank to sit on the sofa, the heat from the fire warming one side of her body and face.

He bent over the flames and ladled out two mugs of the steaming aromatic liquid, the scent of cinnamon, cloves and oranges intensifying.

'Drink this,' he said, handing her one of the cups. 'It will warm you.'

He brought his own cup and sat beside her on the sofa. She had not expected that. She sipped at the steaming brew. It was delicious. 'What is it?'

'A hot toddy. A favourite with miners after a day in the damp and the cold. It is also known as punch.'

His words reminded her of the damp and the cold in the tin mine. She shivered.

He reached over and brought the cup to her lips again. 'Drink it all.'

She took another sip and another and soon it was all gone and her head felt a little muzzy.

He took the cup from her hand. 'How is that?' he asked.

He was right, she did feel warmer, inside and out. Relaxed. Her teeth were no longer clamped together to stop their chattering and her shoulders were not tight. 'Much better, thank you.'

He set the mug on the floor, then he reached out and touched her jaw with the tips of his fingers, urging her with that gentle touch to turn her face towards him. She did not resist, but she kept her gaze on her hands now lightly clasped in her lap.

'Look at me, Mary,' he whispered.

She forced her gaze up to his face. He dipped his head and took her mouth, sweetly, gently, his tightly controlled passion vibrating in the inch of air between their bodies.

He tasted of cinnamon and sweet oranges and nighttime snow. A heady combination, when she was already feeling a little dizzy. His hand linked with hers in her lap, a strangely intrusive sensation, his wide fingers pushing hers apart, touching the sensitive skin in between her fingers. It made her breathe faster. It made her feel languid. Or was it the drink?

Did she care?

She was tired of running. Tired of being pulled hither and yon by her desires warring with her mind. Just once she wanted to experience the delights between a man and a woman.

It didn't mean anything, she knew it in her heart. He was simply seducing her into staying. He wanted to use her for his own purposes. Why should she not do the same? She had no doubt as to his experience as a lover. His touch told her he knew exactly how to make a woman's body hum with delight. She would never marry. So what did it really matter, this virtue, this strict adherence to the rules?

And if she was going to die, perish the thought, should she not have experienced something of the delights between a man and a woman? Discover for herself the joys lauded by poets and romance novels. Not that there was love involved on his part, but there could be great pleasure, according to Sally. He had given her pleasure, already. And she knew, instinctively, there had to be more.

She turned her body, to enable her better access to his mouth, to return his kiss, to twine her free hand around his neck, and kissed him back with all the art she had learned these past few days. The warm slide of tongue against tongue. The movement of lips that stirred her blood and tightened her core and made a rumble of approval rise up from deep in his chest. She liked that she had the power to move him as he moved her, that he was not completely unaffected by her touch. When she speared her fingers through his silky hair, he hissed in a breath. When she withdrew her tongue from his mouth and he followed with his, she captured it with her teeth and he groaned in the back of his throat.

She was also aware of his hand leaving hers and trailing a path up her arm to her shoulder. Aware of its stealthy path to the edge of the robe. Aware of the way he slowly eased it off her shoulder.

Aware with a sense of heart-pounding anticipation.

Each velvet stroke of his fingertips set a new inch of skin on fire. It felt delicious. Wicked. Wanton. And right. So very right. And when he pushed her back into the corner of the sofa, his chest pressing down on hers, his fingers teasing the rise of her breast, she closed her eyes and let the thrills ripple through her body.

Slowly, he broke their kiss, but his mouth didn't stop working its magic. He blazed a path of hot wet kisses across her cheek. His moist warm breath in her ear sent prickles of pleasure racing across her skin. Painful and delightful at one and the same time. She gasped.

He swirled his tongue around the edge of her ear, then nibbled her earlobe. When had her ear become such a centre of delight? Dazed by the sheer unexpectedness of the sensations searing through her body with each touch of his tongue, she lay immobile, breathing hard, waiting for what would come next.

He kissed his way down her throat, lingering to trace the hollow of her throat before moving on to the flesh at the edge of her robe, the swell of her breast.

Shocked to her very soul, she put up a hand to cover herself. He caught her fingers with his and kissed them one by one, until he reached her middle finger and closed his mouth around it, sucking on it.

Darkness edged her vision as something pulled tight inside her. An ache of unbearable sweetness.

'Bane,' she gasped, terrified and fascinated all at once.

Releasing her finger from its hot wet prison, he looked up at her, his eyes alight with fire and a sort of softness she didn't understand. His eyelids looked heavy. His mouth full and sensuous. He looked beautiful.

'Mary,' he whispered. 'Sweetling.' The word made her heart swell too large for her chest.

As he gazed at her, he gently rubbed her fingertip against the peak of her breast, inside the robe, where only the linen of her chemise protected her. The nipple hardened and furled into a tight little nub. It stood at attention. Not with cold, but with longing to be touched.

More thrills chased their way down to her belly. She felt that strange little pulse between her thighs and the jolt of pleasure it caused.

She moaned.

He pressed his lips to the place her finger had touched, kissing and nipping and laving with his tongue. The ache at her core intensified and she writhed beneath him, opening her thighs to cradle his body, seeking the pressure that would relieve the terrible unbearable need.

He unlaced the ribbon at the neck of her chemise and pulled down first one side, then the other to expose her breasts to his gaze. She could only see the top of his head, but she knew what he'd done by the feel of the air and his breath on her skin. By the tightness across her ribs. She tried to cover herself with her hands, but he grasped them in one of his and held them over her head, lifting his upper body to look down into her face.

'Would you deny me such bounteous beauty, my dearest?' he breathed and his expression held such a look of awe as he gazed down at her exposed flesh, at the mounds of her full bosom and at the tightly furled rosy peaks at their tips, she could deny him nothing.

She managed to shake her head and he gave a rough sort of laugh.

'Oh, Mary. You are every bit as delicious as my imagination said you were.'

'And wicked,' she mumbled as her face turned scarlet.

'How can anything so good be wicked?' he said, but his raspy voice was full of wicked seduction and passion. But it was his eyes that gave her pause. They were alive with something more than lust. There was tenderness and…affection. A warmth she had given up hoping to see in anyone's eyes.

She expected her girls to respect her, but she knew she could not command their affection.

But if her heart felt something stronger towards him, a deeper emotion she could not seem to freeze out of existence, there was no reason for him to know. Tonight was just about desire.

She pulled her hands free of his grip and flung her arms around his neck. She kissed his chin, his nose, his cheekbone with a rush of joy. He welcomed her kisses with a smile of such unusual sweetness it made her heart lurch. She had never felt quite so happy. And tears burned the backs of her eyes. His face wobbled out of focus.

His smile fled. 'Crying, sweetling?'

'Happy tears,' she said.

His laugh sounded a little startled.

Too much emotion for a man of his iron control, no doubt. 'It is nothing. Kiss me, Bane. Make me warm.'

His lips met hers and they sank into the heat of passion, his hands wandering her body, the silk of the robe sliding over her skin in a sensual dance. He undid the tie around her waist and it fell open, revealing her skin through her chemise, bathed in firelight.

And when he slid off the sofa to kneel beside her, this time she let him look his fill. Like a wanton woman. She watched his expression as his gaze roved over her from head to heel. A searing glance full of carnal longings. It sent her blood scorching through her veins.

Her thighs fell open at the gentle pressure of his hand. He stroked and kissed the inner bend of her knee, the delicate flesh high on the inside of her thigh and she closed her eyes and let the marvellous feelings wash away all thoughts from her mind. Thought had no place in this miracle of physical delight.

His touch left her. She forced her heavy-lidded eyes open and watched him strip off his shirt. She gaped at the magnificent breadth of him. The wide shoulders, the defined muscles of his chest with a dusting of crisp black curls around his nipples. The ridge of muscles across his abdomen.

So many muscles. So much unforgiving strength.

It would not matter how hard she fought physically, she

could never overcome such power. If she wanted to win, she would have to use her wits.

Right now, she had no thought of their struggle. Just the enjoyment of watching this virile male display his beauty. His hands went to the waistband of his pantaloons where they clung to firm, narrow hips and flanks. He paused.

She looked up at his face and realised he was awaiting her permission. Heat rushed through her body. She gave a quick nod and looked away. Looked at the back of the sofa, at the curtains covering the window, listening to the sound of him stripping off every stitch of clothing.

He gave a soft laugh. 'Coward.'

He picked her up and lay her down in front of the hearth. At her look of surprise, he smiled. 'I don't want you getting cold and that bed seems to sit in a draught.'

She glanced over at the bed and realised that beside the headboard was a sconce similar to the one in her room. Did it also open into a tunnel? For a moment, she tried to recall the map in the book, but when he lay down beside her, one heavy thigh across hers, his mouth plying her with kisses, the thought drifted away. Later. She would think about it later. For now, it was his hands and his mouth and the feel of his warm skin against hers that had all her attention.

The man was a master at seduction. He knew where to touch her, how to make her squirm and gasp. In moments, she was lost in a haze of desire, arching her hips into the thigh pressing down on her mons, moaning at the way his tongue toyed with her breast, making them tingle and ache. And all the while, inside her, there was a growing tension. At first it was an ache. Then it felt like the sweetest pain.

There, where his hand stroked her woman's flesh, delving gently between the hot damp folds. He rubbed and caressed until she cried out in frustration. He slipped one finger inside her, then another.

'So hot,' he murmured in her ear. 'So tight and wet and ready.'

'Yes,' she breathed in wonder at the erotic touch on her most secret place that only seemed to make the tension increase to unbearable proportions.

'Do you like this, Mary?' he breathed in her ear, swirling his tongue in that sensitive place, nuzzling into her neck, kissing and sucking until she wasn't sure which touch was driving her more mad. 'This story between us.'

'Yes,' she whispered. 'Yes,' she said louder when he didn't respond.

'Do you want to find out what happens in the end?'

'Yes.' Of course she did. How could she not? He started withdrawing his fingers and she closed her legs tight, trapping his hand and felt an astonishing rush of pleasure. She moaned at the deliciousness of it.

He muttered something under his breath. 'Relax, sweeting. Let me come over you.'

The words made no sense, but he pressed with his knee, pushing her thighs apart, then when she parted her legs he settled his hips between them, his chest rising above her like the torso of a god, bronzed in firelight, his face strained with some sort of effort.

She glanced down between them and saw that the hard ridge of flesh pressing into her mons was his male member, thick and aroused, its head gleaming darkly where the firelight caught it.

She sucked in a breath.

He didn't move.

The restless inside her, the needs he'd stoked, rose up to claw at her insides.

'Bane,' she pleaded. 'The end of the story.'

'It comes at a price,' he whispered harshly. 'Marriage.'

'What?' She shook her head, thinking to clear her hearing.

'A promise of marriage, or this ends now. I won't ruin you, Mary.'

'You can't ruin a schoolteacher,' she protested, trying to think.

He rocked his hips and sent another pulse of pleasuring ripping up from her belly. She writhed, trying to bring him closer, to ease the torment.

'If you want this, you will promise to be my wife,' he said softly. 'Agree. Or we are done here.' He started to move, lifting himself away with a grimace of pain, but there was no doubting the inflexibility of his decision.

'Yes,' she breathed. And the rush of happiness was almost as painful as his sensual torture. She would have her children, her home and her husband. She wouldn't have love. Not from him. But she had never expected love at all. And her children would love her. And she would love them. And cherish them.

'I didn't hear you,' he said, his breathing harsh and ragged.

'Yes.'

'There's no going back,' he warned. 'No changing your mind in the morning. You will be my wife.'

'Yes,' she said, proudly, more confident than she had been in years. 'Yes, I will be your wife.'

'Thank God,' he breathed and his arm shook as he held himself up on one hand as the other reached between them and guided his hot flesh into her. Large, intrusive, pushing and stretching, while his face contorted with effort as if he was holding back. And then she felt it. Something stopping him. Her maidenhead.

'This might hurt,' he warned gently.

She wanted to laugh at the thought of the pain she'd endured these past few weeks. How could this be that bad? She nodded instead.

He thrust forwards slowly with a low groan and held still.

A pinch of pain caught the breath in her throat. She froze. He froze. They stared at each other, not daring to move.

But the pain soon faded to a memory and all she could feel was him inside her body, large, hot, pulsing.

It felt good. She shifted her hips and felt a stab of pleasure.

He groaned and rocked inside her, small little movements at first, matching the pulse that beat inside them both. It felt delicious. Deliriously so. But not nearly enough.

And then he was kissing her mouth, suckling on her breasts and the tightening that had relaxed started all over again. Worse than before. His hips drew back and plunged forwards, the rhythm steady at first, then increasingly wild, and she could see darkness at the edge of her vision. Blackness beckoned.

A fall into the void.

Terrified, she resisted, her muscles clenching tight as her body strained towards it and her mind pulled her back.

'Let go, Mary,' he whispered in her ear. A devil tempting her into the abyss. 'Let it happen,' he said. 'You will be fine. I promise.'

He reached between them and pressed and circled on that tiny nub buried deep within her folds above their joining. Too much pleasure. Too much sweet pain. She could not hold on.

And she let the darkness take her.

Flew apart. Shattered. And it wasn't dark. It was brilliant with blinding light. And she was falling into bliss.

In a state of languid floating, she felt him tense. Heard his soft deep cry and cushioned his shudders with the cradle of her body. Gave him the same gift he had given her.

His lips found hers and he held himself on trembling arms. Kissing her mouth, her cheeks, her eyelids. 'So grand, lass,' he said in accented tones. 'So damned grand.'

He collapsed at her side, curling around her protectively.

Awed, she stared at the man who would soon be her husband. Handsome. Strong. Terrifying. She'd agreed to wed him based on instinct rather than intellect. He'd forced her to say yes. Even so, a sense of gladness filled her heart. It wasn't a love match. And it was better that way. Less chance for hurt. But they would each gain much of what they wanted from the arrangement.

As long as he gave her children, she could be happy. On that thought, bliss claimed her and she drifted on what felt like warm currents, only to awake a few minutes later being carried.

He lay her down on his bed.

She started to sit up. 'I can't stay here. The servants will find me in the morning.'

'We won't be the first couple to anticipate our wedding vows.' The hot, dark look he sent her way as he pressed her back down on the pillows sparked yet another round of desire. She tried to resist its allure, the pull he exerted on her body and use her mind.

'Betsy will be worried.'

He slipped beneath the sheets and pulled her into his embrace, drawing her head to rest on his shoulder, her hand to drape over his chest. His heart was a strong steady beat in her ear, his skin warm, the scent of him, all dark tones in her nostrils. And her traitorous body warmed.

He kissed the top of her head. 'And what was she to be, when she discovered you gone in the morning?'

'That was different.'

'How?'

'Because I wouldn't have to face her.'

He chuffed a small laugh. It was an endearing sound. Amusement without mockery. 'The servants know what goes on. They won't comment, I can assure you. And you are not going back to your room. Not with so many avenues for you to escape me again. I won't take that risk.'

Risk. The word was like a cold rock dropped on her chest. She gulped in air. She was taking a risk, staying here with him. 'About what happened at the mine...'

He lifted his head to look down at her. 'It's over, Mary. There'll be no more running away. You belong to me now. You swore it and I will not permit you to go back on your word.'

Something he had said didn't make sense. Idly, she placed the flat of her hand on his chest, felt the rough hair and the solid muscle beneath. Heard his quick inward breath as he sank back into the pillows. 'Don't do too much of that, sweetheart. I don't think you will be ready for me again tonight, and, as demonstrated, I don't have a great deal of control when it comes to you.'

Nor she when it came to him it seemed. But... Her brain tumbled like a well-oiled lock. 'I didn't run away at the mine.'

'Don't lie to me, Mary. I found you on the road, re-member?' The rasp was back in his voice.

She rolled on her side, pushing away, so she could see his face, watch his reaction. 'I'm telling the truth.'

He raised himself up on his elbow and pushed the hair

back from her face, staring down into her eyes. 'And I am basing my judgement on experience, sweet. You tried to buy a ticket in St Ives. You walked the path on the cliff. And then there's tonight. Why would the afternoon at the mine be any different?'

'Because I say so.' The look of doubt on his face stirred anger in her breast. 'If I am to trust you, surely you must also trust me.'

He opened his mouth to argue.

'I do not deny those other occasions, but… Oh, what is the use?'

She flopped over on her back and stared up at the canopy. He would never trust her. And she would never trust him. Because she knew what she'd heard. *You stupid little fool.* His words. Even if it wasn't his voice. People sounded different under different emotions. It could have been him. Yet what could she say? Accuse him of trying to kill her now, when they seemed to have agreed to a truce? With their wedding in the offing there was no need for him to be rid of her. He'd have his title and his wealth.

He leaned over her, turning her face towards him. 'All right. Tell me.'

She looked up into his eyes, at the frown, at the jaw already set in uncompromising lines, and knew that, having started down this path, she could not now back away. She had to say something. Come close to the truth, see his reaction.

'I went exploring and got lost.'

The frown deepened. 'How could you get lost?'

'I spoke to one of the boys, working further along one of the tunnels. Then I followed what I thought was candlelight.'

His expression lightened. 'And ended up outside?'

She nodded. 'I thought to go back to the entrance.'

'On the road you were heading downhill. Away from the mine.' He let go a deep sigh. 'As I said. It's over. Let us move forwards from here.' He looked so disappointed she wanted to cry.

'Someone pushed me down one of the old shafts,' she blurted out.

He sat bolt upright. 'What?'

Well, that certainly had his attention. She looked down at where his fist was bunching the sheets. 'Someone shoved me from behind.' Much as he had shoved her that day on the cliff, now she thought about it.

'Are you telling me the truth?'

She looked straight into his eyes, held his gaze steady with her own. 'That is what happened. That's why I was heading away from the mine.' The fear from that day rose up and tightened her throat. 'I was lucky. My bonnet strings tangled with the ladder. I was able to climb out.'

'Your bonnet?'

He sounded incredulous. He would sound that way if he was the one who had pushed her. 'Too bad for you I didn't die,' she said. 'It would have solved all your problems.'

'Too bad indeed,' he said drily. 'You tell a wild story, Miss Wilding. I am surprised you aren't blaming your disappearance on sightings of a ghost or some sort of hobgoblin.'

'A human hand pushed me, not a ghost.' *You little fool.*

He glared at her, his mouth a thin straight line. 'Clearly I should not have let you go to the mine. You are not to be trusted to behave like a sensible woman and stay with your party.'

'Interesting that you were not searching the tunnels, but rather were leaving for home.' There, she had as good as voiced her suspicions.

He frowned, his gaze searching her face. 'I found you on the road.'

'Bad luck for you, I suppose,' she muttered and was surprised when he flinched. It seemed she'd struck a nerve. 'Just like the near miss at the cliff and the lucky escape from the barrel. Marriage must seem a great deal more certain at this point.'

The words hung between them like a sword waiting to strike a death blow.

His face turned to granite. His gaze moved from hers and fixed off in the distance. When he finally looked at her, his eyes were the grey of a winter storm. 'Your powers of deduction are truly astounding.'

No denial. No claims of innocence. All her longing for one person in her life who would care about her balled into one hard lump in her throat. A burning painful blockage that no matter how hard she swallowed would not go back where it belonged in the deep reaches of her soul.

Perhaps if he would just pretend to care, it would not feel quite so bad. She forced a bitter smile. 'Even women are capable of logic when it stares them in the face.' The husky quality in her voice, the grief she hoped he would not recognise, came as a shock. Not even Sally's betrayal had left her with such a feeling of desolation.

'If your logic leads you to the understanding that marriage to me is your best chance of survival, then I am glad.'

She could not control the tremor that rocked her deep in her bones. The threat in his voice was unmistakable.

Chapter Thirteen

'Wharton will have quite a time of it, preparing your trousseau at such short notice,' Mrs Hampton said the next afternoon, as they sat taking tea in the drawing room. 'We should visit her first thing in the morning.'

His lordship looked up from the letter he was writing. 'Only a few things are required. A morning gown. A travelling dress. Send her a note. She has Mary's measurements. We will visit a proper modiste in town after the wedding.'

Mary glowered at the pair of them, tired of the way they decided everything between them. 'I don't need new clothes for a wedding no one but family will attend.'

'You will need appropriate attire for the journey to London, however,' his lordship said. He rose from his chair and went to the window to look out. It was the second time he'd done that in the space of an hour.

'Are you expecting someone?' she asked.

He looked more than a little startled and if she wasn't mistaken his colour heightened on his cheekbones. 'Templeton. He said he would either come himself or send a message. I expected him yesterday.'

'I do hope nothing bad has befallen him on the road,'

Mrs Hampton said, absently. 'What about this one?' she continued, holding up a fashion plate for Mary to see. A dark-blue military-style pelisse over a shirt with a ruffle around the neck. 'It is all the crack according to the *Assemblée.*'

'Too much frill,' Mary said. 'I prefer something simpler.'

Bane went to the hearth and rang the bell. The butler shuffled in a few moments later. His face was impassive, but Mary felt sure his eyes were curious. All the servants must be talking about them spending the night together. 'Yes, my lord.'

'Send word to the stables that I require Henry to take a message to St Ives.' He glanced over at Mary and Mrs Hampton. 'How soon can you have a list ready for the seamstress?'

Mary put her teacup on the table beside her, rose and took the magazine from Mrs Hampton. She flipped through the fashion plates until she saw what she was looking for. 'This one,' she said, showing the older lady. 'And this carriage dress.'

Mrs Hampton reviewed her choices, then nodded. 'Yes. Yes. You are right. You are a perfect height to carry these off.'

A perfect height? No one had ever called her height perfect before and yet there was no trace of mockery in the other woman's voice. 'Then the matter is settled.' She sent a glance of triumph at Bane.

He didn't seem to notice.

'If you will excuse me, Mrs Hampton,' she said, reining in her irritation, 'I find I have run out of reading material. If you need me, I will be in the library.'

'I'll come with you,' Bane said.

She smiled sweetly. 'No need. I won't be but a moment.'

He gave her a look that said he was not prepared to argue. 'No trouble at all.'

She gritted her teeth. All morning he had been at her side, as if he expected her to try to leave the moment his back was turned.

He clicked his fingers and his dog immediately came to its feet.

'That animal should not be in the drawing room,' Mrs Hampton sniffed. 'Gentlemen leave their hunting dogs in the stables.'

'My dog, my drawing room, my house,' Bane said. He bared his teeth in a hard smile. 'And no one in this house has ever suggested I was a gentleman.'

'You are the earl,' the widow said. 'So now you must act like one.'

Mary felt the hairs on the back of her neck prickle. 'He is a very well-behaved dog. I do not mind his presence at all.'

A mocking smile crossed the earl's face. 'I am pleased to hear it.'

Now what had she said to provide him with amusement? Whatever it was she was not going to ask. Not when he was behaving like a shadow. Indeed, after their exchange of truths in bed she had half-expected him to avoid her altogether, since he thought her a liar.

She strolled towards the door and he strode to open it for her to pass through. He bowed as she swept past. She couldn't help notice just how elegantly he did so, or the way her heart fluttered. Dash it all, it was hard to be annoyed when he was being so charmingly attentive.

At the library door, he moved around her to open the door, but remained, with his dog at his side, barring her way, looking down at her with those silvery eyes with an expression she could not read.

'I am sorry if you find my presence wearisome,' he said.

Was that a note of hurt she heard in his voice? She felt an unwanted pang of guilt. She pushed it away. He was playing on her emotions.

'I gave my word that I would not leave, for heaven's sake,' she said. 'But you are making me feel like a prisoner.'

His mouth tightened, and whatever amusement there had been left in his expression, it was gone now. 'You are. Until we are safely wed.'

'After that it won't matter, you mean.'

'It will matter. But not in the same way.'

'Because there is no escape, once we are wed.'

'I will do my best to make sure you do not feel the desire to escape.' His rough voice caressed her.

A delicious shimmer of desire warmed her, and infuriated her, at how easily she succumbed to his sensual wiles. 'I wonder if your best will be good enough.' She bit her lip at the flash of pain in his eyes. She had not meant to hurt him, just to maintain some distance, some control over herself, now he had taken away all her options. Petty, but necessary to her sense of self. Except it wasn't his fault she found herself in this predicament. He hadn't so much seduced her as fulfilled her every spinsterish dream and more.

She deserved whatever fate awaited her, for giving in to those fantasies.

She made to step past him.

'Wait.'

She looked up into his handsome face and once more her chest squeezed painfully with the knowledge he would never love her. She forced herself not to care. 'Yes, my lord.'

His mouth tightened as if he did not like what he was

about to say. 'I have to leave the house, on an errand of my own.'

Her jaw dropped. 'You intend to leave me to my own devices? I am honoured by your trust.'

His expression became rueful. 'You will do as I request and remain here or face the consequences. You have agreed to be mine.' He laid a heavy hand on her shoulder.

The possessive note in his voice gave her a delicious thrill low in her belly. A carnal response to the darkness in his voice she could not help. 'Our agreement is a marriage of convenience. That is all.'

'And as my affianced wife, you are mine to protect.'

'You are the one I need protection from,' she grumbled.

He grimaced. 'Perhaps. But you will not leave the house while I am gone.'

'And if I do?' she challenged.

'You won't.'

He released the door and bowed her in. 'Have a pleasant afternoon, dear Mary. I will see you at dinner.' At his side, Ranger wagged his tail, looking up at his master with complete adoration. She knew how he felt, she just hoped she wasn't quite as obvious. Not when his lordship had nothing to give her in return.

She entered the room and was surprised when the dog followed her.

'On guard, Ranger,' Bane commanded.

Mary swung around. 'You are jesting?'

An apologetic look in his eyes, Bane bowed slightly. 'I am afraid not. Enjoy your afternoon.' He left.

'This is ridiculous. Bane. Come back here.' When he didn't return, she moved to follow him. The dog issued a low growl and lifted its lip, revealing large incisors.

'Down,' she said firmly.

The hairs on the back of its neck bristled.

'Bane,' she shouted. 'Blast.' It seemed she was trapped. Again. What sort of game was he playing? She given into his demands and still he didn't trust her. It hurt. Badly. More than it should, since she certainly didn't dare trust him.

The dog watched her with pricked ears, its red, wet tongue lolling from one side of its very large mouth. She knew nothing about dogs and she did not want to put this one to the test. She moved deeper into the room and it lay down across the threshold with its head on its paws, still watching her intently.

'This is too much.'

The dog whined and thumped its tail on the carpet.

She once more moved towards the door. The dog growled.

It seemed she had no choice but to find a book and read until Bane returned to collect his wretched animal. Was this to be her future with this man? Guarded and watched?

If so, she wasn't sure she could go through with it. Yet what was the alternative?

By the time Bane strode through the door, looking wind blown and purposeful, the candles had been lit, a dinner tray provided and Mary was too furious to read a word of the novel in her lap.

Ranger bounded around his legs in joyful abandon. 'Down, sir,' he said, looking at Mary. 'I am sorry I was longer than I intended. I hope you haven't been too inconvenienced.'

'Apart from being unable to go for dinner or attend the necessary, I haven't been the slightest discommoded.'

Amusement flashed in his eyes, annoying her all the more. 'I am sorry.'

'I see nothing to laugh about.'

He sobered. 'Nor I.'

'Where were you that you must needs leave me here guarded by this animal, a source of amusement for all, especially your cousin Jeffrey?'

'He was here, was he?'

'He came for a book and left without one.'

He patted the dog's flank with a heavy hand. 'Good boy.'

A footman scratched at the door and Bane looked up.

The young man coloured. 'Mr Manners said you asked for me, my lord.'

'Yes, Henry. Please take Ranger to the stables and see him fed, would you please.'

The dog's ears pricked and he attached himself to the footman immediately.

'Cupboard lover,' Bane murmured with a mock glower.

'It's as if he can understand every word,' Mary said as the footman left with the dog lolloping along beside him.

'He does.'

'You still haven't said where you were.'

He frowned. 'Among other places, I went to St Ives to arrange a ship's passage for first thing in the morning.'

'Ship's passage?'

'To London. The sooner we are married the better. I can arrange for a special licence there.'

She swallowed. She had thought she had at least two or three weeks before they were wed. Another woman in different circumstances might have been thrilled by his desire for speed. To Mary it felt a bit like staring into a prison cell. 'Why the sudden rush?'

'I don't like this house. I never have.'

'Because of the ghost?'

'I thought you too sensible to believe in such nonsense.'

She sighed. 'After what happened at the mine, I am not so sure.'

He gave her a sharp look.

'I had the strangest feeling of someone trying to help me.'

'What? After pushing you down a shaft?'

It really did sound foolish when he put it like that. 'You know it has been a long day and I think I would like to retire now.'

'I shall escort you to your chamber.'

'It is not necessary. I can find my way perfectly well.'

'Nevertheless…' He held out his arm.

She could either take it or he would follow her. She could see the determination on his face. And something else, a kind of bitter smile, as if he expected her to reject his offer.

Had other women rejected him, knowing he was low born even though heir to a title? She could imagine they might, in the highest of circles.

She made to place her hand on his sleeve, but he grasped it and drew her close to his side, tucking her hand into the crook of his elbow. A public demonstration of intimacy, even though there was no one there to see it.

It made her feel wanted. A surprisingly warm feeling. It melted her insides, made her want to lean against his strength and let him do with her as he would. And therein lay the danger.

If she came to rely on his caring too much, she would be heading for disappointment, so she did her best to appear unconcerned. To appear as if gentlemen escorted her in such a fashion every day of the week.

'What time do you expect we will leave in the morning?' she asked, feeling obliged to break what felt like far too comfortable a silence as they strolled towards her chamber.

'To leave St Ives on the first tide, we will need to leave here no later than six in the morning. Do you think you can be ready on time?'

'I can. Are you sure we cannot marry from here? I have never set foot on a ship before.'

'Afraid, Mary? I did not think you chicken-hearted.'

'It is the middle of winter. I hear *mal de mer* can be very uncomfortable.'

They had arrived at her chamber door and he turned to face her. 'You are right. But it is the fastest way and, if it is any comfort to you, the weather is set to be fine for the next two days according to the ship's captain.'

She could see from his expression that no objection from her was going to change his mind.

He opened the door to let her in. 'Thank you, my lord.' She dipped a little curtsy.

He gave a short laugh. 'I can see you would rather hit me over the head with your poker. Thank you for not pressing your objections.'

'I can see it would do no good.'

He looked surprised. 'I think you and I will do very well together, my dear Mary.'

'As long as I do exactly as you say.' She shook her head. 'I am afraid that, as a general rule, is not in my nature. Perhaps you should think of another way out of this dilemma.'

'There isn't one.' His voice lost its teasing note.

'Then I must bid you goodnight.' She stepped into her room and was astonished when he walked in behind her.

'What are you doing?'

'Not letting you out of my sight.'

'I promise you, I am not going anywhere.'

He gave her a long considering look and then seemed to come to some decision. 'Before I went to St Ives, I went out to the mine.'

He reached into his watch pocket with two fingers and pulled forth a few strands of fabric. 'I found these.'

She frowned at them.

'Strands of ribbon caught on an iron spike in the wall at the top of one of the deepest shafts in the mine.' His voice was hard and cold.

She raised her gaze to meet his and was surprised at the bleakness she saw in those metallic eyes.

'I'm sorry,' he said in a voice as cold as ice.

She shivered. 'Sorry that I did not fall to my death?'

He grasped her arm and pulled her hard against him, looking down into her face. 'I would not see harm befall you, Mary.'

'Not now we are to be married, at least.'

He swung away with a soft curse, leaving her wishing he was still holding her and hating herself for that weakness.

'I thought your story was a lie,' he gritted out. 'Finding you on the road, heading away from the mine, was all the proof I needed that you were running away.'

Guilt nagged at her, forcing her to speak the truth. 'I was. What fool would stay and risk their life?'

'And you are not a fool.' He let go a short sigh. 'It wasn't me who pushed you.'

A rush of relief rushed through her, followed swiftly by logic and doubt. 'If not you, then who? Only you benefit by my death.'

He winced and scrubbed at his chin. 'I know.'

'Some friend trying to help you? Your friend Lord Templeton, perhaps?'

Startlement entered his gaze. 'Why would you say that?'

'You employed his help to seek information about me.'

'Templeton works for the government. He has access to information and informers. He is right now looking for your Mrs Ladbrook. I hoped she might shed some light on what it was my grandfather was up to with this will. I can assure you he was nowhere near the mine yesterday.'

'Then who could it be?'

'Jeffrey.'

'Your heir.'

'A true Beresford, despite his proclivities. A man my grandfather would have preferred over me, without a doubt.'

Proclivities? She didn't think she wanted to know. 'But how would my death benefit him, when it is you who stands in the way of the title?'

He looked at her for a long moment, as if debating with himself as to what to reveal. He took a deep breath. 'If you die and I am found guilty of your murder, he will inherit.'

The air left her lungs in a rush. If this was true, then neither of them was safe. She paced to the window and back. 'Do you have reason to suspect him?'

'I saw him near the brewer's dray moments before the barrel broke lose. Someone in this house was making those noises in the room above your chamber and he and Gerald hung around the mine as lads enough to know it better than most.'

When she looked at him, she saw there was trepidation in his eyes, as if he feared she would not believe him. Did she? Her heart certainly wanted to. But her mind was a whole other matter.

It sounded logical. But only if he had not wanted her dead. She wanted to believe it, but—

'I think news of our impending wedding made him desperate,' he said.

There was something in his tone which gave her pause. He was looking at her so intensely a hot shiver raced down her back. In two quick strides he was across the room. His fingers formed a cage for her cheeks and they were trembling. His expression was dark, almost murderous.

'Bane?' she gasped.

'I looked into the abyss, Mary. Right into the bowels of the earth. It was impossible that you did not fall to your death.'

The strain in his husky voice was a tangible thing. It swirled around them like the dark centre of a storm as if he held some deep emotion under terrible control.

'Yet here I am,' she said lightly, for it was light that was needed. Something to chase away this terrible darkness.

'Yes. Here you are.' Slowly he lowered his head, his eyelashes shielding his eyes, his mouth hovering above hers, waiting for permission.

And wanton that she was, she wanted to feel the pressure of his lips against hers, to experience the wild sensations his kisses sent rippling through her body. And why should she not kiss her fiancé?

She lifted her mouth to his and he brushed her mouth with parted lips, soft, warm, pliable, wooing. She flung her arms around his neck and kissed him back, hard and demanding, exploring his mouth with her tongue as she had learned so very recently. He growled low in his throat and her pulse jumped.

She clung to him, tasting, exploring, giving in to riotous sensations. It all felt new again. Exciting. Novel. Not different, but fresh. His hand wandered her back in slow widening circles, while her fingers tangled in the hair at his nape.

The warm caressing hand stroked her ribs, her buttocks, and the hand at her waist moved to capture her breast, the thumb gently grazing the nipple through her gown until she thought she would go mad with the tension building inside her.

He was everything she had missed in her life, though she hadn't known it was lacking. Male heat. Masculine strength. He had the power to stir up all the feminine urges she'd denied. He made her flush with heat from her head to her heels. To feel the blood pumping in her veins and her body thrum with desire was exhilarating.

It was a kiss that lasted for ever, yet was over too soon. Their lips seemed to cling and on a groan, he tasted her jaw and nuzzled into her neck.

'Once we wed,' he whispered, 'you will know nothing but pleasure, I promise.'

A promise that made her insides clench.

'Right now, though,' he breathed gently, 'you need to rest. I will sit here in the chair and watch over you.'

'To make sure I do not leave?' She could not help the bitterness in her voice.

He grimaced. 'To bed, Mary. Now. Or I cannot be responsible for what I do. I will give you five minutes to prepare and no more.'

His tone was so dark, so fierce, she undressed quickly and hopped into bed.

A scream. The sound of it echoed in his head. Filled the darkness. He couldn't see, couldn't get to her, but he knew they were hurting her.

'No,' she cried out.

He struggled wildly in the folds of his coat, which they had pulled over his head. It held his arms pinned to his sides. He was panting, struggling for breath, and the one holding him was laughing.

This was his fault. He should not have gone to the mine after she forbade him. Should not have lost his temper. Should not have made her come looking for him.

'Let me go,' he shouted. Tried to shout. The cloth muffled his voice, made it hard to breathe.

And then they were gone. He fought his way out of his coat.

Fought to find his way to the sounds of sobbing.

Free from restraint, Bane shot bolt upright. In a chair. He was watching over Mary, not searching for his mother on a cold Welsh hillside.

The damned dream had returned. Cold sweat trickled down his back. Why now, when he hadn't had it for years?

His gaze sought out Mary. She lay on the bed, still and silent, one arm flung above her head, her beautiful blonde hair tumbling around her shoulders. She looked too delicious for words. Too perfect to be true. And perhaps she was, but he wanted her. And so he would make her his wife in spite of his anger against his scheming grandfather. As long as he kept his distance, didn't allow himself to form an attachment, the marriage could work to the benefit of both. Oh, yes, he could already imagine the benefits as his body hardened.

A woman sobbed. Not Mary. His gaze shot to the chamber door. Another scream ripped through the air. His blood ran cold. Desire fled.

Mary sat up, clutching the sheets to her breasts.

'Its all right,' he said softly.

'The White Lady,' she said, her voice trembling, pointing across the room. Bane stared at the apparition floating beside the red glow of the fireplace. Behind the eerie figure was what appeared to be a gaping hole in the wall.

The ghostly shape faded into the blackness.

Mary crawled out of bed on the other side, clutching that damned poker again.

'What the devil is going on here?' he bit out.

'The tunnel,' she whispered.

'Bloody hell,' he cursed. 'You knew about that?' He pointed at the hole in the wall.

Her eyes widened. Innocence? Or something else? 'There is a passageway behind the wall,' she whispered. 'I thought you knew.'

He grimaced. 'If I had known, I would never have let you sleep here.'

He reached for his discarded coat and pushed his feet into his shoes.

'You are going after her?' Her voice shook.

Fear. She was afraid. A roiling surge of anger ripped through him. His lips drew back from his teeth in a snarl. How dare they terrify his woman? He was going to beat whoever was doing this to a pulp.

She recoiled, staring at him.

Dear God, now she was fearful of him. He fought for control. Remembered who had suffered the last time he let his temper get the best of him and put out a hand. 'We have to put a stop to this, that is all.' There, that sounded reasonable.

She put her poker down on the bed and slipped on her robe. 'The tunnel leads to the chamber above.' She hesitated. 'It also runs along behind your room.'

Horrified, he grasped her arm as she was in the process of tying the belt. She looked up at him, startled. 'Are you telling me you have been in that tunnel?'

She nodded. 'I discovered it by chance. According to the history book it leads down to the sea caves.'

'Smugglers,' he said, as it all became clear. 'The Beresfords were nothing but a pack of pirates and smugglers in Good Queen Bess's day. That's how they gained their wealth and the title.'

She nodded.

'Manners said the tunnels were closed up. Fallen in.'

'Apparently not,' she said drily.

He almost laughed. God, this woman awed him with her pragmatic little comments. 'Stay here. I am going to put a stop to Jeffrey's tricks once and for all.'

'You think it is Jeffrey.'

'Who else would it be?'

'Gerald?' She sounded tentative. 'There is something odd about that boy.'

'He went with his mother to visit friends. Jeffrey was to go with them, but changed his mind at the last, Manners told me.' He pulled on his coat and picked up a candle.

She picked up her poker. 'I'm coming with you.'

That was all he needed. A woman and, in particular, this woman to look after while he chased down a man who wanted them both dead. 'No. Wait here.'

She pushed her feet into her slippers. 'What if he comes back another way? According that history book, there are several entrances.'

The back of his neck prickled at the thought of her being found alone. His chest tightened. He ought to find someone to look after her.

Another shriek issued from the tunnel. The prankster. Or it could be someone in trouble. He didn't want Mary in harm's way. If anything happened to her—

'We are wasting time,' she said, hefting the poker with a determined look on her face.

She wasn't going to stay here no matter what he said. Something warm swelled up to fill the hollow space in his chest. He pushed it aside. Now was not the time to examine what it meant. 'Come if you must, but stay close.'

She nodded her agreement. It would have to do. He picked up the candlestick on the night table and ducked through the wall.

'That way leads to the chamber above,' she whispered, pointing.

The sounds were not coming from that direction. He turned the other way. He could not help feeling amazed by the extent of the structure. Whoever had built this had done so quite deliberately. He frowned. Why had no one told him of their existence? They had clearly been well maintained. He would be having a word with Manners very soon. And his steward. It seemed their loyalties did not lie with their new earl.

He could feel Mary walking behind him, hear her light rapid breathing. She was afraid. Of course she was. What was he thinking letting her come with him? What if something happened and he wasn't able to protect her? A chill crept up from his gut. It wouldn't be the first time he hadn't been able to protect the woman in his care. Bile rose in his throat.

He would not let that happen again. He wasn't a boy and there wasn't a man who could withstand him. Especially not the puny, effeminate Jeffrey. Mary was safer with him than alone. She had to be.

Ahead, the tunnel branched off in two directions.

He looked back and she hesitated for a moment. 'That way goes down to the caves.' She pointed left.

She didn't sound sure.

He turned right. In seconds they came to a dead end. To his surprise, Mary slipped around him and grabbed the sconce on the blank wall facing them. As she turned it, the wall began to shift.

So that was how it was done.

He held the candle higher, revealing a small room. 'A priest's hole.'

'I don't think so,' she whispered, stepping inside. 'Look.'

He followed her and looked around. The little room was lined with shelves—well, pigeonholes—each one containing a scroll of some kind and there were other shelves holding boxes full of papers.

'The muniment room,' he said. 'So this is where all the old papers are. I wondered why there was so little in my grandfather's study. No charters. No letters.' It had been puzzling him for days.

The sound of moaning and rattling chains came from behind them. Mary jumped. He put an arm around her shoulder and realised that for all her brave outward appearance, she was trembling.

'You should go back,' he said. 'Leave Jeffrey to me.'

Her expression turned mulish. 'I'm coming with you. I intend to give that young man a piece of my mind.'

Bane could not help the smile that formed on his lips at the image of her slicing at the little worm with the edge of her tongue. It would indeed serve him right. Once more they plunged into the tunnel and took the other fork.

At the next corner, the draught blew out his candle. He cursed softly as Mary clutched at his coat. Bane let his eyes adjust, but there really wasn't any light at all. It was pitch black. Just like the mines he loved. The only way to move forwards was by feel. 'Keep hold of me,' he whispered.

The ground began to slope steeply downwards. They were going deeper and deeper into the earth, and the sound of the sea was getting louder. After a while, the floor flattened out. The tunnel must have widened out, too. On his right he could still touch the wall, but to his left, no matter far out he reached, he could feel nothing.

Aware that Mary had a good grasp of his coat-tails, he felt his way forwards, testing the way ahead with his foot before taking a step. He had no wish to tumble down a hole or into the sea.

A light glimmered off to the left. It went out instantly. Even so, it was there just long enough to show they were in a natural cavern.

He turned to face Mary. 'How much of these caves did that blasted book show?' he murmured directly into her ear, inhaling the scent that was uniquely her.

'I didn't take much notice of the caves,' she muttered. 'But I think there was only one leading out to the sea.'

'We are going back.'

'What?'

'We have no light. No weapon. And we have no idea where we are. I am not chasing a will o' the wisp when I have no hope of catching him.' He made to step around her to head back the way they had come. His foot slipped off the edge of a rock and slid down. His heart jolted as he came to rest one leg knee-deep in water with Mary clutching his arm. He cursed under his breath, but thanked providence it wasn't any deeper. He could have pulled her down with him.

'Bane,' she cried out.

'I'm fine,' he said. 'You can let go now.' He scrambled back up the rocks to her side. 'This is why we have to go back.'

A glowing figure appeared in front of her. 'Boo!'

Mary screamed.

Bane curse as he looked over her shoulder at what was

clearly a person wearing a sheet and carrying a lantern beneath it. 'Jeffrey, you idiot. What game are you playing?'

'I am the White Lady,' the apparition moaned. 'It is your turn to die.'

Chapter Fourteen

The light grew brighter, blinding Bane until his eyes adjusted. The figure behind the lantern was masked by the glare of the light, but he had no problem making out the pistol pointing at Mary. His stomach fell away.

'What the hell are you doing?' he growled. 'Put that thing down before you hurt someone.'

'Turn around and continue on.' There was no ghostly voice this time.

'Gerald,' Mary exclaimed. 'Stop this at once.'

Gerald? Now that was a surprise, but she had suspected the younger man.

Gerald laughed and it was an eerie sound that echoed off the cavern walls. 'Do as you are told. Turn around,' he said. 'Bane, you go first. Watch your step, the rocks are slippery.'

'It would be easier to see if you gave me the light,' Bane said, hoping the boy would be stupid enough to try it.

'Don't worry, you'll have plenty of light in a moment. Walk straight ahead and you will be fine.'

He lifted the lantern higher and Bane was able to make out the path ahead. They came to an outcrop of rock and the path disappeared around it.

'Stop,' Gerald commanded.

Bane did so. He reached back to where Mary was holding on to his coat and gave her hand a squeeze, offering comfort, hoping she would realise he was biding his time, waiting for an opportunity that would allow him to deal with this mad man.

His gut clenched. Fear that he would fail Mary, as he had failed his mother. No. He wasn't a weakling boy held down by a full-grown man. He just needed patience. To wait until the time was right.

'Against the wall, both of you,' Gerald ordered.

They shuffled back.

He passed by them, but since he had the pistol shoved against Mary's chest, Bane could not risk an attack. He could see that the pistol was cocked and the lightest pressure on the trigger would cause it to fire.

And then he was past them. 'Here.' He handed Bane a lantern and stepped back. 'Walk straight ahead.'

'It seems you have thought of everything,' Bane said, holding the lantern up.

'I wasn't expecting both of you,' Gerald said. 'Just Miss Wilding. But this is better. Much better. Don't try anything, Bane. Miss Wilding will confirm I have my pistol pressed to her neck.'

Mary gasped.

Bane's blood froze. He stifled a curse. He was going to make this man pay.

The skin across Bane's back tightened as they headed into yet another narrow tunnel. A draught of cool air blasted through it and when they reached the end and it once more opened out, Bane could see why. This cave led out to open water. He could see the waves washing into the mouth of the cave a few yards away.

They were standing on what looked very much like

a quay with a boat lying on its side on a narrow strip of sand. It was tied to a ring set in the rocks.

Judging from the way the seaweed grew up the walls, when the tide came in, where they were standing would be underwater.

'You weren't thinking of going for a midnight sail?' Bane said lightly. 'I don't think Miss Wilding is very fond of boats.'

'You didn't care about that when you booked her passage from St Ives,' Gerald said. 'But actually, no, the only one going sailing is me. You will be staying here.'

He waved the pistol. Bane prepared himself to jump and bring the little worm down.

The pistol steadied on Mary once more and Bane unclenched his fists. He did not want to give advanced notice of his intentions.

'Miss Wilding,' Gerald said, 'would you be so good as to take the lantern from your fiancé?' His voice dripped with sarcasm.

Bane handed it over, glad to have two free hands, but he didn't like it that it made Mary an easier target. She looked as pale as a ghost in the lamplight and her eyes, her pretty blue eyes, were large and frightened. He wanted to tell her not to worry, that he would think of something, but he could only give her an encouraging stare.

'See those chains beside your feet, Bane?' Gerald continued. 'The one with the manacles attached.'

Coldness bored into Bane's gut as he looked at the manacles. 'I see them.'

'Kneel and fasten one to your wrist.'

'No,' Mary said, her face full of horror. She'd guessed, like Bane had, the purpose of those chains. 'This is absolute nonsense. Gerald. You cannot do this. Don't you realise murder is a hanging offence?'

Gerald tittered. 'What a preachy schoolmarm you are. Just like my tutor, until I found a way to be rid of him.' He grinned. And the evil in that smiling angelic face made a shiver run down Bane's back. More than oddness resided in his cousin, he realised.

'Mary is right,' Bane said. 'You can't get away with this. And when the crime is discovered they will think it was Jeffrey.'

Gerald frowned. 'Why would they think it was him? Not that they will think it was murder. I have it all planned. They will just think you fell in the sea and drowned. You should have drowned anyway,' he said, flashing a look of hatred Bane's way. 'For years everyone thought the woman and child pulled from the sea the day your mother ran off was you.'

Bane wondered if he should threaten him with Templeton's expected arrival, but he had the feeling he needed to keep that card close for the moment. 'Any suspicious death of a peer comes under scrutiny and Jeffrey is the only one who benefits by my death.'

'Put your hand in that manacle. Now. Or I will shoot Miss Wilding.'

'And how will Jeffrey explain a bullet wound to the authorities?'

Gerald frowned. The pistol wavered. Then his face cleared. 'I'll tell them you shot her to get the money. And when I tried to protect her, you fell in the sea.'

Bane cursed. The lad might not be right in the head, but he had a chillingly cunning mind.

'Do as I say. Now. Or she dies.' He lined up the pistol on Mary's chest. Mary was looking at Bane in mute horror, expecting him to do something. Anything he could do right now would get her killed.

He did not want to put his wrist in that manacle, to willingly chain himself to a wall and leave himself helpless. He felt sick at the thought. But there was no other option, if he was to keep Gerald from firing his weapon. Gritting his teeth, he knelt on the cold hard rock and closed the iron around his wrist.

It was tight, but it wasn't yet locked.

Gerald grinned as if he'd read his thoughts. He held up the key. 'Catch it. If you drop it, I will shoot her in the head.'

Cursing inwardly, Bane caught the key and turned it in the lock. His insides rebelled at the sound.

'You can throw it back,' Gerald said. 'Be careful, I wouldn't like Miss Wilding to suffer for your poor aim.'

'Let her go, Gerald,' Bane said. 'She is a pawn in all of this.'

'She is a witness.'

Surreptitiously, Bane tugged on the chain. It seemed solidly attached, but that didn't mean one good hard tug wouldn't pull it free. 'She would probably just as soon marry Jeffrey as me. She was only doing it because I forced her.'

Gerald glanced at her.

Bane noticed she'd shifted, moved away from the wall and… Oh God, she still had the damned poker hidden in her skirts. If she tried that, he'd shoot her for certain.

'You know, Gerald,' he drawled, 'if you kill her, the money will be tied up in Chancery for years. Why do you think I didn't do it? Jeffrey won't thank you for it.'

'What?' The boy faced him. 'What are you talking about?'

'If she dies before she marries, the money goes to the Crown.'

'No. You are wrong.'

'I can assure you I know what I am talking about. Why else would I offer for her?'

The pain on Mary's face clawed at his chest, because she believed him. And it wasn't far off the truth. He would never have given marrying her a thought if it not for the money. He hadn't wanted to marry anyone. He only wanted justice for his mother.

'It's a trick,' Gerald said, glaring at him. 'Put your other hand in the manacle.'

'It is no trick.'

'Do it,' Gerald yelled, his voice rising.

The boy was getting anxious. Too anxious. Bane did not want that weapon going off by mistake and injuring Mary. His stomach lurched as he used his chained hand to close the manacle around his other wrist.

Gerald bent and locked it.

Bane lashed out with his foot at the gun as the key turned. He missed. But he managed to knock Gerald's arm, destroying his aim.

'Run,' he yelled.

Damn the woman, she wasn't listening. In awe and horror, he watched as she swung the poker. It hit Gerald's wrist. The gun flew out of his hand and skittered across the ledge. Bane willed it to fall into the sea. Dear God, the sea… While they had been bickering, the tide had been coming in. The boat was already afloat.

Gerald howled with pain and rage. He grabbed for Mary, who dodged him.

'Run, Mary,' Bane shouted, yanking on the chains, the iron biting into his wrists. 'Run. Save yourself.'

An agonised look crossed her face, then she turned and fled.

Gerald nursed his wrist for a moment, then picked up the pistol. He turned on Bane. 'I'll get her. And I'll make her marry Jeffrey. And it will be a proper Beresford who inherits the title. Not a bastard. My grandfather never wanted you as his heir.'

'I already inherited,' Bane said conversationally, judging the distance between them, trying to get under the lad's skin, to get him closer. A couple of feet and he'd have him. 'There will never be another Beresford heir.'

Gerald swung at Bane with the pistol and, chained as he was, he had no way to avoid the blow other than by turning his shoulder.

Pain exploded in a bright white light and his world went dark.

His head not only ached, but it felt like it was stuffed with wool. His ears were filled with the sound of rushing water. Was he cupshot? He opened his eyes. To blackness. And the smell of the sea. And the sound of waves. Water washed over him. Cold. Bringing him wide awake. He coughed and spat out the salt in his mouth. His mind cleared. Realisation colder than the air around him.

He'd allowed that little worm Gerald to chain him up. He shuddered as he realised he was helpless.

Fighting the insidious sensation of fear in his gut, he yanked on the chains. They'd looked rusty and old, but, no matter how hard he pulled, they didn't give.

Another wave rushed in and he fought to stay upright on his knees. This time when the sea receded, the water lapped around his legs. The tide was coming in fast. Fifteen minutes. That was all he had left of his life. Unless he could break the damn chains.

The thought of Gerald hurting Matry pierced his heart to the point of anguish. He had to get to her. Make sure she was all right. Feverishly he tore at the chains holding him fast. Pain gnawed at his flesh, but he barely felt it.

He took a deep breath, tensed every muscle in his body and pulled with all of his strength.

Pain was his only reward. He roared his anger and it echoed back at him. He sagged against the rocks, to recover his strength. To try again.

Sick horror filled his gut. Mary. He'd failed her, just as he'd failed his mother.

For days he'd tried to ignore his growing attraction. To keep himself aloof from emotions, as he had taught himself to do. After watching his mother die slowly of her injuries, because of him, he had known he could never again expose himself to the pain of losing someone else. Overcome by guilt, he had sworn he would never allow himself the privilege of another's love. He didn't deserve love.

He still didn't. But Mary, with her quick humour and courage, had made him want more than vindication for his mother. She'd made him want her, when he had known all along that he shouldn't. And now he'd failed her, too.

If only he could know she'd escaped. If he knew that for certain, he wouldn't care about the sea encroaching higher with every cold wave.

Because he loved her more than he loved his own life. He loved her.

The thought filled him with despair. He'd carelessly put her in terrible danger. Again he yanked on the chains.

A glowing figure in white floated towards him. The seawater had affected his brain, because what he was seeing was the White Lady. There was no mistaking the feminine figure outlined beneath the filmy robe and her long hair floating behind her.

His heart pounded wildly. Was this the signal that he was about to die?

'Bane,' she called out.

Not a ghost. But, oh damn, he wished it was. 'Mary,'

he pleaded desperately. 'I told you to leave. Go before he finds you.'

'I—I hit him over the head with the poker,' she said, crouching down. 'I—I think I killed him.' Her voice wavered badly. 'I have his pistol.'

Relief washed through him. Dear God, never had he met such a courageous woman or one so frighteningly resourceful. 'Do you think you can shoot at the pin holding me fast to this wall without killing me?'

She chuckled. 'Probably not. But I have something better.' She put down the lantern and reached for his hands. 'I have the key.'

The next wave was coming. He could hear it rushing into the cavern. He held his hands steady while she fumbled with the lock. 'Whatever you do, don't drop it.'

'I'll try not to,' she said, her voice grim.

The first shackle fell away. But he could see the wave rolling towards him in the light from the lantern. 'Get back,' he said, hating the idea of her moving away from him, but terrified that the next wave might carry her off.

Instead of doing as he said, she continued jiggling the key in the lock. And then it was open. He leaped to his feet and picked up her and the lantern and ran from the onrushing wave.

'Oh,' she said when he put her down. 'That was…remarkable.'

Cold and shivering, he leaned against the wall of the cave. 'Where is he?'

She took the lantern from his numb fingers. 'I hid in the muniment room and tripped him with the poker as he ran by. Then I hit him over the head and pushed him inside. I barred the door with the poker. Just in case.' She winced. 'But there was blood on his face.'

A very clever woman, his Mary. His? His heart stilled.

His mouth dried. He would be lucky if she agreed to speak to him again after the way he had endangered her life. And he wouldn't blame her at all.

He put an arm around her shoulders. 'Let us make sure he is no danger to us or anyone else, then find some dry clothes and a warm fire.'

She nodded, but her eyes were huge, her face pale and her expression fearful. He cursed the day he was born for causing such a look on her face.

Gerald was screaming invective when they reached that part of the tunnel. He'd managed to get the door open a fraction, but he barely seemed rational and was tossing papers and boxes around as if they were live things he was trying to murder.

Bane hurried Mary past and got her back to his chamber. He rang for his man and then sent him for her maid and a bath.

'I can't bathe in here,' she cried.

'You are not going back to a room that has a secret entrance,' he said. 'You can rest easy, I won't disturb you. There are many things I need to take care of before morning. But not until I am sure you are well protected.'

There was a strange look on her face. He wanted to ask her what she was thinking, but he didn't have the right. He had taken far too many liberties already.

A sleepy-looking Betsy arrived, followed by two footmen with a tin bath and another two with buckets of water.

Bane skewered the maid with a look. 'Take care of your mistress. She has been through a great deal this night and deserves every consideration.'

Betsy's mouth gaped. She dropped a curtsy and hurried through the door. Bane turned and left before he was tempted to remain, to help Mary bathe and see her safe to bed.

By letting his attraction for her overcome rational thought, he'd cause her a great deal of harm. She could have died.

And it would have been his fault.

The very idea almost sent him to his knees.

More guilt on his shoulders, heavier even than the death of his mother. Only this time he had a chance to atone.

It was almost mid-afternoon by the time Bane was able to seek out Mary. She'd slept until well past noon, he'd been told, and she was now in the drawing room.

Unable to resist looking his fill unnoticed, he paused outside the open door. She was sitting quietly gazing out the window, her hands folded in her lap, her thoughts clearly elsewhere.

So beautiful. An island of calm in a frenetic world. Only he knew the passion residing beneath the quiet exterior. Only he knew the wildly seductive woman below the unruffled surface.

Guilt assailed him. No true gentleman would have taken advantage of her innocence the way he had. He'd forced her into making a decision before he had all the facts. He'd wanted to believe she was up to some trick with his grandfather. He'd wanted to believe seduction was fair play, because he wanted her in his bed when in his heart he'd known better.

He was lowest kind of cur.

And when she found out the truth, how he had put her life in danger for his own selfish ends, he wasn't sure of her forgiveness. Nor did he deserve it.

He cleared his throat.

She jumped. Then flushed pink.

'My lord.' Only a tall, elegant woman like her could carry off that regal incline of her head.

'Miss Wilding.' He bowed.

Her eyes widened. A wary expression crossed her face. She smiled coolly. 'You have arranged everything to your satisfaction?'

'Yes. Gerald and his mother have been escorted by the doctor to York. She convinced me to allow Gerald to live out his days in an asylum there. Apparently this is not his first episode. His grandfather always put it down to an excess of sensibility. His mother suspected it was more, but didn't want to believe it.'

'I feel sorry for her. He…he won't be badly treated, I hope.'

He'd been ready to give him a quick end such was his anger at the danger inflicted on her. 'If that is your wish.'

She turned her face away. 'I hardly think my wishes are important.'

'He tried to kill you.' This time he could not keep his anger from surfacing.

'And you,' she said softly.

He waved a careless hand. 'If you can be magnanimous, then so can I.'

'And Jeffrey?'

'Like Mrs Hampton, he always knew Gerald was highly strung. He treated him with kid gloves and jollied him along. It never occurred to him that Gerald would act on his grandfather's continual complaints.'

'You believe him innocent, then?'

'I do. His horror and abject apology for not seeing what was going on were most convincing. You see, Jeffrey has money troubles. He was hoping to turn me up sweet for a large sum of money. The will made it all very difficult, as he had said to his cousin. He feels guilt for adding fuel to the fires in his cousin's head, but he would have stopped him if he had realised what he was doing.'

'So it is all settled.'

'Yes.'

He couldn't help looking at her, at the turn of her neck, at the faint pink blush on her cheeks, the bright sky-blue of her eyes. Because this might be the very last time he got to see her. She'd saved his life, while he'd done nothing but put hers at risk. Every time he thought about it his gut tightened and his blood turned to ice.

'I have to apologise to you for my behaviour these past several days,' he said.

Her gaze shot to meet his. Her chin came up. 'Your behaviour?'

His heart squeezed. She didn't trust him. She never had and with good reason. 'I have not treated you with the respect and honour you deserve.' He took a deep breath. 'I suspected you of colluding with my grandfather's machinations.'

'To what end?'

He looked at her, the heaviness in his chest almost unbearable. 'I didn't know. But I suspected there had to be something that would deprive me of my rightful inheritance. Something that would be revealed once we wed.'

A small crease formed in her brow. 'Yet you insisted we marry?'

Because he'd decided he could deal with any plan of his grandfather, once he had his instrument under his control. Liar. He'd wanted Mary in his bed.

She deserved so much more.

She certainly deserved better than a bastard for a husband who had not protected what was his. His fists opened and closed. Fear squirmed like a live thing in his gut. He pushed his roiling emotions behind a wall of ice the way he'd learned to do as a boy. At some time in the future they might bear closer examination, but not now, when it would take all his strength to do the right thing.

Squaring his shoulders, he strolled into the room. Her quick smile warmed him like the midsummer sun, but he shielded his heart in icy determination.

'What is wrong?' she asked.

Already she understood him too well. 'Word from Templeton has arrived.'

Her gaze sharpened.

'The will is undeniably flawed. He signed his father's name, not his own. Two names reversed. So small a mistake, it took ages for anyone to spot it. Whether it was intentional or because of infirmity, we will never know, even though I suspect the latter. Whatever the case, it will not stand.'

She gazed at him for a long moment, beautiful, clear blue eyes revealing the working of a bright intelligence. He could almost see the implications tumbling through her mind.

'I am not then an heiress who must marry within the year?' she finally asked.

'But we will marry,' he said. 'The settlements will be generous, you can be sure.'

He waited, his mind, his whole body, alert for some sign as to her response to his announcement. He didn't expect this to be easy, or go well.

A small crease formed between her finely drawn brows. Her gaze dropped to the still hands in her lap, effectively hiding her thoughts. He wanted to counsel her not to speak precipitously, not to rush to judgement, to consider the advantages, but he had been forcing her to his will from the moment they met. No longer. He didn't have the right.

She had saved his life.

What he wanted, what he hoped, was that she could conclude that what he suggested was the right choice, the sensible choice.

'Why?' she said to her hands. She lifted her gaze. 'Why should we marry?'

She demanded he argue his case after all.

'Surely the reason is obvious.'

A blush said she understood his meaning perfectly well. He let go of a sigh of relief. He'd feared she'd balk. Feared it badly enough to hold his breath like a schoolboy longing for a treat.

She shook her head. 'I won't do it.'

For a moment, he didn't believe what he heard. Then realisation hit with the force of a blow, shattering his soul to nothing but shards that pierced his heart in the aftermath.

He strode to stand before her, gazing down into her lovely, sorrowful face. He loomed over her, letting her see his disbelief. But not the damage. Never that. 'You are not thinking clearly,' he said.

She rose to her feet, tall, magnificent, her flashing eyes almost on a level with his. An angry goddess about to smite some lesser mortal.

And after the way he'd behaved, it was just. But he wasn't going to let her go without a fight. 'Honour demands—'

'Your honour, not mine. As I told you before, I do not move in circles that bind me to your notions of honour.' A flicker of comprehension passed across her face. 'And besides, if the will is broken, then you can no longer claim guardianship. You cannot keep me against my will, or force me to wed you.'

Oh, his Mary was indeed clever.

Only she was not his. And never really had been his. He should have known better than to think, to hope, she might yet find him of some worth. Still, he could not let her go without one more attempt to find common ground.

'Hear me out, at least,' he said.

Her eyes were as cold as the grave. 'Very well.'

'The tables have turned, yes, but it does not mean we should not marry. I am no woman's first choice of a father to their children, with my own parentage in doubt, despite my mother's denial of wrongdoing.'

'You doubt her.' She spoke flatly.

'I just don't know. She fled. If she was innocent, why would she not have stood her ground?'

'Sometimes that is the easiest way for a woman.'

He'd made her flee, too. He heard the condemnation in her voice. 'Think of the advantages. I am wealthy. I can provide for you. Protect you.' He could see he wasn't making any headway from the hard expression on her face. He started to panic. 'Build as many schools for orphans as you decide are required.'

For that he earned a small smile. It was a start. A chink in her armour. 'I'll give you free rein. Your own allowance. You don't have to see me from one year to the next, if you don't want to.' He would do his level best to make sure that didn't happen.

She took a deep breath. 'It is not enough.'

Dumbfounded, he stared at her. She turned and walked away, out of the door, out of his life.

Left him standing there feeling as if he had a hole in his chest the size of a cannonball. He looked down just to be sure he was still in one piece.

Damnation. Impossible, headstrong, wilful woman.

And he'd thought she was the only truly sensible female he'd ever met.

He ought to lock her up until she saw reason. Except he'd tried that already. He could not hold back the small smile that tugged at his lips.

Now what the hell was he to do?

Manners scratched at the door and came in, disturbing his thoughts.

'What?' he snarled, then closed his eyes and grappled his temper into submission. 'I beg your pardon, Manners, what did you require?'

Manners acknowledged the apology with a twinkle in his eyes. 'Miss Wilding has requested the carriage for first thing in the morning. I told her that our carriage was with Mrs Hampton and that the earliest I could arrange for a hiring would be the day after tomorrow. Did I do right?'

He could refuse to let her leave. Again. What would that get him, apart from her hatred? No. If leaving was what she wanted, if that would make her happy... Happy. The word painfully jiggled the shards in his chest. If leaving made her happy, he forced himself to continue, then that was what must happen. 'Arrange it.' He had one more day to find a way to change her mind.

The butler bowed himself out.

Happy. The word came back to lash him anew. She deserved to be happy. Between him and his predecessor, they'd destroyed her life. If he couldn't do anything else for her, he could help her put it back together the way she wanted.

Finding this Mrs Ladbrook might be the key. But if Templeton couldn't locate her, no one could. Then he would give her a school of her own.

Nearby. Where he could keep an eye on her. A school and a salary large enough to keep her in luxury. He would then have the excuse to ride over and see her from time to time, to inspect his investment.

His throat dried. She might not welcome visits from the bastard earl.

All right. He would have his reports second-hand. He would know she was safe, and from a distance he could protect her from harm.

The ache in his chest eased slightly.

And what if she found a man she did want to marry? What then? The thought of another man with the right to engage her wit in conversation whenever the mood took him, the right to touch her silken skin and arouse her passion... No. He would not think of his needs. This was about her happiness. Nothing else mattered.

Something burned behind his eyes.

He felt like a boy again, mourning his mother. Only this time, he knew it was different. There was no anger to balance the pain. No one else to blame.

'You sent for me, my lord?'

Bane put down his pen and looked up. How was it that when she walked into a room she made it come alive? Or was it only him who came alive?

At this moment she looked worried. Expecting he would prevent her departure on the morrow, just as he had prevented it today, no doubt. She thought him that kind of cur. And he didn't blame her.

'Please, sit.'

She did so, sinking into the chair in front of his desk with natural elegance, her long slender limbs bending to her will, when he would much rather they would bend to his, her face calm and still, her eyes a deep shadowed blue.

Perhaps he shouldn't bother her with this, but she wouldn't thank him for making her decision for her. 'I found something among the papers Gerald tried to destroy. You might find it of interest.' He passed over the piece of parchment he'd read with astonishment only half an hour before.

Swiftly, she scanned the yellowed paper. A gasp left her lips as she raised her gaze to meet his. It was filled with wonder and disbelief. 'But this is…' She looked at it again.

'From your father. It was he who consigned you to the earl's care, in payment for some earlier favour. I am assuming our marriage was what was promised.'

'Oh,' she said, her whisper husky, her eyes still fixed on the words. The paper trembled in her fingers. 'Oh.'

Tears tracked down her cheeks.

He'd made her cry. He'd thought she might be interested. Or even pleased. Tears he had not expected. He wanted to hit something. Better that than giving way to the pain at the sight of her anguish.

He got up slowly, afraid he might make things worse. 'Mary,' he whispered. He came around the desk to her side, put a comforting hand on her shoulder and was glad when she didn't pull away. He dropped to his knees, put his head close to hers. 'Mary, please. I would not have shown you this if I thought it would upset you.'

She swallowed and choked on an apologetic laugh. 'You don't understand. I'm not upset.'

With her shoulders hunched and one hand covering her eyes, she looked the very picture of misery. 'You are crying.'

She raised her head and her watery gaze met his. 'Don't you see what this means?'

'Your father undertook some sort of service for the old earl and this letter calls the favour in.'

She shook her head. 'No. I mean, yes, that is what is says. But it also says he loved me. He says *my beloved daughter.* In his last moments in this life, he thought of me, his beloved daughter.'

He frowned. 'Of course he did. You were his child.'

A tremble quaked her body. 'I didn't know. I understood he had sent me away when my mother died. That he didn't want me. To know that I was loved…' Her voice cracked and broke. She buried her face in her hands.

Bane remembered all the hugs and sweet kisses on his brow from his mother when he was young and swallowed the hot hard lump in his throat. He'd known without even thinking about it that he was loved. He'd known love in its purest form, even if he had lost it too soon. For years, he had shut himself off from its memory. Built walls of cold anger to keep the guilt at bay. The guilt for his part in his mother's death. Now those walls were shattered, leaving him with his memories and vulnerable to her hurt.

'Mary,' he whispered. He swallowed again, for the words had been so long closed off. He cradled her face in hands that felt awkward and over large. 'My darling. Look at me.' A flood of emotion washed over him. Hope. Joy. And, yes, sweet warm love. They constricted his throat as her gaze met his. 'Of course he loved you. *I* love you.'

He stilled, shocked by the sound of what he had said. Shocked by the fact that he had dared to put his feelings into words. 'I love your wit and your courage. I love your beauty. But most of all I love you.'

Her mouth trembled as her gazed searched his face. 'Please. I don't need your kindness.'

'When have I ever been kind to you?' He brushed his mouth against hers. His lips tingled at this briefest of touches, wanting more. 'It is I who needs kindness. All morning I've been plotting ways to keep you close, building a cage from which you could not escape. But I just couldn't do it, sweet. It seems I can't keep you against your will. I want you to be happy.' He groaned. 'But God, I don't want to lose you.'

'Oh, Bane.' She flung her arms about his neck and sobbed against his shoulder.

He'd made her cry yet again. He was an idiot. He'd made things worse. Awkwardly he patted her back. Forced himself not to wrap his arms around her and kiss her until she forgot his promise to let her leave. He had wooed her with seduction once, he would not lower himself to doing it again.

Slowly her sobs subsided.

He handed her his handkerchief and stood up while she dried her eyes.

'You meant what you said about letting me leave?' she asked in a shaky whisper and the glimmer of a smile.

He nodded. The damnable lump in his throat did not allow for speech, but his eyes drank her in and he realised this would likely be the last time he would ever have a chance to be this close to her.

'And if I wanted to stay?'

His heart stopped beating. He swallowed. 'Stay?' God, was that croak actually a word?

She stood up and, as always, he marvelled at how perfect was her stature, how elegant her neck, how feminine her figure. He had never seen her look more lovely, though her nose was red from weeping and her eyes still misty with tears.

To his surprise, she placed her hand against his cheek. Without thinking, he turned his face and kissed her palm before her hand fell away.

He felt its loss keenly.

'I lied,' she said so softly he had to lean closer to hear her words. 'To you. To myself. I told myself I was trapped in this house by a man I didn't trust with my life.'

'You had every reason—'

She stopped his words with a finger to his lips. 'My heart knew what my mind did not. It always knew to trust you. If not, I would have found a way to leave that very first day.' A small smile curved her lovely mouth. 'I think I fell in love with you the moment I saw you standing in the shadows like some dark avenging angel.'

Warmth trickled into all the remaining cold places in his heart. Her warmth. Her generous spirit. 'You are saying you love me in return?' he asked cautiously, fearing he had misunderstood.

Her smile broadened. 'Yes, Bane. I am saying I love you.'

He felt his way forwards with care. 'Then you mean to stay? To marry me?'

'If you truly love me and want me.'

He crushed her against his chest, feeling the pounding of his heart against his ribs. But did she really know what she was getting into with him? 'I almost got you killed. I wanted to keep you safe and I almost got you killed the way I did my mother. If I had done the same to you, I would have gone mad.'

She pushed back to look at him, a question in her eyes.

All the old guilt rushed back. 'I don't deserve your love. I don't deserve anyone's love.'

'You don't get to choose who loves you.'

'You would not, if you knew the truth.' Painful though it was, he forced himself to remember that dreadful day when his life changed for ever. 'I was ten. We had an argument. I ran off in a temper to the mine with some of the local boys. She hated me going anywhere near it, but the other boys always taunted me about being a coward and it seemed like a good way to get my own back. It got late and she came looking for me.'

He inhaled a deep ragged breath. 'We walked home in the dark, her trudging along behind me, because I was angry that she'd shamed me before my so-called friends. We were set upon by thieves. Big men. They held me down and they beat her. And there was nothing I could do. I could hear her crying out and the blows...' The sickening sound rang in his ears. 'I felt so helpless. She died of her injuries weeks later and not once did she berate me. But I knew. I knew it was all my doing. My temper that caused her death. I swore it would never happen again.'

'So that is why you always seem so cold and controlled.'

Her understanding was extraordinary. He let go a sigh. 'Always, until I met you.'

She smiled softly. But he hardened himself against his longing to kiss her. He wasn't done.

'I very nearly caused your death, too! What if you had died? I froze out the world after the death of my mother. Life would be unbearable if anything happened to you.'

'What happened to your mother wasn't your fault. Nor was what Gerald did.'

'I know that. Yet in my heart I failed my mother and I failed you. How can you trust me to keep you safe?'

'I don't need you to keep me safe, I need your love.'

The truth of it was blinding. He almost fell to his knees at the revelation. Yet even as the fear was vanquished, more doubts surfaced.

'I'll never be fully accepted in society,' he forced himself to warn her.

'I don't care about society. I only care about you.'

'What about children?'

'I want children.' She tipped up her face to kiss his cheek. 'Don't you?'

'Yes. I want your children. But...but I don't know

whose blood runs in my veins. I could be a Beresford, as my mother swore, or the son of a villain.'

'And I am the daughter of a vicar. The mixture will be interesting, I am sure.'

He looked at her beautiful mouth with longing. 'You are determined, then?'

'Am I ever anything else?'

No, thank God. He kissed her until he was dizzy with wanting her in his bed. It was all he could do not to carry her off to his chamber and make sure this was not all a dream. Make sure she could never change her mind. But there was a better way to do that.

'We will take that passage to London, first thing in the morning, and I will obtain a special licence.'

'The banns will be read and we will be married in the parish church for all your people to see, as already arranged, according to my father's wishes.'

'You don't know your father's wishes.'

She looked down at the note in her hand. 'Yes,' she said softly. 'I do.'

Tears burned behind his eyes at the tenderness in her voice. 'I don't want to wait weeks to have you in my arms, in my bed,' he groaned. 'but if that is your wish…'

Her arms came up around his neck. She kissed his lips, a small press of her lips against his, before she drew back with a smile. 'There is absolutely no reason for us to wait until we are married, is there?'

'You are a wicked woman.'

'I'm a blue-stocking, remember.'

Right then, with his blood pounding in his veins, he couldn't remember a thing except his need to be inside her. He picked her up in his arms and strode for his chamber, knowing only one thing. She was his and he was the luckiest man alive.

Epilogue

‘So Beresford, I finally get to meet your lovely wife,’ Templeton drawled.

Bane narrowed his eyes as his friend, the blond darling of the *ton* and heir to the Marquisate of Mooreshead, bowed over Mary’s hand. He’d given this ball at his newly renovated London town house, invited the *ton,* in order to introduce her to society. He could hardly complain that so many of them, including his oldest and most trusted friend, had come. Most of them were curious to see who the bastard earl had married, no doubt. Still, he did not have to like that his best friend and well-known rake, Lord Templeton, was eyeing his wife like a wolf who had just spotted dinner.

As usual he’d come late to the party. There were only a few more dances now supper was over and the last of the guests would depart.

Gabe caught his glare and laughed. Damn, the man was far too handsome a fellow with a smile on his lips, even if he was one of His Majesty’s most dangerous spies.

‘I wish you both much happiness,’ Gabe said.

‘Thank you, my lord.’ Mary dipped a curtsy. She looked beautiful tonight in a gown of pale-rose silk, her hair arranged artfully by Betsy, her height lending her the elegance of a queen. Pride filled him, every time he looked at her, along with the desire to glare at any male who approached.

'Do you plan to return to that pile of rocks in Cornwall?' Gabe asked.

'In time,' Bane said. 'It needs some major renovations before we will feel comfortable there.' Like the closing up of passages behind the walls.

Mary nodded her agreement.

'Before you do anything to the house, would you be willing to lease it to me? For a year or so? Its inconveniences might prove very useful to my enterprise.'

Mary didn't so much as blink. They'd agreed they would keep no secrets from each other and, after receiving Gabe's permission, he'd told her all about his friend's work for the Foreign Office.

He sent her an enquiring look and she nodded. 'I owe you for finding my friend Mrs Ladbrook.'

Bane had wanted the woman to pay back the money she had salted away, but Mary wouldn't allow it. A woman alone had to do what she needed to survive. Besides, they were friends.

She turned to Bane. 'Since you will be busy making your mark in Parliament, and working for better conditions in the mines, and I have an idea for a school for miners' children I would like to raise with the denizens of the *ton,* I don't see why not,' she said. 'We will need its return when we begin our family.'

A family was her dearest hope, he knew. But he hoped it would not happen too soon. He liked having her to himself.

'Then it is agreed,' Bane said to Gabe.

'May I request this next dance, Lady Beresford?' Gabe

asked, with a sly look at Bane and a charming smile for his wife.

'Mary is promised to me,' Bane said quickly, unable to keep the possessive note from his voice.

She shook her head at him.

'You are,' he said and swept her into the waltz with a warning glower at his friend. As they moved around the floor, he was overcome by a wave of contentment.

'Are you happy?' he whispered in her ear.

'Incredibly. Unbelievably. There is only one thing missing.'

'Children.'

'Your children,' she whispered close to his ear.

His groin tightened. 'I am sure no one would miss us if it is your pleasure to try again.'

A shiver passed through her frame. 'It is always my pleasure.'

He manoeuvred her closer to the door and then whirled her out into the hallway. Giggling like children, they ran up the servants' staircase to their chamber.

'You, sir, are wicked,' she said, leaning her back against the closed door.

She looked wanton and quite delighted.

His heart swelled as he pulled her close. 'I am glad you are pleased, my dearest heart,' he breathed softly against her neck, feeling her soft swells against his length with a powerful shudder of anticipation of the love and bliss he would find in her arms.

* * * * *

COMING NEXT MONTH from Harlequin® Historical

AVAILABLE FEBRUARY 19, 2013

INHERITING A BRIDE
Lauri Robinson

Clay Hoffman knows a thing or two about money-grubbing females, so when he finds one posing as his new ward he's determined to get beneath every delicious layer of her disguises. Discovering she's telling the truth, Clay is torn—he should be protecting her, not thinking about making her his bride! All he knows for sure is that he's inherited a whole heap of trouble!

(Western)

THE ACCIDENTAL PRINCE
Michelle Willingham

Karl von Lohenberg is without a country, a title—and a bride if he lets Serena get away. A ruthless man, he takes her to a secluded island, hell-bent on seduction. Only, he discovers a broken woman behind the prim princess facade. The time they spend together mends her spirit and touches his soul, but how will she react to his deception?

(Victorian)

THE RAKE TO RUIN HER
The Ransleigh Rogues
Julia Justiss

Known as Magnificent Max, diplomat Max Ransleigh was famed for his lethal charm until a political betrayal left him exiled from government and his reputation in tatters. He seems a *very* unlikely savior for a well-bred young lady. Except that Miss Caroline Denby doesn't want to be saved...she wants to be ruined!

(Regency)

TAKEN BY THE BORDER REBEL
The Brunson Clan
Blythe Gifford

As leader of his clan, Black Rob Brunson has earned every dark syllable of his name. But having taken hostage his enemy's daughter in a fierce act of rebellion, he is tormented by feelings of guilt and torn apart with the growing need to protect her—and seduce her!

(Tudor)

You can find more information on upcoming Harlequin® titles, free excerpts and more at www.Harlequin.com.

HHCNM0213

REQUEST YOUR FREE BOOKS!

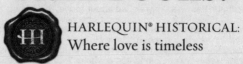

HARLEQUIN® HISTORICAL:
Where love is timeless

2 FREE NOVELS PLUS 2 FREE GIFTS!

YES! Please send me 2 FREE Harlequin® Historical novels and my 2 FREE gifts (gifts are worth about $10). After receiving them, if I don't wish to receive any more books, I can return the shipping statement marked "cancel." If I don't cancel, I will receive 6 brand-new novels every month and be billed just $5.19 per book in the U.S. or $5.74 per book in Canada. That's a savings of at least 17% off the cover price! It's quite a bargain! Shipping and handling is just 50¢ per book in the U.S. and 75¢ per book in Canada.* I understand that accepting the 2 free books and gifts places me under no obligation to buy anything. I can always return a shipment and cancel at any time. Even if I never buy another book, the two free books and gifts are mine to keep forever.

246/349 HDN FVQK

Name	(PLEASE PRINT)	
Address		Apt. #
City	State/Prov.	Zip/Postal Code

Signature (if under 18, a parent or guardian must sign)

Mail to the Harlequin® Reader Service:
IN U.S.A.: P.O. Box 1867, Buffalo, NY 14240-1867
IN CANADA: P.O. Box 609, Fort Erie, Ontario L2A 5X3

Want to try two free books from another line?
Call 1-800-873-8635 or visit www.ReaderService.com.

* Terms and prices subject to change without notice. Prices do not include applicable taxes. Sales tax applicable in N.Y. Canadian residents will be charged applicable taxes. Offer not valid in Quebec. This offer is limited to one order per household. Not valid for current subscribers to Harlequin Historical books. All orders subject to credit approval. Credit or debit balances in a customer's account(s) may be offset by any other outstanding balance owed by or to the customer. Please allow 4 to 6 weeks for delivery. Offer available while quantities last.

Your Privacy—The Harlequin® Reader Service is committed to protecting your privacy. Our Privacy Policy is available online at www.ReaderService.com or upon request from the Harlequin Reader Service.

We make a portion of our mailing list available to reputable third parties that offer products we believe may interest you. If you prefer that we not exchange your name with third parties, or if you wish to clarify or modify your communication preferences, please visit us at www.ReaderService.com/consumerschoice or write to us at Harlequin Reader Service Preference Service, P.O. Box 9062, Buffalo, NY 14269. Include your complete name and address.

HH13

SPECIAL EXCERPT FROM
HARLEQUIN® HISTORICAL™

Introducing the merciless Karl von Lohenberg in
Michelle Willingham's latest Historical romance,
THE ACCIDENTAL PRINCE...

"Why are you really here?" she demanded. "And don't
tell me it's because my sister sent you. You didn't care
enough to come and see me more than twice in the six years
since we've been betrothed."

"I think you know why I came, Princess," he said smoothly.
"To make sure you weren't eloping with some other man
instead of me." He removed his hat and set it beside him.
The cold rain had dampened his face, and his clothing was
soaked from the bad weather.

Serena kept her hands folded primly in her lap. "Your
Highness, let us be honest with one another. We were only
betrothed because my father wanted to secure the alliance
with Lohenberg. After we are married, what we do with our
lives won't matter. I don't believe for a moment that you
have any interest in me."

"You're wrong." He reached out and lowered her hood,
brushing his fingertips against her damp cheek. In her
eyes he saw the startled shock. "I find you very interesting
indeed, Princess."

He could see from the look on her face that she wasn't
at all looking forward to their union. Whether she disliked
him or was afraid of him, he couldn't be certain. "Our marriage
can be more than political."

She turned her face to the window, the melancholy sinking in. "Sometimes I wish I could live like an ordinary woman, just for a few days. Free to make my own decisions." Her voice held a note of misery, as though she believed herself a prisoner.

"Is it such a hardship, wearing diamonds and silks?"

"Sometimes," she admitted.

When he saw her shivering, Karl reached beneath the seat for a blanket. He passed it to her, and she huddled within the wool, struggling to get warm. Outside, the rain continued, and he could see his breath within the interior of the coach.

She stared outside the coach and said, "This isn't the way to my grandfather's lodge."

"We can't go there," he admitted. "If we do, they'll find you within a few hours."

Her face paled. "Then you really are abducting me."

"Yes." He made no apology for his actions. "You'll still have your holiday away from the palace," he reassured her. "And I'll bring you back within a week."

As my wife.

**Be sure to find out what happens next in
THE ACCIDENTAL PRINCE
by Michelle Willingham**

Available from Harlequin Historical in March 2013!

HHEXP0213

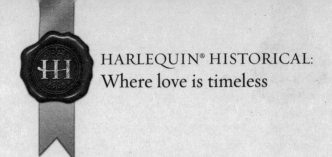

HARLEQUIN® HISTORICAL:
Where love is timeless

COMING IN MARCH

Inheriting a Bride

BY FAN-FAVORITE AUTHOR

LAURI ROBINSON

Stubborn and sassy Kit Becker is determined to access her inheritance, no matter what it takes. Clay Hoffman wishes he could give it to her, just to get her out of his hair, and heart.

Find out what happens in this Rocky Mountain story of mistaken identity, family obligations and secrets!

Available March 2013 from Harlequin Historical

HARLEQUIN® HISTORICAL:
Where love is timeless

ONCE A RAKE...

Known as Magnificent Max, diplomat Max Ransleigh was famed for his lethal charm until a political betrayal left him exiled from government and his reputation in tatters. He seems a very unlikely savior for a well-bred young lady.

Except that Miss Caroline Denby doesn't want to be saved…she wants to be ruined! To Caroline, getting married is tantamount to a death sentence, and meeting the rakish Max at a house party seems the answer to her prayers…. Surely this rogue won't hesitate to put his bad reputation to good use?

Look for THE RAKE TO RUIN HER by Julia Justiss in March 2013—the first book in The Ransleigh Rogues miniseries!

The Ransleigh Rogues
Where these notorious rakes go, scandal always *follows….*

Max, Will, Alastair and Dominic Ransleigh—cousins, friends…and the most wickedly attractive men in Regency London. Between war, betrayal and scandal, love has never featured in the Ransleighs' destinies—until now!

Don't miss this enthralling new quartet from Julia Justiss, starting with Max's story.

Book #2 THE RAKE TO REDEEM HER by Julia Justiss is available in April 2013.